CW00927096

~

SPIRIT WALKER
Warwick Gibson.

Content 88,000 words.

Also by Warwick Gibson
The Traveller Series
(modern thrillers)
The Navscar Trilogy
(science fiction)
The H'Roth Trilogy
(science fiction)

~

Spirit Walker
Copyright © 2024 Warwick Gibson.

ONE

Mono stirred restlessly in his sleep. An old dream had come back to haunt him. He was somewhere in the Eastern Marches, and he had taken up his future role as Regent of the prosperous Marchlands region. It was something his father wanted, but something Mono had sworn he would never do.

He turned to the north, toward the Scaffold Mountains. Then his vantage point soared higher, and he could see beyond the orderly rows of mountain peaks. His heart beat faster, as he looked across the great desert beyond. Something was wrong with Xianak, the sprawling capital of the ancient empire on the other side of the desert, but he couldn't say what it was.

A voice whispered something in his ear, and he looked to the west. He saw the Independent Kingdoms as they ran to the Trading Seas. Then he was somewhere else. He saw an old stone keep, abandoned at the foot of a mountain range. Something glowed at the base of it, something oddly familiar.

He looked down at his body. One leg stood in the Wild Marches to the west, and one in the Eastern Marches. He straddled Middle March between them, and the great Southern Sea stretched endlessly behind him.

A darkness drew over the city of Xianak. Some force he did not understand was marking the ancient empire as its own. One day soon it would descend upon the surrounding regions, destroying everything in its path.

How long did the free peoples of the Karnatic League have? How long until everything changed forever? Then the dream was gone, and he subsided into a fitful sleep.

Much later, the light of dawn filtered into the room. It came through shutters closed over rough windows devoid of glass. The gloominess of the room slowly lifted, and dark shapes became recognizable things.

The four walls looked sturdy. They were made of logs chinked with mosses from the forest. An elaborate construction of poles rested along the top of the logs, and supported a thick reed thatch.

There was a fireplace at one end, built out of earth sods. The sods crumbled during winter fires, sending little cascades of dirt down onto the hearth, but the fire hadn't been lit in months.

A simple construction of poles tied to a frame stood beside a pallet bed. It took Mono's clothes, and anything else he wanted to keep off the sawdust floor. His worldly possessions were on show for all to see, but anything like a cupboard was out of the question. It would be far beyond the reach of a poor-mouth smallholder like himself.

Opposite the frame was a cooking pit and a tiny kitchen area. To the left of that was a sturdy wooden door. It stood in the middle of the end wall. Life here was very basic, but it had taught Mono one thing. A simple life, a natural diet, and plenty of exercise, had made him happier than he had ever been.

The first bright rays of the sun had not yet appeared when a tapping sound began in one corner of the room, just under the reed layers of the roof. In the opposite corner, the figure on the pallet bed stirred slightly.

The sound launched itself along the top of the wall, and down an adjoining section of chinked logs to the kitchen area. It increased in volume as it did so. As it passed the roughly shaped metal cooking pots they clanged loudly against each other. One fell into the wooden sink with a crash.

Mono woke with a start, and reflexively flung out an arm in the direction of the noise. A cold, blue fire lanced from his hand. It froze the intruder in the act of spilling a container of salt into the porridge pot.

The sprite battled the power in the thought form around it. Its changing shape appeared as a kind of negative inside the coalescing ball of pale fire. At last it succumbed, and appeared in its true form.

Even half asleep, Mono was too powerful for it.

The last of the dream slipped out of his mind, going with his blessing. The first few times it had happened he'd tried desperately to understand the dream, but without success. Now he found it best to bury the memory in the activities of the day.

"What did I tell you about bothering me before the sun shines on the turnagain?" yawned Mono from the bed. The beaten copper disc on the outside of the door sported several semi-precious gems. The power in it confused woodland creatures that might try to gain access to the hut. That usually meant the rats, mice and climbing creatures common in the forest. On a deeper level it kept out anything unearthly, and of the night, as well.

"Mono say Demetrius to cook breakfast," began the gnarled sprite, before Mono crooked his fingers. The creature doubled over, making a high-pitched, keening noise.

"Prince Monhoven the Fourteenth, Keeper-designate of the Eastern Marches," it gasped. "Fourth in line to the Throne of Power, Order of the . . ."

Mono cut it off.

"Prince Monhoven will do," he said coolly.

The forest sprites were almost impossible to train. They were even worse in the half-dawn, before sunlight sharpened their limited intellect. Mono had often thought of adjusting the turnagain to keep them out altogether, but they were useful messengers, and they could handle some of the daily chores around the hut.

All the sprites in this area shared a collective memory. What he told one the day before would be done, after a fashion, by another the following day. This one had disclosed its name, which was rare, but understanding why sprites did things was an impossible task.

"Return to the forest, Demetrius," he commanded, "until I call you."

The sprite faded from view, looking sulky and defiant. Mono would make the spirit call to bring it back when he was ready, he thought sharply, and not a moment before.

But then he caught himself getting angry, and felt chastened. Why was he getting angry at a sprite? It was a force of nature, like the wind. It was incapable of deliberate annoyance. How would he ever rule the Eastern Marches – not that he wanted to – if he couldn't even rule himself?

His anger had been a problem from his early years, and it was a problem that wasn't going away as he got older. Rising from the pallet he tossed aside the rough, quilted cover. He was upset now, damn it, and he might as well get up.

He made his way to the recessed nook that served as a kitchen, and cleared away the mess the sprite had made. Then he tipped a little water into a pot at the side of the cooking pit. He would normally boil the water to make his breakfast, except today was a special day, and he didn't have time to light a fire.

Extending his spirit senses, he swept the surrounding area for any creature, human or otherwise, that might be drawn to a small flash of power. Finding nothing, he put his hands around the pot and brought the water to boiling point. Snatching his hands away from the sudden heat, he added a handful of grains.

After his morning wash there would be a meal of rough but nourishing porridge waiting for him. It would be something to break his night's fast.

He moved to the stout door at the front of the cottage, raised the latch, and stepped out into the new day. The turnagain on the door jingled faintly. It was reminding him that it had turned away at least one unwelcome intruder during the night. Mono thought of the small insignia on the back of it. A tiny mountain cat, the emblem of the Karnatic League.

Thoughts of the League stirred an old emotional wound. When would he find his place in his father's sprawling federation of kingdoms? What would his role there be? He pushed a sense of confusion from his mind.

He always enjoyed the morning. He liked the first rays of the sun on his shoulders, and the feel of cold water on his face and hands. He kept a basin of water under the thatched eaves especially for the special moment each day.

Plunging his head into the basin, he rubbed his face with his hands and then lifted his head clear. He wiped his eyes with the front of his long sleeping shirt. The burnished metal plate on the wall reflected the first of the sun's rays into his eyes. He saw his chubby features and mousy hair, and twisted his face in annoyance. How, how ... *ordinary* ... he looked. There wasn't enough hair on his chin to shape into anything stylish, or on his cheeks to hide his baby face.

On the positive side his time in the forest had bulked him out a little. It wasn't exactly muscle, but he was getting some shape to his awkward frame.

He sighed. He would never be as tall as his father, and he knew he didn't have what it took to succeed in the intrigues of the court. That suited him fine. He was only fourth in line to the throne anyway, not that he cared one jot who ruled the kingdoms of the Karnatic League.

The old man could lead the League forever, as far as Mono was concerned. His father had always wanted reliable, substantial, sound behaviour from him. If that was the case, he must be from the unreliable, insubstantial, and unsound branch of the family. Yes, that was who he was, the unsound prince.

He decided he liked the idea of the unsound prince, in fact he liked it very much. He paused for a moment before plunging his face back into the cold water, in celebration of the fact. Then he thought again how lucky he was to be this far from the palace. He dried his back with a length of soft cloth. He had been sent for the gods knew what reason to a forgotten place on the edge of nowhere.

Well, the joke was on them. He liked it here. He had friends in the village who treated him like one of themselves. That was worth more than anything to Mono. In the beginning he hadn't given a damn where he was sent for his transition years, the time in which he was expected to undergo his 'regency training' away from the Golden Palace.

There were reasons for that. Everything had gone a dull, cotton-clad grey after his mother had died. It hadn't helped that he was so young, or that her death was a pointless hunting accident. The hopelessness he had felt then had got worse when his father wouldn't talk about it. Mono had never felt so alone.

He had been his parents' first, and only, child. There were any number of uncles and aunts, but they were scattered across the Karnatic League, doing their bit to hold the sprawling federation together. You could say my childhood wasn't much fun, he thought grimly. He took some satisfaction from the sheer understatement of the words.

He plunged his head into the cold water again. At least here, in the rough country of the Wild Marches, he had begun to take an interest in life again. Shaker's Hope was so different to the Golden Palace. Life was all foppery and pretence there, with the court meandering endlessly along. There wasn't any real competition for the throne, so the chances of change in the League any time soon were slim. It seemed nothing would break the thirty years of his father's iron rule.

Still, it had taken a Monhoven to consolidate the sprawling tangle of southern kingdoms into one cohesive body. Kingdoms that had wasted their time in endless disputes and blood-letting for centuries. He had to admit he took some pride out of the fact it had been Monhovens who had done that.

At the head of the broad valley stood a prominent hill, its slopes covered in dense forest. Two imposing ridges stretched out from it and ran down either side of the valley. One of the ridges curled round a cottage in the middle of a cleared area. Further down the valley similar clearings merged into a much larger space, and then a village. It was a farming area, centred around Shaker's Hope.

On one of the ridges an ancient tree, its core rotted out after centuries of majestic life, quivered uncertainly. The sky darkened, and a squall came. It lashed the tops of the forest and tore at the great tree. The giant groaned as its roots slipped through the tight grip of its mother the earth. Then its centre of balance moved too far, and it toppled forward.

At the precise moment the sound of the crash reverberated round the valley, two men appeared in the shade of a much smaller tree on the opposite ridge.

"Always use a method of distraction, Sergeos," murmured the older one, leaning heavily on his staff. He was restoring his energy, and he needed to. Transporting two of them from the Golden Palace to this obscure spot on the fringes of the Karnatic League was no mean feat. Few others could have done it.

"Many a spirit walker lost his life because he wasn't prepared," he continued.

"Or because he or she didn't leave their anger at home," added the one who was, apparently, Sergeos. The older man smiled, and nodded.

"Have you picked up the boy yet," he said, breathing more easily now. He began to straighten up.

Sergeos had indeed been trying to locate him. "Nothing," he said, puzzled. The boy's spirit sense should have stood out like a beacon fire in the valley below.

The older man chuckled. "He's changing so fast between visits we can't keep up. Now he's learned how to shield himself." There was a moment's pause.

"I expected nothing less," he said quietly.

"But he's so young to master such a thing," said Sergeos, astounded at the thought. "Besides, *Alfas*, how do you know he has made that step?"

The Legatus had tried to discourage him from using the honorific, meaning 'great one', but for Sergeos it just felt right to do so sometimes.

"Because I see him," said his companion, and pointed to a cottage on the edge of a clearing. It was barely visible on the other side of the valley. Sergeos squinted at the clearing, and engaged his own farsight. As the clearing enlarged before his eyes he saw a young man, standing in front of a rough hut.

Yes, the spirit master was good alright, he thought, impressed. No one would argue with that. And he should be that good. He sat on the Throne of Power. He was Legatus, ruler of the Karnatic League, and he was Combat Prime, head of the Priatic Order of Mysteries. No one in the history of all the kingdoms had ever held both those positions at once.

Then again, no one had ever hammered the kingdoms into one tightly bound federation before. All three Marches, the tangled mountains of the Scion Kingdoms, and the nomadic tribes of the High Steppe. It was an honour for Sergeos to accompany him, and to learn what he could from such a master.

Ultrich Monhoven opened his hand as he turned it palm up. It was an odd, fluid gesture that seemed to have no purpose. Sergeos felt his skin prickle, and knew the Combat Prime was strengthening the spirit shield that hid them from outsiders.

"Is there anything in particular you want us to include in our report on the prince?" enquired Sergeos.

The older man looked troubled.

"We are only here to observe," he said at last.

Sergeos was surprised. He had assumed it was going to be a routine report on the prince's progress. What could possibly merit a change of plan?

Ultrich put up his hand, to forestall more questions.

"This will take some time," he said. "I think we had better make ourselves comfortable."

Down in the valley, the self-anointed unsound prince was finishing his breakfast.

He had been famished. Preparations for the village market had taken three days, and the work had been arduous. All the same, it had been good to spend time with his friends, and he had put his body to work with a will.

The empty plate went into the sink, before he called the sprite from its place in the forest. He used a gesture remarkably similar to his father's, though he didn't know it. A winged seed floated in through the open door, and Mono smiled. The sprite wouldn't be far behind it.

Or was the sprite hiding in the seed? He looked at the winged seed suspiciously, his brows coming down low over his eyes in an unusual display of forehead agility.

There was so much he didn't know about sprites, but he was relentless in all matters of the supernatural world. From the moment he had arrived in his new home he had been determined to learn the secrets of everything in the valley. And he was succeeding.

His own examination of the mysteries was much more satisfying than his abortive training at the Priatic School of Mysteries, though his studies in Karnassus had at least helped him get out of the Golden Palace. He had been an average student. There were times when he was sure the tutors let him pass simply because he was a Monhoven.

It was different here in the valley, and he was becoming sure of one thing in particular. There were rules behind the tricks and incantations the spirit masters used. Something that directed the way they controlled nature, and commanded the lower orders of spirit beings. There was a pattern to the Priatic Order of Mysteries, and he was going to find it!

For one thing the Order's methods seemed to take so long, and he was sure that wasn't necessary. The trouble was that he needed to be outside the system to see it. How could he become more not Mono?

Something pulled on the rough fabric of his breeches, and he looked down to see the sprite. It looked up at him enquiringly. He smiled ruefully at being caught out. Winged seed it was not.

He set the forest wisp to work, cleaning the porridge pot and the wooden ladle. Then he gave it instructions to air the lumpy mattress on the pallet, and make some attempt to block a number of thin slits in the walls. Some of the moss chinking had fallen out in the summer heat. Re-packing was needed now autumn had arrived.

He normally wouldn't mind doing these things himself, but today was market day!

He grabbed a few small coins, and a tightly woven overcoat that was warm and almost waterproof. Checking he had everything he needed, he headed for the door. As he closed it he wondered whether it was wise to leave the sprite unattended. Would he find the hut in worse condition, rather than better, when he got home?

He set out at a fast walk for the village. Before long he passed his makeshift lumber camp on the right. He thought again about the tree he had prepared for felling the day before.

Perhaps it would be better to get several trees ready at once. Then he could get some of his neighbours to help him, so it was all over in a day. But then he would owe each of them a day's labour in return, and he wasn't sure he could spare that much time.

He certainly needed the money from the wood though. He was determined not to go running to his father's people for a raku more than they'd given him when he first arrived.

He had cleared the brush from the overgrown clearing when he first came to the cottage, and soon discovered the area couldn't sustain enough animals to make a living, or produce a worthwhile grain crop. It seemed there was no choice but to carve more land out of the forest, hard work though that was.

Still, he had to take his smallholding seriously if his presence in the valley was to be believable. He didn't like deceiving people he had come to think of as friends, but he rarely thought of it as deceit these days. His life here seemed infinitely more real than his other one, in the capital city of the League. Karnassus now seemed very far away.

His father's clan council had given him the smallholding when the tenant, a soldier serving in the League armies, had been killed in the line of duty. The man had left no descendants, and it had been an easy matter to forge a letter that left everything to one of his brothers in arms, who in turn gifted it to his 'son', Mono. Not that he was called Mono here of course.

He still thought of himself as Mono. Not Prince Rossi Monhoven, the name he couldn't stomach, but just Mono. It was an unconscious acknowledgment of his lineage, though he didn't see it that way.

Mono turned onto a forest track, and into a tunnel of green under the trees. It wasn't long before he broke into another clearing, with another cottage to one side. Following the track along the side of the clearing, he plunged back into the forest.

It was darker here. The trees were bigger, and more densely thatched overhead. The gloom made him uneasy, as if there was danger in the darkness. He looked around, but saw nothing.

A faint glow came through the trees to one side. He figured there was a clearing further over, lit by the morning sun. For a moment he saw an odd shape of black and red through the trees. Then it was gone.

He walked on, and his mind rationalised the shape into several strangely garbed figures, all walking away from him. He realized with a start they were very like something he had seen in his dreams lately. But the forest was still, and quiet, and that made him question whether he had seen anything at all. After a moment's indecision he set off along the track again.

The sense of danger faded as he strode along, and he shook his head. He dismissed what he had seen as imagination. Things he saw in dreams stayed in dreams, he told himself. They didn't turn up in daily life.

It wasn't long before he came out of the forest and made his way past a row of cottages. They had been built side by side on a larger tract of land. It was a beautiful autumn morning, and an idyllic setting. The gentleness of the day slowly worked its magic on Mono, and he felt his spirits lift as he walked along.

The clearings eventually gave way to open land, and the first post and rail fences appeared. These were used to keep animals in, or in some cases out, of the fertile holdings around Shaker's Hope. There were a few men and women already in the fields, tending to necessary chores. They would be back inside soon, preparing for their part in market day.

Then the fields got smaller, given over to vegetables and fruit trees, and buildings loomed ahead. The track became a proper lane, and ran along the back of some stores that opened onto the main square. Mono was headed for one of the hunters' dens, where anything from skins to basic foodstuffs could be traded for coins or produce. He had arranged to meet his friends there.

He turned up the short path to the back entrance and found the den already open. He pushed his way through the hanging cloths that kept out flying insects, and a tall youth his own age called to him from the front of the shop.

"Hey there, Mudge, didn't expect you for a while yet!"

"You calling me a slouch, Jago?" he replied, feigning indignation. "Remember what happened last time you forgot your manners."

"Yep, I paddled your backside good and proper," came the reply.

Mono burst out laughing. Jago was his best friend in the valley, and as with many friendships they took a lot of liberty with the truth. Particularly when they were trying to outdo each other. Mudge was his name now, Mudge Wheeler, and it was a perfect name for a village surrounded by forest on the edges of the Wild Marches.

Mudge let his friend's comment pass – for now – and looked around the shop for the others.

"Where's Bear?" he asked, thinking it odd that Bear wasn't around. His friend usually ran the store when his father was busy elsewhere, as was the case today.

He was unsure about Bear's unusual name, or the story that Bear and his father had killed the mythical animals when they were many days west in The Wilderness. Bear's sister Shyleen wasn't there either, which was good. She always managed to look cool and elegant, and Mudge never knew what to say around her.

"Don't know," said Jago. Then he added, "Colma's gone to get something for me, and Luce is right behind you." Mudge spun around, and nearly collided with Andalucia.

A mischievous gleam shone in his eye, and he put on an offended air. "Trying to sneak up on me, huh," he said. "Think you can outfox us'n dumb country boys, do you?"

"It wouldn't be hard," she retorted. "You're deaf as a post, and that's when you're trying to hear me coming."

"Ar, well then, let'm lowly peasant carry the box for the l-a-a-a-d-y," he said, mocking her with the long title. Then he tried to take the box she was carrying over to Jago.

The peasant and lady routine always got a rise out of Luce. Mostly because it was unfair. She had the good fortune to be very down to earth, despite being the daughter of the mayor. A fierce tussle ensued for control of the box, which Mudge was winning.

Then Jago said, "cut it out you two. If you want to wrestle with her, Mudge, ask the mayor if you can walk out with her."

Mudge let go of the box like it was red-hot, and they both blushed furiously. The thought of walking out together must have occurred, subconsciously at least, to both of them. There was a strained silence until Colma walked in.

"Come on, you three," said Jago. "Bear wants to open the store in a few minutes, and I need help to get everything set up."

When Bear did turn up, a little later, Shyleen was with him. After a quick inspection of their efforts, Bear showed his appreciation with a nod. Jago was fast proving useful running the hunters' den when Bear was away, and moments later it was time to open the store for business.

Mudge took a seat at the back of the den. He was happy just to be present, and to join in the excitement of market day. His friends were with him, and that was what counted most.

He felt for the first time in his life that he belonged. There were a few awkward moments sometimes with Luce and Shyleen, but he didn't feel complete without the girls around either. Such were the mysteries of life. At least in this place he was simply Mudge Wheeler, one young man with a smallholding among many smallholders. Not Mono, and definitely not Prince Monhoven, and that felt good.

He worried that he might snap at one of his friends, showing something of his spoilt childhood at the palace, but that seemed less and less likely these days. Though he could still make a fool of himself when he felt unfairly accused of something.

He had decided that his temper had something to do with his mother's early death. Strangely, he felt responsible for her passing. He knew how stupid the thought was. He was only a child at the time, and nowhere near the hunting accident when it happened.

It hadn't helped that no-one, then or since, had told him any of the details. He felt himself steam up at the injustice of it, and made an effort to relax. What had happened to his mother seemed destined to remain a mystery of the past.

Fortunately, Jago asked him to pick up some spearheads and wheel rims from the smithy, and the errand gave him something to do. He snapped a mock salute before hurrying out into the sunlight and turned right.

Senovila's smithy stood by itself in a small field away from the square. This was a wise precaution, since smithies were well known for burning down. A stallion and several mares kept the rampant grasses and tatty scrub around it under control.

When Mudge had arrived in Shaker's Hope Senovila had been the first to take the boy under his wing. Mudge had really appreciated that. He hastened to see his friend, and mentor, once again.

TWO

The square was still mostly deserted. Mudge was halfway across it when he heard a disturbance ahead of him. A man's voice was raised in anger, and was suddenly choked off. Followed a moment later by the sound of several women screaming.

Then there were people running toward him, and his friends appeared outside the store, looking for the source of the commotion. In the distance, Senovila came charging out of the smithy. He had a square-headed hammer in one hand and a battleaxe in the other.

Looking in the direction of the noise, Mudge could eventually see what was happening. He stopped in his tracks. Three black-clad figures with red masks and ornate headpieces were striding rapidly in his direction. They wore long pleated skirts that brushed the ground, and they were callously murdering anyone in their way with long, curved swords held in either hand.

One of them raised a piece of carved amber enclosed in a loose net of gold, and swept the square with it. He turned it towards Mudge, and it flared into life. The three figures snapped their heads around, and began to run toward him. Their chilling cries curdled his blood.

Senovila was closing in on the black figures from behind. Then a spear hurtled toward the figures from the direction of the store, to be knocked contemptuously aside. Mudge felt something happening behind him, a prickling sensation similar to when he called a sprite.

One of the figures threw a knife that whistled past on Mudge's left, and the prickling sensation stopped abruptly. Then Jago burst past him, wielding a sword taken from the store. His first blow was deflected downward, and Mudge watched in horror as the sword held in the other hand opened his friend from hip to shoulder. Jago tumbled to the ground.

Then Bear and his father were next to him, swords drawn.

"Back up, boy," said the older man harshly, and they began to walk him back toward the store, but the trio were on them too quickly. Mudge continued to walk backward, trance-like, as the two men left him and tried desperately to keep the first of the attackers at bay.

As if in a dream he saw Senovila throw his axe, and the third figure fall face down with the axe blade buried in its back. The second attacker ran back and slid his sword under the swinging arc of Senovila's hammer. It cut across the smith's biceps, making him curse and drop the hammer. The swordsman flicked his sword back once more and ran Senovila through the heart. The shock of the sudden impaling showed on his friend's face.

Pulling his sword free from the toppling form, the swordsman whirled about and ran to help the attacker driving Bear and his father back. He stopped to dispatch one of the villagers, who tried to take him from the side with a short stabbing spear. Then he was in front of Mudge. One of the long, curved swords whipped round to take him in the neck.

Something clicked inside Mudge then. He felt in one moment all the anger he had tried to control for his whole life. Then he felt his outrage at what these . . . things . . . were doing to his friends, to his village. And he realized he was going to die.

So be it, he thought calmly, but someone was going to pay for this.

He reached up at a speed he didn't know he had, and caught the blade as it travelled toward him. He was surprised there was no pain. The metal of the blade felt odd. Malleable, eager, somehow alive.

He called up what spirit power he had, and sent it into the sword – though he knew that calling a forest sprite was a far cry from killing an experienced swordsman. The blade flashed like molten metal, and the swordsman tore his hand away from the other end, leaving most of the skin on his hand behind.

Mudge looked at the sword, now hanging in the air between them, and nudged it with his mind. It spun, decapitating his assailant. Sword and body toppled slowly toward the ground together.

Mudge looked at what he had done in surprise. Then the world seemed to speed up again. The body of the swordsman hit the ground, and the head rolled away from it. Mudge looked up, and saw the last of the attackers caught between the spears of angry villagers and a vigorous attack by Bear and his father.

The black-clad figure plucked something from its belt, and pushed it into the mouth behind the mask. Its body went rigid, then arched backward. It stayed upright by willpower alone for a few seconds, before it toppled onto the ground and was still.

Villagers poured into the square, wailing over the crumpled forms of their own people. One by one the dead were brought into the back of the store to be laid out, under the watchful eyes of Bear and his father. It was clear the body count was going to be high.

The victims all bore sickening wounds. The more faint-hearted of the living left the shop to sit along the wide veranda and collect their thoughts. Mudge forced himself to confront the still shapes of the friends and neighbours he had lost.

The first five bodies on the long trestles were villagers he knew only vaguely, but next to them lay Pieter Waldrow and his wife Valmar. Mudge had liked them both. They were good people. It was they who had first confronted the intruders, and paid for it with their lives.

Then there was Jago, white and motionless on the long table. And beside him Andalucia.

The loss of his closest friends wasn't registering yet. It was just a vague numbness that he would feel later. The loss of Andalucia in particular didn't make any sense. She was one of the few forces for good in the world. It seemed unfair that death had not respected that.

Then he realized she had been constructing a spirit veil for him. That had been the prickling sensation in the square. But the knife the attacker had thrown had taken her in the throat, and she had died instantly. How had she known what a spirit veil was, he wondered vaguely, and how to construct one?

Nonetheless, she had died bravely, trying to defend him, simply because he was her friend. It was too much of a revelation, and Mudge had to look away from the ruined body. He felt completely wooden, hardly able to move his arms and legs, so he left the back room of the store and made his way into the square.

He could see the bodies of the attackers where they had fallen. A funeral pyre was already being put together outside the village. No one thought the attackers worthy of burial and sacrament.

Mudge found Shyleen on the verandah, and they embraced naturally. It was amazing how grief removed any sense of embarrassment. Colma made his way dispiritedly in their direction, and the three of them clung together for a long time.

Bear finished laying out another of the villagers inside the store. Then he came out and stood with them. Six of us, thought Mudge, with everything to look forward to, reduced to four. Jago and Luce hadn't even lived yet! Tears filled his eyes.

The last of the fallen were carried past, and Mudge realized shakily that Senovila was not among them. He said so to Bear, who put his finger to his lips in an odd way. Then he said quietly, "wait here until I get Ochren."

When the older man returned, he motioned for Mudge to follow him. The young man shrugged, and trudged dispiritedly after him. They made their way toward the smithy.

It seemed odd to Mudge that Senovila had been laid out in the smithy, and not with the others in the store. Still, he had suspected that the smith was from another land. Perhaps this was a foreign custom. Senovila himself was dark skinned. Though that could be explained by his work in the smithy, around the charcoal fire and the strange fluxes for working metal.

His wife was another matter altogether. She was short, rather round, and almost excessively plain. She spoke the common tongue roughly, and talked to her husband in some Xaanian dialect Mudge couldn't understand. It was rare for inhabitants of the powerful but increasingly decadent empire to the north to make their way this far south.

Ochren led the way through the smithy, and into a room at the back. Senovila had been placed in a great armchair on one side of the room. A thick wad of bandages over his heart bulked large under his shirt.

His wife had cleaned him up nicely, though his skin was now pale and waxen. Mudge wondered if their customs would allow her to bury him with the rest of the villagers.

Arnima, for that was her name, looked absolutely haggard. More, it seemed to Mudge, than even grief could bestow on a person. He was moved out of his own pain for a moment to consider her loss. She and Senovila must have been a couple for many years.

As he turned back to look at Senovila, he saw the smith's chest rise and fall in a ragged breath. Startled, he spun round to look more closely.

"Ochren, he's alive," he hissed.

"I know," said Ochren evenly.

"But he was dead, I saw it myself," said Mudge, unable to hide his disbelief.

"He was," said Ochren. There was a long pause.

"It's Arnima's doing," added Ochren at last.

"There's much you don't know about your time here, Mudge Wheeler, but it's not up to me to tell you these things. Senovila will answer your questions – when he's recovered from his ordeal."

"Yes, when he has recovered," said Mudge softly in wonder. Ochren patted him on the shoulder, and made his way back through the front of the smithy. He was going to make arrangements for the dead at the store.

What sort of creature was Arnima, thought Mudge, if she could bring back the dead? The idea astounded him.

Then he remembered Luce casting a spirit veil, and he wondered how she had known about that. He stopped for a moment, as his heart contracted painfully at the thought she was dead. Then he forced himself to carry on with his line of reasoning.

People with a connection to the spirit world were rare. That there were two of them, Arnima and Andalucia, in the one valley didn't make sense. His mind flicked to Ochren and Bear, who had managed to hold their own against the first swordsman. They were skilled fighters, far too skilled for the villagers they were supposed to be.

Then he understood. These people were all there to protect him. His father had planted these people in Shaker's Hope years before he arrived in the village as his bodyguard. But somehow, word of his presence had got out, and those black-clad swordsmen had come for him.

He remembered the amulet of amber and gold, and how it had flared into life when it was aimed at him. Now it made sense. They were assassins, trying to weaken the Monhoven line. They were trying to destroy the heirs to the throne, and he wondered if there had been other attacks.

But it meant he had caused the death of every villager that now lay on trestles at the back of Ochren's store. And it also meant he had killed his closest friend, and the first girl he'd ever had real feelings for.

Was that what it meant, he thought, to be of the Monhoven line? To bring death and destruction? Would those closest to him always have to live in fear? It made him feel sick to his stomach.

On a ridge at the head of the valley, two figures were using their farsight to observe him closely.

"Is that enough death for you," snorted Sergeos sharply. He didn't know why they hadn't intervened during the attack on the village. He couldn't believe that the Legatus had refused to protect his own son, and his frustration had finally overwhelmed his respect for his teacher.

Sergeos' farsight was stretched to its limit, following what was happening inside the smithy, but he was able to see most of it. Ultrich, he had no doubt, was seeing it all. In his mind that damned the Combat Prime even more.

When Ultrich spoke, his voice was steady. "He is still my son, Sergeos, but you forget that sometimes duty comes before kinship." There was a long pause, while Sergeos struggled to bring his feelings under some sort of control.

"But why?" he exploded in time.

"Why?" said the Legatus slowly. "Which of a hundred threads of destiny do you want to examine? He is already a man, and he must now make his own choices. We cannot control events from behind the scenes for him. If we did, the rest of the world would know he was weak. And more importantly his heart would know he didn't have it in him. He would never develop the confidence he is going to need, and need very soon.

"We saw him claim his power today, and it had to be called up by a matter of life and death. It would not have happened if we had stepped in."

Ultrich's voice softened. "How do we manipulate the spirit world, Sergeos?"

Sergeos looked across at him, a breeze rippling along the ridge and flapping his robes momentarily. What was the Combat Prime talking about?

"We harness the shards of power left over in hidden places from the creation of the world. We have to awaken them, tie them to our will, and then tell them exactly what we want them to do. It's ritual, pattern and ceremony. All very elaborate, and all very slow.

"Did you see the boy perform any ritual? Do you detect any spirit totems on him, any power he used that was bound to something he carries?"

Sergeos thought about it, and shook his head.

"He connects straight to the source, Sergeos. He thinks and it is done."

"What is this 'source', *Alfas*? There is nothing in the Mysteries of the Priatic Order about this." The Combat Prime leaned heavily on his staff, as if all this wearied him.

"Nonetheless, it exists, old friend. Outside our world perhaps, but it exists. The original power that created the world."

His voice dropped to a whisper. "And just possibly, it might be our ally in the terrible battles to come."

"What battles?" Sergeos forced himself to say, a feeling of unease coming over him.

Ultrich dropped his head onto his chest, and his voice, whether he intended it or not, sounded hollow, something echoing in a graveyard.

"A dark power will rise in Xaan, Sergeos. At first the people will embrace it, thinking it will restore the former glories of their empire. By the time they realize they are nothing but slaves, it will be too late.

"The power that will rise in Xaan is allied to an ancient evil. One from the forsaken realms, a sorceress from the dawn of time. If she is not stopped, her soulless legions will eventually find their way into this world."

Ultrich paused for a moment.

"If my son doesn't grow into the power within him, there will be no other who can match her."

Sergeos was speechless. He was barely able to take in this sudden revelation. Eventually he dropped his head in surrender. If the Legatus said it was so, then it was so.

It seemed that Ultrich too felt he had said enough. He gathered his energies, ready to transport the two of them back to the Golden Palace. As he concentrated on the task a rockfall cascaded down a slope on the opposite side of the valley. When it settled into place, the two men were gone.

In Shaker's Hope the following day, Senovila was much improved. Mudge could hardly believe the change in him.

"Ah, the old girl knows what she's doing," said Senovila from his armchair. His voice was filled with affection. Arnima beamed with pride, and looked for a moment like a young girl again. There was no doubting the deep bond between the unlikely couple.

Senovila rose, a little unsteadily, from his chair. With Arnima fussing about him, he made his way to the front of the building. When she had him settled comfortably in a chair in his beloved smithy, Arnima left him with Mudge.

"Just wanted to see everything was all right out here," said Senovila, looking round with a practised eye at his tools. Nothing, apparently, was out of place. "And there are some things Arnima doesn't need to hear just yet. Women worry unnecessarily sometimes."

Mudge nodded, though he wasn't sure what that meant. Senovila had taken a chair along the back wall, and it allowed him to see the foundry and the main entrance at the same time. Mudge sat on a bench next to him, finding a spot amongst a tangle of metal implements that needed various amounts of repair.

"Those men, they were assassins, weren't they?" blurted out Mudge at last. "They were looking for me." His voice caught. "All those people died because of me."

Senovila was silent for a long time.

"There are no easy decisions in leadership," he said at last. "Which choice would you have taken. The risk that a few might die now, or the greater certainty that thousands will die later?"

"What do you mean?" said Mudge. "How could thousands die?"

There had been peace in the League since his father had united the kingdoms, and that was before Mudge was born. He had no concept of death on such a scale. Senovila looked away. Mudge could see he didn't like being the bearer of bad news.

"War is coming, my young friend," he said at last. "This little skirmish was the start of it. Others of the Monhoven family, all those in line for the throne, will have come under attack as well. Or soon will be."

Mudge started. He hadn't thought much about the rest of his family, his aunts and uncles and cousins. Holy gods, were they alright? How would he find out?"

"Take it easy, Mudge," said Senovila kindly. "The Legatus keeps me up with the news, and I'll let you know how your family are."

Mudge was aware that his father could do that. A spirit hawk covered vast distances instantaneously, and spoke in his father's voice. Still, it meant Senovila was a lot closer to the Legatus than he had first thought. He was more than just a soldier sent to guard Mudge's life in Shaker's Hope.

"You're the Legatus' man," said Mudge quietly. Senovila nodded. When he said nothing more, Senovila sighed.

"You want to hear the whole story, I see. Well, I guess you deserve that."

He made himself comfortable in his chair.

"I was a commander in the royal guard at Xianak," he began. "The High Council of Xaan sent a company of our best soldiers to kill your father. I was their leader."

Senovila sighed again. "It was a long time ago, and I was young. Do you understand?"

Mudge rather doubtfully nodded.

"Your father was travelling along the border of our country on his way to the Independent Kingdoms on a diplomatic mission.

"He was at the start of his adult life, well before he became Legatus. But the High Council of Xaan was alarmed at the way he was uniting the southern kingdoms behind him.

"I didn't know it at the time, but he was already Combat Prime of the Priatic Order. Though my company outnumbered his bodyguard two to one, he was just too powerful. In the end all of my troops had been killed or captured, but he and I fought on. He wouldn't let any of his bodyguard intervene. It was just man on man.

"There was one moment," . . . here Senovila rolled his eyes in disbelief . . . "when I swear my sword went right through him like he was a wraith. Or maybe he tricked my mind into believing that. But he couldn't best me. Then he asked me how I'd got the spirit cloak I was wearing.

"I had no idea what he was talking about. I just thought I was fast, very fast, but eventually I could see that something was slowing his attacks.

"Then I began to understand what must have happened.

"I'd met Arnima at the healing tents. She had patched me up after one of the worst battles I had ever been in. I thought I was going to die.

"She was a skinny wee thing then, but I spent a lot of time in her care. It took a while, but we fell in love. Maybe there was more than a bit of gratitude on my part for her saving my life, but in the end I could see we were a good match.

"I knew she had powers of some sort. Gods' death, I should have died after that battle, but she healed my wounds somehow. So I figured this spirit cloak thing must have been her work. It was her way of protecting me."

Senovila paused, and looked straight at Mudge.

"Then your father did an unusual thing. He let me go. He told me there was evil coming to these lands. To the southern kingdoms and Xaan alike.

"If I wanted to, I could start a new life in the south preparing for what was to come, or I could return to Xaan. He told me to go away and think about it.

"I talked it over with Arnima, and we accepted his offer.

"The rest of the story you know, or must have guessed. When you were sent here your father's people were already waiting for you."

Mudge was silent for a while. At least Senovila wasn't hiding anything from him, and that was a welcome change. Most of his life seemed to be a collection of missing segments and unknown things.

He was also thinking about Senovila and Arnima. He wanted a relationship like they had one day, though he worried that he wouldn't know what to do when it arrived. His mother had died when he was young, and he had few recollections of her talking and laughing with his father.

He was touched for a moment by one precious thought. His father had never married again. Perhaps that was an indication of how much his mother had meant to him. At least it was something, when he had too little proof of a happy family life in his past. Then he forced his mind back to the conversation with Senovila.

"Ochren and Bear, both my father's people?" he said. Senovila nodded.

"Tell me about Andalucia," said Mudge guardedly.

"Ah," said Senovila. "Her mother is a spirit walker your father sent here, and she brought her daughter with her. Then she met and married the local mayor. I'm not sure how much he knows about all this."

Mudge nodded. He barely knew Luce's parents. They seemed to keep to themselves, apart from their duties on the council, but the mother would explain the daughter's powers. They didn't always transfer to the children of spirit bearers, but it was likely. It would also explain her training, at least to the extent she could cast a spirit veil.

"But why all this protection for me?" he said at last. "And why the assassins? I'm a minor prince destined for a dutiful life as a Regent of the Eastern Marches. It's probably the League's oldest and most loyal dominion."

Senovila just looked at him, until the silence became uncomfortable.

"I'm not going to rule the Eastern Marches?" said Mudge uncertainly.

"Very good," said Senovila.

"So I have another destiny?" said Mudge.

"Which will take you where it takes you," said Senovila, with an air of finality. There was a long silence while Mudge digested this.

"Do you prefer your new life over your old one?" he asked the old smith suddenly.

Senovila laughed at the unexpected question. "In Xaan I was an aristocrat, Sien O'Villa. I was involved in politics and character assassination. Here I am Senovila and I work with metals. I think I like it better here. Having Arnima with me helps. Home is wherever she is.

"And above all, your father may yet be the salvation of us all. He's a very capable man, Mudge, and a good one."

Mudge wasn't so sure about that, but he was left with a great many things to think about.

THREE

Mudge stayed with Ochren and Bear at the trading store that night. The bunk room at the back of the store had become familiar to him over the last two years, but there was a lot different this time round.

The bodies of the slain villagers lay on trestles in the front room, though the period of mourning was almost over. The store had been filled that day with people saying goodbye to friends they had known forever. People who had been an inseparable part of the village family.

The night, when it came, was eerily still. Mudge didn't mind the bodies lying on the other side of the wall from him. They were good people, and he feared no evil from them, alive or dead.

The next day he woke early, and was up as soon as it was light. There was activity in the sprawling kitchen at the back of the store, and he made his way there. Ochren kept a well-stocked kitchen. He was used to traders using his place as a base, or villagers making preparations for a hunting expedition.

Mudge slotted in beside Bear, mixing grains for the traditional breakfast. Shyleen was running back and forth taking wooden bowls and spoons to another room. Mudge smiled at her dishevelled look.

There were smears of batter across her working shift. Curls had escaped from the hair she had pulled back tightly behind her head. She was finding it hard to look cool and collected under these conditions.

Then he remembered, with a start, his discussion with Senovila yesterday. The whole Ochren 'family' had been planted in the village. They had been chosen for their skills, and sent here to be his bodyguard. That meant Shyleen probably wasn't Bear's sister, and maybe neither of them were related to Ochren. Mudge wondered idly what Shyleen's skills as a bodyguard were.

"Everything is ready for the burials," said Bear, coming up alongside Mudge in the kitchen. He handed over a bag of salt to use with the grains.

"We also need to collect ash from the funeral pyres and add it to the fertiliser stocks," he continued. Whatever was left from the bonfires that consumed the three assassins would be scraped up and put in the ash pits. The villagers knew the benefits of sprinkling wood ash across their fields before the spring rains.

Mudge mused wryly that at least in death the assassins would be put to some good use, their bodies helping to restore the fertility of the land. Then he was struck by something, and lowered the bag of salt to the table. He stood motionless for a long time, looking off into space.

"Sprite got you?" said Bear, conjuring up a tale told to the village children. Sprites were supposed to prey upon children who were lazy. They sent them wandering off into the woods, entranced by visions, or the smell of food.

"I can't do it, Bear," he said, suddenly certain of the fact. "I can't just carry on doing what we've always done, pretending everything is normal."

Bear stopped stirring the grain mixture, and listened attentively.

Mudge was struggling with his feelings. He knew he had been happy at Shaker's Hope. He had begun to discover what it was to be himself, and he had made good friends here. 'Used to have' good friends here, in the case of Jago and Luce, he reminded himself bitterly. It hurt so much to think about them now.

"We have to do something. We have to fight back!" he said suddenly.

He lifted his head to look Bear squarely in the eyes. "Spirit knows I'm no damn good at anything, really. But I'd rather die trying to put this mess right than do nothing. Jago and Luce would have done the same for me."

Bear was smiling now. He slapped Mudge firmly on the shoulder. "Glad you agree, then," he said. "We leave tomorrow morning."

Bear lifted his hand away, barely able to stop himself from laughing as he went back to the grains he was preparing.

Mudge's brain whirled as he tried to make sense of what Bear was saying. What were they going to do, run away from Shaker's Hope? Or take the fight to whoever had ordered the assassination attempt? But how would they do that?

He made an attempt to stop his runaway thoughts. There was more than himself to consider here. Senovila had said the whole Monhoven line had been targeted, and he was still waiting to hear from the smith if any of the assassination attempts had been successful.

Mudge realized the whole League must be mobilizing to counter the threat from Xaan, but that didn't tell him what Bear and Ochren had in mind. Where were they going in the morning? Was Senovila part of it?

He forced himself to think more slowly. Bear and Ochren were his father's men, so they would do what they were told to do. What would the Legatus do in this situation?

Mudge felt a cold chill run down his back. It hadn't taken him long to work out where they were going. It was what his father had always done. They must be going straight to the heart of the problem, and by the fastest possible route. That meant they would be crossing the mountains, and heading straight for the heart of Xaan. Ultrich Monhoven never waited for events to come to him. He struck first. He bypassed the posturing and the empty displays of enemy might, and struck at the heart of his enemy's power.

It was an all or nothing gambit that had served the Legatus well. Mudge hoped fervently that it would work just as well for the group leaving in the morning. He didn't like the fact, but his father's plans tallied perfectly with his own need for vengeance.

It was a strange little party that left Shaker's Hope the following day. Senovila had harnessed the horses he kept round the smithy, and fitted them out as pack animals. They had a type of netting slung on either side of a long saddle.

Mudge had always thought of them as farm horses, slow but enduring. Now he saw them more closely, he realized his mistake. These were warhorses.

They lifted their feet impatiently when he approached, eager to meet the next challenge. They were heavily muscled, and precious stores of metal had been used to make boots that covered their feet to the top of their wide hooves. One kick would kill a man.

Senovila must have brought the horses from Xaan when he came to Shaker's Hope, or their sires before them. Mudge didn't have the farmer's eye for guessing their ages.

When he looked around there were dappled green outfits everywhere. Bear, Ochren and Shyleen were no longer hiding what they were, elite rangers in the Karnatic Defence Forces.

The oddly patched greens of their clothing made them invisible in forest or scrub. Senovila was being outfitted in the same colours by Arnima, much to his annoyance. Whether the annoyance was at the uniform, or Arnima fussing about him in the presence of the others, was hard to tell.

"Who's going to want to skewer an old smith like me?" he protested. "They'll just think I'm the cook or something. Anyway, I'd like to see them try!"

A triumphant gleam shone in his eye as he balanced himself on his feet and recalled the many victories of his youth. Mudge conceded it would still take a great deal to stop the old warrior.

"You know how archers like to pick out someone in different colours," said Arnima firmly. She looped a pair of breeches around Senovila's hands and tied them off to stop him waving his arms around. Then she checked the fit across his shoulders. Senovila subsided, embarrassed that she had so easily trussed him like a chicken.

Mudge was surprised to see Colma in brown and russet clothing. He was not, apparently, one of the rangers. He had, however, been hunting with Bear and Ochren often enough for them to trust him in the wilderness, and Colma had been adamant from the start that his friend's weren't going anywhere without him.

Arnima was also going. Mudge had half expected that. She was middle-aged and a round little thing, hardly suitable for the rigours of the weeks and months ahead, but the bond between her and Senovila was unbreakable. He decided her strange 'healing skills' might come in handy too.

A trader couple, Mareet and Liam Cathart, completed the group. Mudge had seen them around Shaker's Hope before. He had thought it odd they used the place as a base to trade from.

Most of the traders he knew did a much wider circuit, hoping to trade the products of one region to another. That way they got the best prices. Now he understood that the Catharts had been checking who came and went around Shaker's Hope, and which people in surrounding villages had been asking about this village. It had been part of the way they protected Mudge.

Mareet seemed to take pains to look ordinary. Mudge figured that was part of her role. She seemed so much part of the background that people forgot she was there. Then she would overhear secrets not meant for her. Or pluck a blade from her sleeve, and use it before the target realized an enemy was that close.

Liam said little. Like her he seemed to fit into his surroundings wherever he was, and he could have been taken for a man of few words in any village.

Mudge remembered Liam walking round Shaker's Hope with his head down, his eyes vacant. Now, he was completely different. He strode like a man with purpose. His eyes flicked up just once to weigh up Mudge, then snapped back to more important things.

When the little party was ready to go, Mudge counted nine travellers including himself. Some had packs, but most had bulky waist harnesses that left their arms free. They waited patiently as Mudge struggled into the last of the packs. It seemed odd they had to carry so much when they had horses, but the reasons were soon made clear.

"Idea of mine I've been wanting to try out," said Senovila enthusiastically, as Mudge fell into step beside him. "A lightweight cart that can be carried in pieces on the back of two horses. When there's a group of us, and so much mixed terrain, it could be just the thing!"

Mudge realized there was an inventor inside his smithy friend, and he had to admit the cart idea would make sense when they came to level ground. Senovila must have seen a dozen ways to improve things when he was a commander in the Xaanian army. Now he had a chance to try some of them out.

"I can see wheels, and an axle," said Mudge, "and a few boards over there, but where's the rest of the cart?"

"Ah," said Senovila. "We have to build that out of what we find in our travels."

Mudge nodded. If they could get the cart working, and hitched to the horses, they would cover a lot more ground. Though that wouldn't happen until they were through The Wilderness, and onto the flats of The Gap. It was the most direct route north, and the fastest way to get to Xaan.

"I thought the burial service went well," said Mudge, his voice catching despite his determination to make light of the matter.

"Never easy saying goodbye," said Senovila bluntly. Mudge realized the smith must have lost a lot of people over his years as an army commander. Senovila's experience of death seemed to lessen his own losses, but Mudge refused to get hardened by it. He suspected Senovila's bluntness was just a cover for his own deeper feelings too.

Jago had died for him, and that was a debt he could never repay. So had Luce. But on top of that there had been a special connection to Luce he would never be able to explore now. He missed all those days and years ahead, the opportunity to find out where that special connection might have led them. He had to make the deaths of his two friends mean something.

The day was beginning to warm up when Senovila sought him out, and drew him away from the others.

"You wanted to know about your family, boy," he said, and Mudge's ears pricked up. They had been so busy over the last day and a half he'd almost forgotten Senovila's promise.

"They're all alive," said Senovila, and Mudge felt a huge sense of relief. His father must have sent Senovila a spirit hawk with the news.

"Your uncle Evant Monhoven was badly wounded, but he'll live. It was an attack much like the one we had here. He's king of one of the Scion Kingdoms isn't he? Elsewhere the assassins were stopped before they did any damage to the royal line."

It was clear that whatever was stirring in Xaan had made a co-ordinated attempt to remove the leadership of the Karnatic League. That would have reduced the League to a collection of self-governed kingdoms, which would have been easy to conquer one at a time.

"The attacks were just what your father wanted," said Senovila, and Mudge stared at him in disbelief. Ultrich would never want his own family attacked, surely. He knew his father well enough to know that. But Senovila went on to explain.

"It brought out all the enemy agents inside the League," he said, "and the Legatus was ready for them. None of them, as far as we know, got away. Let Ottar Bey chew on that for a while!"

The head of the Xaanian Council had died less than a year ago in mysterious circumstances, and many of the members of the Council had also been killed in the same 'accident'.

One of the nobles, Ottar Bey, had been trying to get onto the Council for some time, and no one knew where he was getting so much gold from to pave the way. He was able to take advantage of the power vacuum to put his name forward. Then he was made First Elect in similarly strange circumstances when his main rival died. It was fast and underhand work, and Senovila muttered about something unholy stirring in Xaan.

"Ultrich is certain Ottar Bey was behind the assassination attempts here," continued the smith, "and Xaan has started picking fights with the nearest of the Independent Kingdoms. I'll bet Ottar Bey is behind that too."

The trail climbed into the ranges of The Wilderness, and soon became little more than a hunter's track. Horses and people alike were reduced to single file, and the horses with their heavy loads had to be coaxed up the worst stretches of steep, crumbling track.

They were not the only members of the party that had to be coaxed. Arnima was puffing and wheezing before she'd been two minutes on the steep slopes. Senovila offered his arm so she could lean on him, but she pushed him away and struggled on.

She was furious with herself for holding them up, and close to tears. Liam tied a rope to one of the pack horse's saddles, and handed her the other end. It was a simple and effective solution. Arnima continued up the track, more dragged along than climbing, and the travellers rested often.

The little party came out onto a broad ridge just before midday, and Ochren called a halt. Mudge suddenly realized that Shyleen was no longer with them. In fact, he hadn't seen her for some time. Bear didn't seem concerned though.

"She'll be back soon," he said, as he took a large upside down metal funnel from one of the packs on the horses. He set the contraption on the ground, and Mudge watched him feed dry twigs into the base of it and set them alight. It was time for a quick boil up, and a miniature heat haze soon appeared over the top end of the funnel.

"No smoke," said Mudge, looking at the metal funnel. Bear smiled.

"Standard ranger issue," he said quietly. "Lots of small twigs, dry as you can get them. That's the secret."

Mudge looked up to see Shyleen standing beside them. He jumped up, startled.

Bear laughed out loud. "Stop sneaking up on the boy," he said. "He's got enough on his mind without you scaring the spirits out of him as well."

"I wasn't scared!" replied Mudge indignantly. Shyleen shrugged non-committally.

"She's a scout," said Bear, dropping a cap with metal arms on the funnel. He filled it with the water he wanted to boil.

"Any ranger is capable of doing a good job as a scout, but Shyleen's the best. She senses things, even when she can't see or hear them."

Mudge opened his spirit sense a little, and quickly closed it again. He had seen a connection between Shyleen and her surroundings that had nothing to do with her senses. A hazy spider web of light trails that extended from her into the trees around them, and it went out further than eyes or ears ever could.

"I believe you," he said, with a small shiver. It was bad enough trying to come to terms with his own power, he didn't want to know there were others around him with equally strange abilities.

Now that Mudge could see Shyleen in her ranger's uniform, he realized the camaraderie between Shyleen and Bear was the closeness of those who train and work together, not that of a brother and sister.

"Is Ochren your father?" he blurted out, looking at Bear. Bear looked up at him slowly, then looked at Shyleen. She nodded.

"Yes," said Bear. "It's unusual for two members of the same family to be rangers. If it does happen, they're not normally allowed to work together.

"Family bonds can be stronger than the rules rangers have to live by, and that can get people killed. But Ochren asked for me to be allocated to him on this assignment." He shrugged. "I have certain, ah, unusual skills he thinks may be useful."

Mudge turned his gaze toward Shyleen. She shook her head. He hadn't thought she was Ochren's daughter, but there had been something about the way Bear and Ochren had fought together at Shaker's Hope that made him think they were of the same flesh and blood.

Then Mudge remembered Luce and her mother. They had both been spirit walkers. Apparently that wasn't as unusual as rangers working together. Whichever way you looked at it, all these people had put their lives on the line for him. He was still unbearably embarrassed about that.

From the top of the ridge Mudge could see the wide depression in the hills that had Shaker's Hope at its centre. He couldn't see the village itself, though the fields were visible.

Beyond the depression the hills smoothed out into the rich, flat country of the Wild Marches. Though life had became pretty settled, and tame, since Ultrich had brought the Marches together at the very start of the Karnatic League.

The small party was moving into the heart of The Wilderness now. Somewhere ahead of them were the cultivated fields of little Wensh, and the border with giant Beltainia, the closest of the

Independent Kingdoms. Mudge wondered if areas like The Wilderness would continue to be wild forever, or would become tamed like the Wild Marches.

When it was time to set off again, Mudge could not resist one last farewell look in the direction of Shaker's Hope. He felt miserably nostalgic, and wondered if he would ever see it again. He had been catapulted into the middle of things he didn't understand, and any number of unknown forces could swat him like a fly. Still, he knew that fear was a choice. He put his fears firmly behind him, and fell in behind one of the horses.

Bear and Mudge trudged along together until the track started to descend off the ridge. Then Mudge found himself next to Colma. He noticed the young man's awkwardness at his presence as he walked beside him.

Ochren must have told Colma who Mudge really was, and what the assassination attempt meant. That was fair, since he was coming with them into the unknown, but it seemed Colma was having trouble knowing how to deal with Karnatic royalty.

Mudge thumped him on the arm, and said, "remember when we put field mice in the pockets of Shyleen's overalls after she'd changed for market day, and Luce found them. She went through the roof! Then she blamed you, and wouldn't believe that 'nice new boy' could have done anything so horrid?"

Colma snorted to himself, and a grin appeared on his face.

That's better, thought Mudge.

"We have to stick together," said Mudge in a whisper. "We're the only ones who aren't some sort of super soldier that can make a weapon out of a soup ladle and kill ten men with it."

A solid thump landed squarely between his shoulder blades. "I can hear that, you know," said Bear, pretending to be angry. They all laughed.

"But what, er, exactly, should I call you?" said Colma.

"Call me Mudge," said Mudge. "That way no one will know who I am, and since I look the least like a prince out of all of us, they'll kill you lot while I sneak off."

Colma thumped him on the arm while Bear put a stranglehold around his neck. Mudge begged for mercy until Bear let him go. But Colma was looking a lot more relaxed, and Mudge knew he'd done the right thing. Senovila could have told him right then that he was his father's son all the way down to his toenails. His father was aloof in affairs of state and 'one of the boys' when the chips were down. Certainly when he was part of a team facing down a threat to the League.

Mudge, on the other hand, wouldn't have wanted to hear that.

The travellers trudged north for hours along the valley floor, until at last another track turned west again. As they laboured up the next ridge, Mudge wondered when they'd make camp. It was getting dark, and they hadn't started an evening meal yet.

Near the top of the ridge his questions were answered. The track ran along underneath a limestone overhang on their left. At one point in the limestone a fair-sized cave ran off into the darkness.

"That's us for the day," called out Ochren, and the little party slowed gratefully to a stop. Shyleen descended from one side of the ridge, carrying two plump, heavy birds. She had taken them out of a tree with carefully placed arrows.

"Tame as all get out!" she exclaimed. "Hardly anyone hunts this far in. The woods are full of easy pickings."

Bear had his funnel-shaped metal stove out and fired up in a matter of minutes. Mudge noticed Liam had one working as well. Arnima coiled the rope that was pulling her up the slope across the horse's packsaddle, and sat down, breathing heavily. But it wasn't long before she was up and helping Mareet and Ochren prepare a meal. Mudge was impressed. At this rate she would trim down and shape up in a matter of weeks.

They spent their first night in The Wilderness in relative comfort. The cave was dry, and held in the warmth. A hastily made bed of ferns and bracken allowed each of them a good night's sleep, and Shyleen and Bear took turns on lookout.

Just before dawn Mudge woke inside one of his dreams. He was growing insanely tall again. He looked around, and saw a bright day had risen over the Marches. His vantage point rose until he could see the Independent Kingdoms over The Wilderness on his left, and the city of Xianak over the Scaffold Mountains to the north.

This time, the dream was different. A giant black figure was standing triumphantly astride Xianak, while armies poured forth from the east, west, and southern gates of the great city.

Mudge had seen his father's maps, and he knew where the trade routes ran across the land. The army heading west would fall upon Beltainia first, and then the rest of the Independent Kingdoms. The army heading south would attack the hill tribes of the High Steppes. His mother's people.

The troops travelling west would overrun the coastal port of Mishvart in less than a week. If Mudge was guessing right, they would slaughter the jungle tribes on the other side of the Galleon Straits. Then they would take over the gold and silver mines in the hills.

Mudge woke as the dream began to fade, and was pleased to find every detail still fresh in his mind. He looked around. Dawn was just beginning to coat the forest in a soft grey, and he could see Senovila next to Ochren at the mouth of the cave. He hurried over to talk to them.

The information he had learned from the dream might be something his father already knew, but he wasn't going to take any chances. Senovila could send a message faster than anyone if he could call Ultrich's spirit hawk. Somehow, too, they had to get troops onto the High Steppes to support the hill tribes, and it looked like they didn't have long.

FOUR

"The Legatus will want to hear about this," said Senovila, looking off into space. "He needs all the information he can get. War is a game of strategy on a grand scale, and details can make all the difference!"

Senovila sounded worried, and Mudge wondered why.

"I can't get the Legatus' attention any time I want to," said the old smith. "Mostly I leave it to him to contact me. He checks in when it's been a while, or he's got new orders for me.

"You're going to have to contact him yourself, boy," said Senovila. He looked straight at Mudge in a way that said they had no other option.

Mudge felt the ground open under him. He'd got a sprite to do the dishes, more or less, and he had been lucky against one assassin, though he wondered if one of the others hadn't helped him out. Now they wanted him to send a spirit hawk? The thought of imminent humiliation sent waves of fear coursing through him.

"Ah, that's asking a bit much of me, really," he managed to croak. At least I've got the courage to tell the truth, he thought.

"I'll make you a staff," said Senovila helpfully, and hurried off to look for a young sapling. Ochren went with him.

Mudge wondered gloomily whether a staff might just increase his limited powers a bit.

"Staff's an old fakir's trick," said Senovila in a whisper to Ochren. They were cutting a staff out of a tough-looking sapling further up the trail.

"It doesn't make a bit of difference, but we have to get the boy to try. Ultrich said it might come to this."

Ochren nodded thoughtfully. As a ranger captain he just took orders and gave them to others, but it looked like Senovila's world was more complicated. It must come from being closer to the

Legatus, he thought. It would be an interesting life, being in charge of the Legatus' son.

Senovila hurried over to one of the packsaddles. He had finished working the sapling down to the heartwood. Now he dug around in the bag of bits that went with the axles for the cart, and came up with some flat straps of metal.

"These should do nicely," he said. Then he lifted out a small, round-headed hammer. Ochren set to work slimming down the wooden ends to take the metal sleeves.

Mudge thanked them solemnly when they presented the staff to him. Inwardly he didn't think it would help much. Still, he was going to respect their efforts.

He motioned for the two of them to follow, and climbed a small promontory on the ridge. He wanted as few people around as possible when he failed at the task.

When they arrived at the rocky top of the promontory, he turned in the direction of Karnassus. The Legatus was most likely to be in the Golden Palace, in the heart of the great city. It would make things easier if he could sense his father's presence before trying to make contact.

He took a deep breath. The staff felt heavy and reassuring in his hands. He closed his eyes and concentrated. There was nothing. He tried again. This time he thought he registered a faint scent at the edge of his senses.

It reminded him, perhaps, of the astringency in the air after a lightning strike. It was silly to say spirit power had an earthly smell, but he had always thought of it as being like lightning and cinnamon.

There were other barely distinguishable smells, all at the very edge of his senses. Each one denoted a power of some description. He thought one of them was Shyleen. Another had no smell at all, but he knew it was there, and he knew it was Arnima.

Mudge concentrated on a growing smell of lightning and cinnamon. This was his father, or at least a concentration of spirit walkers close to his father. He might even have stumbled on the inner sanctum of the Priatic Order of Mysteries, not far from the Golden Palace.

Whoever it was, they would have to mark the receiving end of the message. Opening a spirit trail, and sending a spirit hawk along it, took a lot less energy when there was a clear destination. From the vantage point of the ridge, if he gave it everything he had, they might just be able to detect him.

He took a firm grip on the staff, and 'knocked' as hard as he could at the awareness he had sensed in Karnassus.

A window blinked opened in the air in front of him. Mudge stepped back, startled. This wasn't how spirit walkers were supposed to send spirit hawks.

On the other side of the window his father appeared, bent almost double. He slowly straightened up. His hands were over his ears, and there was a look of pain on his face. Ultrich blinked several times, and then focused on the window in front of him. He recognized Mudge.

"Hell's teeth, Rossi," he grunted. "We're not on the other side of the Galleon Straits!"

The Legatus looked around, and spoke quickly to someone Mudge couldn't see. Then he turned back to his son.

"One of my army commanders is flat on his back with blood pouring out of his nose," he said grimly, "and one of my city councillors is halfway down a tree in the garden. Thank the gods he went through an open window, and not into a brick wall."

He turned away, and spoke again for a moment. Then he turned back to the window.

"Though it looks like both will live," he said, in a more normal voice.

Father and son stared at each other through a portal that made nothing of the hundreds of leagues between them. Ultrich examined the edges of the roughly-shaped opening, hanging in the middle of the room. He sniffed at it tentatively, recognizing something unique in the power that sustained it.

"A spirit hawk would have done," he said, making light of the situation.

Mudge was still struggling to accept that he had done this.

"What do you have to report?" continued Ultrich briskly, businesslike once more.

Mudge recounted his dream, then at Senovila's urging detailed their progress through The Wilderness.

Ultrich listened attentively.

When Mudge had finished his report, he asked after his uncle Evant. Then it was time for him to close the window.

"Do what Senovila tells you," said Ultrich, in a kindly voice. "He knows what he's doing."

The Legatus paused. "I have every faith in you, my son," he said at last, his voice a little rough. He was clearly unused to giving words of encouragement.

Mudge let the contact lapse, and the window began to waver, like a picture built of smoke. Then it floated away on the breeze.

He sat down on one of the rocks at the top of the promontory, shaken by the strange turn of events. He had never felt such absolute power pour through him, and it was terrifying.

"Your family are okay, then," said Senovila, sitting down next to him. "That's good to hear."

Mudge turned to him.

"I almost killed two of the Legatus' staff, and I tore a thumping great hole in the spirit world. What's good about that!"

"You've just got to learn to control your abilities," said Senovila evenly, "and, more importantly, you have to learn how to control your emotions. We all go through that particular lesson. I did. The Legatus did. It's not going to be any different for you."

"So what if it all goes wrong while I'm 'learning' this stuff," said Mudge cynically. "What happens when I start killing people by mistake?"

Mudge was catapulted onto his feet before he realized it. Then he was dangling in the air in an iron grip.

"You are going to learn discipline," said Ochren's bull voice next to his ear in a flat, hard tone of command.

"Like every warrior going to war, you are going to learn to put yourself second, and your comrades first, until the whole team thinks like one living, breathing organism.

"Each of us brings different abilities to the team, and you *will learn* how to temper and control yours. Now stop bellyaching and find something useful to do!"

He dropped Mudge unceremoniously on the ground and walked away. Senovila helped him to his feet.

"The Legatus said he had every faith in you, boy," he growled. "Now act like you believe it!"

He followed Ochren, leaving Mudge alone in the forest to regain his composure – and then decide whether he was outraged or humbled.

Senovila and Ochren rejoined the others, to find that breakfast was nearly over.

"Finish up and get ready to move out," Ochren told the travellers curtly. The others started to pack things away while Senovila followed Ochren over to where the horses were tethered.

"You were hard on the boy," he said, as he greeted the horses affectionately. He started to feed them some oats.

"Did I do the wrong thing?" said Ochren, re-distributing the weight on the packsaddles to even them up.

"No," said Senovila at last.

"You're too close to him," said Ochren. "It's better if I'm the one that stays on his back. That leaves you free to build him up. Two separate jobs, see?"

Senovila grunted. He had to admit Ochren was right. Someone had needed to snap Mudge out of it. If Ochren hadn't done it, he would have.

"There's something else," said Senovila quietly, and Ochren looked up.

"Ultrich didn't expect the boy to reach this level so early. He thought sending a spirit hawk would have been just within his capabilities. What he did went far beyond that."

"It did, didn't it," said Ochren with a smile. "I'm glad the little nobblenose is on our side!"

He thought about it for a minute. "Probably brought on by the death of his friends. Now he wants to protect what's left of them, and the power inside him is responding to that need."

Senovila looked up. He hadn't expected the bluff ranger to think that deeply into the situation.

"I think you're right," he said, looking worried, "but that much power, arcing over half the Karnatic League, will have attracted a lot of attention, and it won't just be from friends."

Ochren finished balancing the last packsaddle as he thought about what Senovila had said.

"You think we've drawn the wrong sort of attention to ourselves?" he said.

Senovila nodded.

"Xaanian spirit channellers, or maybe the power behind them?"

Senovila nodded again.

"So, what can we do about it?" said Ochren bluntly.

"Leave that to me," said Senovila. "I'll talk to the boy, but you and your team need to be on guard against more mortal threats.

Best you be prepared to get us out of sight and hunkered down at a moment's notice if we run into anything."

Ochren nodded gravely.

"It's begun a lot earlier than I had expected," said the head ranger heavily. "I had hoped we could get to Tashigot Keep without trouble."

Senovila slapped him on the back. "Apparently not, my friend," he said. Then he smiled. "I thought trouble was your middle name."

Ochren smiled back. "And it is, you old war dog. You can count on that!"

Still, getting to the keep was going to be a problem. It was on the other side of the Scaffold Mountains and at the Beltainian end of them. There was no obvious pass cutting through to it, but it was the most direct route to Xianak. They would just have to find a way through the mountains when it was time.

The rest of the morning passed uneventfully. Mudge kept to himself, and Senovila thought that was probably best. Colma and Bear kept Mudge company when they could, though they mostly walked in silence. Even Shyleen walked with him for a while, when she got back from scouting ahead.

They put a good stretch of The Wilderness behind them during the morning. Ochren wasn't entirely happy with the northerly valley they were in. He wanted to veer a little more east, make a more direct line for The Gap, but the going was easier in the rough track along the valley floor that they were following.

The group halted a little before midday. Bear started examining a cut above one of the horse's hooves, and then Shyleen came running through the trees faster than Mudge would have thought possible.

She cleared a fallen log like a deer in flight, and rattled off something to Ochren as soon as she arrived. She pointed urgently, sending the rest of them under the trees as fast as possible. They scrambled for cover, leading the horses as they went.

Mudge could feel something with his spirit senses now, an animalistic seeking of prey that soared above them. It had a deep hunger for the kill, and he knew the creature was after them.

It was unlikely Shyleen had used her spirit senses to detect this one. She had probably seen it clear a ridge ahead of them, and had time to get back. He was aware of how lucky they had been.

Mudge wondered what he should do. He was terrified that anything he tried would give their location away, but then the carnal hunger above them grew stronger, and he knew he had to do something.

He cast a spirit veil, keeping it small. He was gratified to see a faint blue shield form overhead. The next step was to refine it. He softened the edges, and blended it into the forest world about them.

They heard a long, rippling crack as air bent over enormous wings, coming in fast. Then Mudge felt the awareness above them flare into a killing frenzy. For a moment he thought his spirit veil had been too late, but then the creature above them seemed to lose direction, and he felt its disappointment. There was the vast thump of a wingbeat, and the creature receded, following the valley to the south.

Mudge kept the spirit veil in place for another minute or two, and discovered he was shaking. The airborne hunter had come so painfully close to killing them all. Senovila had been right, it was his emotions that were his greatest enemy. The old smith had given him good advice, and that meant he had a lot of work to do.

Senovila patted him on the shoulder. "I take it that was some of your work, boy," he said, smiling. "Got to tell you we're all mighty grateful for that." Mudge looked up, and acknowledged the praise. Then Shyleen gave the all clear. Senovila took a couple of paces and stopped, then turned back.

"The Legatus couldn't have done better," he said, with a wink, and hurried to the horses. Mudge wasn't sure he wanted to hear that, but it was time to get back on the trail. The little party was more than halfway through The Wilderness now, and that meant The Gap had to be a bit more than a day away. It would be time to assemble Senovila's cart when they got down on the flats.

Once they found the flats it wouldn't be long before they came across the Great Trade Route, and headed east until they found Attica. The crossroads town lay in the first of the Scion Kingdoms. They would stock up there for the next leg of the journey, the leg into Xaan. They made good time for the rest of the day, but it was only when they were holed up in another cave for the night that they breathed a collective sigh of relief. There had been no further signs of the flying creature.

That night Mudge had a new dream, and it had nothing to do with the evil rising in Xaan. He noted too that his dreams were infused with a growing sense of power, a power that had its source inside him. He had more control now, and sometimes the dreams let him go where he wanted.

This time he was somewhere above The Wilderness, trying to track the creature that had hunted them during the day. Was it still close by, looking for them? Or was it resting somewhere for the night?

He thought he detected a trace of it. A tiny sign from something that seemed out of place in the forest, but it faded and was gone. How was he going to do this? Then Jago and Luce were beside him.

They seemed joyous, happy, in the way of old friends who were reuniting. They urged him on, helping him in his search for the huge flying creature. He found another faint trace, this time emanating from a rocky crag on one of the highest ridges. In his dream he used his farsight to home in on it.

Bathed in the dim light of a half moon, something littered the rocks. It looked like the remains of goats, or mountain sheep, or the great Ibex of the tall crags. Several animals, at least, had been ripped apart in this place in the last day or so. The creature's spoor lingered, but the area was not bedevilled by the beast itself at the moment.

Mudge felt a sense of relief. He looked further, but there were no traces of it elsewhere in The Wilderness, and that was encouraging. It unsettled him how fast it had appeared after he had opened a tear in the spirit world. There had to be a connection, but that fact didn't seem to bother Jago or Luce.

Then the high crags and bloody remains receded, and he found himself over more familiar terrain. He saw the place where he was sleeping with the others, and wondered if he would be able to see Bear or Shyleen on watch.

Then Luce took his hand, and he smiled. She hugged him, and took a favourite scarf from around her neck. She tied it around his shoulders, and Jago thumped him on the arm, then hugged him in turn. His eyes shone with joy at their meeting.

Mudge was filled with a great happiness. He found himself sinking lower, returning to the cave. He looked up a last time and waved. The next thing he knew a heavy boot was rolling him over on his back, and Senovila was shaking him.

"We're damn near ready to go, boy. Have you been up all night dancing with sprites? You're like someone dead."

Mudge roused himself groggily. He knew he'd been dreaming again, but he had no idea for how long. Then he remembered what the dream had been about. Luce and Jago were still alive! Maybe it was just as ghosts, but they were still here, in this world, and they had helped him in his dream.

He sat up, and something caught round his neck. He looked down, and saw Luce's scarf. He sat motionless for a long moment, astonished, and then he lifted up one tail of the yellow material to examine it. This was getting altogether too strange.

He took the scarf off. It was real enough, one that Luce had worn often. A simple rectangle of yellow cloth edged in blue. It was folded along one of the long diagonals, giving two tails that would fall in random places around her shoulders.

Turning a thought form into a scarf was unheard of among spirit walkers. Maybe it was easier for the dead, maybe it was something he had done to help her. Perhaps it was part of the bodily form someone got if they elected to stay behind in the world for a while.

It was too hard to think about, and Mudge stuffed the scarf into a pocket so he could hurry over and get something to eat. Ochren was almost ready to lead the group up the next ridge, and into their last day in The Wilderness.

The ridges were becoming less daunting now. The valleys were opening out, turning broader, and more inclined to host scrub than trees. The winds that funnelled through The Gap made the region colder, and less hospitable for plant and animal alike. But the next valley wasn't like anything like that.

Lush, dense foliage soared up to impossible heights from the valley floor. It was unnatural, and it started at a sharply defined line that crossed the valley. They could see a scrubby, open ridge behind them, yet down in the valley the trail stopped at an impenetrable wall.

"Shyleen, backtrack and check that last valley," said Ochren, searching among the party for the scout.

"She's already gone," said Bear. "There was an old tree not far back covered in vines. She'll get a good look from there."

Ochren nodded. He encouraged initiative.

A few minutes later Shyleen came into view on the trail behind them. She shook her head. The extraordinary wall of foliage went as far left and right as she could see.

"Hell's teeth!" swore Ochren. "Don't want to go through it, can't go round it. What in the name of all the saints is that stuff?"

He made the trail sign for them to take a break.

Mudge had a sinking feeling. Some of the lessons from his teachers at the Priatic Order must have sunk in, despite his complete lack of interest.

"Mesoans," he said resignedly.

The others looked at him.

"A – kind of – original race of people. Here when the gods formed the world," he said. He was searching his memories frantically, and wishing he had paid more attention to the subject.

"They move around, generally going where there are no people. It looks like they're here in The Wilderness for the moment.

"Wherever they are the plant life grows like this. It's part of what they are, and what they do. They still have that 'becoming' thing, the 'could be this or could be that' potential that was around at the start of the world.

"Though it's a stretch to call them people," he ended lamely. "A force of nature perhaps."

"Mesoans," echoed Ochren, incredulously. He snorted, then turned his mind to ways of overcoming the problem.

"Will they let us through their land?" he said, at last.

Mudge blew out a breath. "Don't know," he said.

"Well, someone has to go ask them," said Ochren. The rest of the little party looked at Mudge. He got a strong sinking feeling.

"And yes, we think it ought to be you," said Senovila, smiling as he said it.

Mudge didn't feel like smiling at all.

FIVE

Senovila and Bear accompanied Mudge to the solid wall of vegetation in the valley below them. It didn't take long, and then they were staring up at the strange, moving homeland of the Mesoans. Mudge was immersed in his own thoughts. Each day was getting more complicated than the one before it, and there was more than a little despair in this realization.

He had travelled in the dream world, but it had somehow turned out to be the real world. Then, incredibly, he'd met Jago and Luce, and all that had happened before sun up. Now the travellers had run into mythical creatures he didn't actually believe in, and it wasn't even halfway through the morning.

Mudge shook his head. It was hard to figure out how to react to this. There wasn't enough time to adjust to all this, to any of it.

"Trust your instincts, boy," said Senovila, and a heavy hand settled on his shoulder. "Don't slow yourself down with unnecessary thinking."

Do I look that lost? mused Mudge, but he was grateful for Senovila's words.

"Just do what feels right," continued the smith. "Not what feels easy, or saves your skin, or gives you a chance to show off. Just make sure you can live with yourself afterwards."

Mudge thought that sounded about right. Easy to say when he didn't know what was ahead, or what his choices were going to be. Bear murmured his own words of encouragement.

Mudge looked at the Mesoan homeland more closely. The path ahead ended in an impossibly lush burst of growth. A rampart of green disappeared into the scrubby forest on either side of them. There was no way in.

"Well, it looks like you're on your own from here," said Senovila. "We'll wait here until you come back, you can rely on that."

Bear reached into a pouch on the belt around his waist. He gave Mudge a metal ball with a spout on one side and two little fins at the top.

"Blow on this if you want help. It's standard ranger issue. Makes a piercing sound that carries a long way." Senovila nodded his approval. It was a good bit of practical help.

"Good luck, Mudge," he said at last. "Keep your wits about you." Mudge nodded. He took the metal ball and put it carefully in one of his pockets. It didn't matter that the others weren't coming with him. He didn't think the rangers, or any material force, would be of much use in the Mesoan world.

He looked at the wall of green again and told himself it didn't look that dangerous. Then he smiled grimly. It didn't matter what it looked like, he had no choice. Squaring his shoulders he marched resolutely into the unnaturally green vegetation.

In the meantime, on the other side of the Karnatic League, Ultrich assembled his war cabinet in the chart room at the Golden Palace. The chart room was always his base in times of conflict, ever since he'd first united the three Marches.

He smiled ruefully at the memory. Then, he had been barely old enough to serve in the armies he commanded, but his ideas had worked. The Karnatic League had slowly taken shape.

He had taken special steps to see the war cabinet wasn't interrupted. The stone building sat close by the palace, in the grounds, and the chart room had been strengthened by means both practical and esoteric. In fact Ultrich had added spirit links of his own, connections that led to some very unpleasant places. Anything that attempted to follow the spirit trace his son had left behind would be in for a nasty surprise.

As part of his plans he had put his greatest concentration of spirit walkers on high alert. Teams of spirit walkers at Prias, on the coast, were now scouring the spirit world day and night. Ultrich would know if his enemies stirred anywhere in the League, or beyond it.

However, much of what lay ahead of them would be won by conventional forces, and for that he needed commanders with a good grasp of strategy. That was why the war cabinet was meeting today.

"If our information is correct, gentlemen, we have very little time in which to act," began the Legatus.

"The main body of Xaanian troops is somewhere on the Desert Trade Route, and may already be at the borders of Beltainia. We haven't yet heard from commander Yeltar, but we know he can be relied upon. He will mobilise his forces at the first sign of trouble, and send us a messenger."

Heads nodded round the table, and there were rumbles of agreement. The war cabinet were all confident the Beltainian commander-in-chief would lead his people well.

Previously head of the cavalry forces, Yeltar had taken over as People's Guardian more than twenty years ago. It had been a black day when unknown assassins wiped out the Beltainian royal family, but Yeltar had led the Independent Kingdom very ably since then and the country had grown strong under his leadership. Yeltar had hunted down the bandits that had been the country's main problem, and firmed up control of its borders. Beltainia, the largest of the Independent Kingdoms, had thrived under his leadership.

"Unfortunately," continued Ultrich, "the situation in Beltainia is only one of our problems. Another army is marching south toward the High Steppes. If they overcome the hill tribes it's only a matter of time before they'll be through the Scaffold Mountains.

"If they get through the mountain passes they'll overrun the Scion Kingdoms, and then they'll be at the borders of the Marches."

There was a moment's silence. The war cabinet was wondering how the Legatus would take this news of the impending army. His wife had come from the hill tribes, and after her sudden death he had never remarried. The High Steppes were his second home, and the news must be a crushing blow. Ultrich, however, wasn't dwelling on that.

"A third force has arrived at Mishvart, and is preparing to cross the Galleon Straights to the Gold Coast. One of our spirit walkers, living as a fisherman at the docks, has been watching the ships embark."

There was some uncomfortable fidgeting round the table at the mention of spirit walkers. These were practical men and women. They were warriors, and commanders of armies, and only two of them, Sergeos and Cinnabar, were spirit walkers. The idea of spirit hawks, that crossed vast distances instantly and spoke with a human voice, made the rest uneasy.

Ultrich noticed the fidgeting, but let it pass. These were people who saw war as a science, but in other areas could be quite superstitious. A spirit hawk was a force, a repeatable experiment within a body of knowledge. As such it was a science. Unfortunately, most of his commanders couldn't bring themselves to try and understand it.

He was grateful Cinnabar was there. A noblewoman who had also studied at the Priatic Order of Mysteries, she gave some legitimacy to the Legatus' use of spirit walkers in his war cabinet.

"Half the ships are empty," he continued smoothly, "and we have to ask ourselves why that is. I think they intend to take control of the gold and silver mines on the Gold Coast by force, and use those mines to help fund their expansion.

"But, and this is a new twist, there is a rumour they're going to round up the men from the villages and bring them back to Xaan. I think they intend to press-gang them into their armies.

"This may be part of the answer to a question that has been bothering me. The forces Xaan has already fielded are much greater than we anticipated. Where are they getting the extra numbers from?"

The Legatus looked around the room. His commanders looked uneasy at the idea of an enemy with greater numbers. The Karnatic League, with a little help from the Independent Kingdoms, had always seemed a match for Xaan. In fact they ran war games occasionally that assumed this very situation. But if the Xaanian army was much larger than expected, the battles were going to get increasingly lop-sided.

"I think their strategy is to rely upon mercenary soldiers and press-ganged villagers," said the Legatus, "all paid for by the mines on the Gold Coast. If that's the case we may find the going tougher than we expected."

Heads around the table nodded a reluctant agreement.

Ultrich paused. He had one more unpalatable bit of news for them. "I suspect many of their current numbers are made up of Wild Men from the Northern Wastes."

This got a reaction. The cold, barren lands north of Xaan were a freezing hell. The population who lived there were savage barbarians. They had a primitive language few understood, and they lived in caves and sod huts. It was an addition to this war that unsettled the League commanders.

"The Xaanian First Elect, Ottar Bey, must have been preparing for these invasions much longer than we thought," said the Legatus. "It's the only way he could have fielded three armies this big, this quickly." Then he looked around the room. "While we are woefully unprepared," he added.

There was much shuffling of feet. Sergeos had been with the Legatus since they were boys together. He was the one that had the courage to ask the obvious question first.

"Why did we not know about this? What's the point of having spirit walkers if they can't tell us what's happening?" he demanded.

Since he was a spirit walker himself, Sergeos was free to say what the commanders were thinking.

Ultrich was troubled by the question. Though not because he thought the spirit walkers had let the League down. He was troubled by the answer he had to share with them.

"I have discovered an ancient power behind Ottar Bey," he said quietly. "Something like our spirit walkers, but much older, and much stronger.

"It is something without rules of behaviour, and without a conscience. It will lay waste to everything it touches until it gets what it wants. And what it wants is control of all the known world, and the slavery of every citizen of every nation. At the very least it wants to reduce the League, and the Independent Kingdoms, to a rubble that cannot threaten it.

"So far this power has been able to cast a veil over what Ottar Bey is doing in Xaan. That is why our spirit walkers haven't given us more warning. It also means that things we normally rely upon in a time of war may not work out the way we expect them to.

"This is a battle for our freedom that will be fought as much in the spirit world as on the ground, I'm afraid."

The members of the war cabinet were even more troubled by that revelation. War was a business where numbers and knowledge made all the difference. When there was uncertainty, when you couldn't trust the information you were receiving, it was hard to know what to do. Commanders could end up sending soldiers into battle blind to what lay ahead, and that got troops killed.

"I think we should leave the spirit stuff to our spirit walkers," said the Legatus firmly. "They're just starting to come to grips with this, and I think we can expect some improvements in that area." He didn't say that his greatest hope for a breakthrough was his own son.

"We've all got jobs to do," he continued, "and we have to trust the spirit walkers to do theirs." He looked around his war cabinet to see what the reaction to his words would be. They weren't happy with this new reliance on spirit walkers, but they had learned to trust Ultrich's leadership over the years.

"We also have to leave the defence of Beltainia to Yeltar for the moment," he finished. "Mobilizing the entire League is going to take time. I say we take the troops we've got, and stop the Xaanian army heading our way at the High Steppes."

The Legatus hesitated for a moment. He had always tried to be fair. Anyone suggesting he was running the League to serve his own purposes would feel the full force of his wrath. On the other hand his war cabinet, hell's teeth the whole League, knew his heart lay in the High Steppes. Perhaps he needed to say something.

"We have to stop the Xaanian armies overrunning the Scion Kingdoms," he said quietly. "Our best fighters come from there, and we can't outfit troops with armour or weapons if we lose the mines in the mountains.

"That means we have to stop the enemy on the High Steppes. We might hold out in the Marches for a while if they broke through, by trading for metals from the Independent Kingdoms and the Tengue Dynasty to the south, but that's a big risk, and an unnecessary one, do you understand?"

Heads nodded vigorously around the table. Porteous, the army commander from Middle March, rose out of his chair. His thickset build, grey hair, and straight-backed bearing added dignity to his words.

"No one thought otherwise, your eminence," he said gravely. He was letting the Legatus know the war cabinet stood solidly behind him. Ultrich was silent for a moment, then bowed his head in acceptance of their loyalty.

After that the war cabinet settled down to the task at hand. They built up a plan to move their troops to the other side of the Scaffold Mountains in record time. Then they tore the plan apart and rebuilt it. Then they did it all over again. Slowly, as they tested it, fixed it, and retested it, they developed confidence in what they could achieve in such a short time. They would be ready to meet the Xaanian war machine.

Within days troops were being marshalled at key points throughout the League. It wasn't long before a steady stream of battalions and supplies converged on Rotor Valley Pass, because it was the only way to move large numbers of soldiers and supplies through the Scaffold Mountains.

Ultrich's spirit walkers became increasingly busy. They needed to conceal troop movements from the enemy, and block Xaanian spies on the ground.

It was much later in the day when the Legatus finally told his commanders to go home and get some rest. The war cabinet had made good progress, but they would be needed back in the chart room, well rested, for the evening shift.

Once they were gone, Ultrich got up and stretched. Then he settled himself back in his chair. One more thing remained on his mental checklist, and for that task he would send himself. It would be a bitter-sweet journey, but he was looking forward to it.

He hadn't seen his wife's family for almost a year, so a visit was overdue. What he would be doing this time, though, would be asking a lot more of them than could reasonably be expected. He wanted them to give up the High Steppes, and join with the League forces to defend Rotor Valley Pass. It would be a hard sell.

Ultrich smiled. Krell, his father-in-law, was still the most powerful chieftain of the hill tribes after all these years. If Ultrich could get his support, the others would follow.

He liked the old man. It would be a joy to ride with him and his people once more, even if it was to war. If the war cabinet could work out the details of the High Steppes campaign tonight, he would set off for Krell's camp first thing in the morning.

Back in The Wilderness, Mudge was pushing his way into the imposing wall of green that stretched left and right in front of him. It gave way as he eased his shoulder into its depths. Lush, leaf-laden branches closed behind him, and then he was gone.

Bear shook his head. It felt like Mudge had stepped out of the known world, disappeared without a trace, but what had he stepped into?

Inside the tangle of greenery, Mudge forced his way onward. He wondered at the density of the stuff. It was more than a thicket, but it didn't have the abrasiveness or resistance of a hedge. At least it was soft, like a constricting blanket.

He found it reasonable going, if he ignored the great effort each step was taking him. Reasonable going or not, he had only taken a few steps before he was completely lost. He looked up, hoping to see the sky through the trees above, but the greenery had closed over him like a roof.

He wondered how he could see at all, since the sun was now completely hidden from view, but light appeared to be emanating from the plants around him. Or out of the air itself, it was hard to tell.

Mudge focused his mind, hoping his spirit direction would work in this place, but he detected nothing ahead of him. He was deliberating whether to push on in the direction he was facing, or try a new direction, when he heard music. It was unlike any music he had ever come across, but it quickened his step and lifted his spirits. It made him feel glad in his heart, as though anything was possible. The apprehension he had begun to feel disappeared, and for that he was grateful.

Though the music was faint, he reasoned it was coming from somewhere further on and deeper in. That encouraged him to continue pushing onward through the dense growth. As he did so, the sound of the music slowly increased. Still, it was hard work, and it wasn't long before he stopped for a rest.

While he stood, breathing heavily, he noticed the greenery had a life of its own. It was swaying from side to side. A faster rhythm entered the harmonies of the music, and the leaves shivered appreciatively.

Mudge turned side on, and went back to forcing his shoulder through the greenery as best he could. At least he seemed to be making better progress now. A bush moved out of his way, and for a moment there was a small, open space. He stepped into it, and looked around.

The plant life was moving somehow, following some intricate dance of its own. By timing his steps he was able to connect the occasional open spaces, and move faster. He pushed on, and noticed more changes.

For one thing the open spaces became more common, and when he looked up there was now a deep purple and red, almost black, sky above him. There was a scattering of stars in it, and they were unnaturally bright, He also noticed that there were very few of them. Mudge felt a strange newness to it all. He wondered if he was present at the birth of the world.

Then the ground took on a variable consistency. At times he seemed to be wading through it, at others he was floating above it. The last was a most unnerving sensation, and it was becoming harder to avoid the trees that now moved around him with a life of their own.

It seemed the trees were lost in the complicated movements of the Great Dance, the music of life that pulsed everywhere in the Mesoan homeland. A substantial boulder floated past. Mudge had to resist a boyish urge to climb on board and see where it took him.

He decided he had come far enough. He was here to contact the strange inhabitants of this place, not wander about aimlessly. But his voice, when he called out, sounded discordant. It jarred with the rich harmonies of the music. He persisted for a while, but there was no reply.

It was becoming difficult to stay upright on the moving ground and avoid the trees at the same time. He managed to extend his spirit senses into his surroundings, but he couldn't detect the familiar smell of lightning, or cinnamon, that indicated a spirit presence. In fact he detected nothing that was familiar to him. That, more than anything else, drove home that he was no longer in his own world.

Driven by increasing desperation, Mudge tried to impose a little order on the whirling energy around him. He sensed a resistance to what he was trying to do, but he continued to imagine an orderly world, a place where the ground stayed level, and things didn't go whirling about.

At a certain point there was a momentary shock wave, an upheaval that threw him off his feet. When he pushed himself upright again, the world had returned to normal. Normal for him, that is; with level ground, and trees that stayed in one place. Probably not normal for the Mesoans, though.

Mudge found himself in an open glade, and he waited nervously to see what would happen next. It didn't take long for something to come looking for him now. The space about him began to fill with wisps of light.

Mudge tried talking to one of them, but there was no response. Then one of the floating wisps came closer. A tendril of mist reached out and touched him on the arm. The tenuous column in front of him coalesced into a solid form, and Mudge found himself looking at a perfect copy of himself.

Another one touched the first, and began to coalesce in the same way. Others joined in. The effect spread, like ripples spreading in a pond, until Mudge found himself surrounded by dozens of copies of himself.

The one closest to him looked up and smiled, if a little uncertainly. It seemed to be having trouble with the mechanics of Mudge's body.

"How did you create this clearing in our world?" it asked.

"Nothing must be allowed to stop the Great Dance," said another emphatically. Then they were all talking. The first raised a hand, finger extended, and the others fell silent. The double in front of Mudge raised an eyebrow enquiringly.

"I don't know," said Mudge uncertainly. "It was just too unsettling for me the way it was."

There was great consternation among Mudge's many replicas. The babble of voices continued until the double in front of Mudge once again raised a finger imperiously.

"You do not wield such power of your own accord," it said, enigmatically. "It is something from outside of your world, and your time, that permits this."

It paused, and turned to its fellows. Mudge waited apprehensively while the soft murmur of voices rose and fell around the clearing. The one who had assumed the role of speaker for the others turned back to Mudge.

"Normally we avoid your people," it said heavily. Then it stopped to reflect on what it had said. It seemed to reach a decision. "However, you have been sent to us for a reason, even though we dislike such contact with your world."

Mudge's double gestured, and a long bench of rock rose out of the ground and dusted itself off. The double sat, and indicated that Mudge should join it.

"Tell me what is happening out there in the world, and why you have come to this place," it said. Mudge thought he detected a certain uneasiness in the way it asked the question.

He told his double about the power that was rising in Xaan, and the party of travellers from Shaker's Hope. How they were trying to make their way northward, toward Xaan.

His double made some sharp comments to the Mesoans behind it, using a language Mudge did not understand. Then it asked him about his relationship with the Legatus, who it seemed to know. Mudge tried to explain his ambivalent ties to the throne, and his double seemed to understand.

There was more discussion, but it felt like no time at all had passed when it raised its arm abruptly.

"Enough," it said.

It stood up, and Mudge followed its lead.

"We will assist you where we can," it said, "though existence in your world is very damaging for us." It paused for a moment.

"For now I think we will make things a little easier for you and your companions," it said.

The trees began to move again. The ground split into several layers, like sheets of paper sliding on top of one another, until Mudge wasn't sure which one he was on. He stayed where he was, in case he found out he wasn't on any of them, and began to feel a little seasick.

The Mesoans became indistinct, and their outlines dissolved into a spreading mist. Mudge reached out a hand and touched one as they began to drift away from him. There was a momentary sensation of coolness, then a wall of vegetation rolled over him from behind.

His recollections of the next minute or two were a blur. He remembered odd, distorted images, and bumping along in some direction or other. He was suspended between an entire forest that was passing over him, and a ground that had a somewhat cloudy consistency. Then the Mesoan homeland was gone.

After a moment Mudge found his feet, and swayed dizzily. As his insides settled back into place he lifted his head, and found he was back on the trail, while the imposing wall of vibrant green was receding into the distance. Mudge's world appeared out of the receding greenery as if they both occupied the same space, but in different ways.

He stood up, and wondered where he was. He hallooed loudly, but there was no answer. Then he remembered the metal ball he'd been given, and dug it out of his pocket. It appeared undamaged by his time in the dense undergrowth, and he blew a long blast. A moment later he heard a faint answer from further up the valley.

Mudge worked his way up the trail, in the direction of the sounds. More answering whistle blasts guided him. It wasn't long before he could hear Bear's voice close by, and then he could see the two rangers waiting for him. As soon as they saw him they came running down the trail, pleased to see he was still alive.

"What did you do?" said Bear excitedly. "The whole forest just up and moved! It was incredible, and I've never seen anything like it. Whatever you said to them, it must have worked!"

Bear and Ochren half carried Mudge up the path towards the rest of the little party, plying him with questions as they went. Mudge gave some general answers, but didn't dwell on the details of what had happened. Then he suddenly realized how tired he was. This world might weaken the Mesoans, but living in their world didn't do him much good either.

The rest of the travellers were waiting for him at the top of the ridge, and he was touched at their concern. Colma hugged him, and lifted him off the ground, following that by thumping him on the arm. Arnima almost smothered him in her ample bosom. Then Senovila was pumping his hand and clapping him on the back.

"Well done, boy. Well done indeed! We might be able to make Tashigot Keep in reasonable time now – and we owe it all to you!"

Mudge downplayed the whole thing, and after a while they stopped asking questions about what had happened. When he had eaten something, and had a long drink from the water supplies, he began to feel a little better.

Once they had reorganized, the travellers set off down the trail. It wasn't long before they found themselves on the valley floor, amid a widening corridor of grassland. This was the first really open land they had seen in The Wilderness, and their pace picked up. Once they had finished their midday meal, Senovila insisted on making up his portable cart.

There was a lot of detailed work needed before all the parts went together smoothly. It took Senovila most of the afternoon and he had help for all of that time. The tray had to be made from woven lengths of supple branches, and that was the most difficult part.

Senovila was determined to get some distance behind them before they stopped for the night, so at his insistence they climbed gingerly aboard what looked like a rather fragile machine. Happily, it took the weight without complaint. Senovila flicked the reins lightly and the two horses started off at a steady walk. The cart followed, bumping and swaying behind them.

"I can't believe it works," said Bear to Ochren. He got a clip across the back of the head as Senovila turned around with a scowl.

"It beats walking," said Shyleen amiably from the back of the cart. She had found enough room to stretch out, and was enjoying the gentle swaying.

It was a much happier band that camped further along the valley that evening. They should be able to manage a good distance on the following day, if they didn't run into any problems with the cart. That would take them out of The Wilderness and onto the Great Trade Route by midday. From there they should make Attica by nightfall.

SIX

They travellers were up at first light the next morning, and finished breakfast quickly. Senovila sent Mudge and Colma out to collect more supple branches to weave into the bed of the cart. The tray they had built the previous day had started to sag alarmingly.

The two of them returned with armfuls of thin branches and began to weave them into the existing framework. Shyleen, Liam and Mareet left to scout the valley ahead, and Bear turned up with a large bush fowl and a clutch of eggs.

"Lunch," he said briskly, then wandered over to help Arnima and Senovila pack. Ochren headed off to fill up the water bags, and it was a little after sunrise when the last of the packs were thrown onto the cart.

With both horses in high spirits, and the floor of the valley getting smoother, they made good time. The travellers took it in turns to walk beside the cart, lessening the load the horses had to pull. The exercise also helped to keep the rangers in good condition.

Arnima had toughened up on the trail. She was able to push herself along when it was her turn to walk, though it helped that she could rest an arm on the cart when she got tired. As far as Ochren was concerned, Senovila's lightweight, portable cart creaked a little too alarmingly, so he walked most of the time.

"You keep an eye out for that infernal flying thing, boy," said Senovila. He was voicing the lingering concerns of them all. The fearsome flying creature wasn't an enemy they wished to meet again.

Mudge was working on it. His spirit senses were unfolding a little more each day, and his confidence was growing. He could see, almost like a map in his mind, that the skies over The Wilderness were clear of threats. No trace remained of the winged creature, whatever it had been.

Ahead of the cart he thought he could detect Shyleen, Liam and Mareet. They were making their way along the left side of the valley as they scouted ahead. He sent his mind out further, and found nothing but a handful of smallholdings and subsistence farms ahead. They huddled in the valley just before it opened out onto the Great Trade Route.

When he had finished, Mudge brought his attention back to his surroundings. He was walking alongside the cart, with Bear next to him. The others were resting on the tray, or up front guiding the two horses. Then he suddenly felt exhausted, and leaned on the side of the cart. He was learning just how much energy spirit work took out of him.

But the little group made good progress. They continued to change places on the cart on a regular basis until, at last, Senovila announced he could see the Great Trade Route ahead. A rough hut appeared on their left, then a larger house with outbuildings. Mudge nodded. His spirit sense had picked up the smallholdings correctly.

Shyleen, Liam and Mareet appeared out of one of the houses. They had been quizzing the locals on anything unusual they had seen in the area, and now they fell in beside the cart and passed on an all clear message.

"Short break," announced Senovila later, as they reached the Trade Route proper. He stopped the cart, and took some feed forward to the horses. Mudge noticed again how Ochren left the leadership of the group to the old smith.

He had no doubt the situation would change if the rangers needed to take charge of the little party. All the same, he liked the way there were no set levels of command. They all contributed something, and they all seemed to know when to leave the decision making to others. It felt good. Better than the rigid command structure his father used to run the League.

Then he realized he was being unfair. He could understand why a large organization like the League might need rules, and structure. Mudge wondered how much his thoughts came from the fact that his father seemed to have no time for him. It was a challenging idea, but then he hesitated. Maybe he would look at it again on another day, but not today.

After the break, they made good time on the smooth surface of the Great Trade Route. The Legatus had understood early in his career the need for wagons to travel quickly between towns. Otherwise goods spoiled and traders missed the best prices, and taxes were lower. So every village in the League was levied a certain number of 'worker days' each month to maintain the Trade Routes.

Villages prospered under the system, and people could see the advantage of keeping the roads in good order. Potholes were filled in with a mixture of stones and clay, and water was carefully channelled away from the road surfaces. Some stretches of road were raised above marshy areas completely. It certainly made for fast travelling.

The cart left the poorer soils and grazing lands of The Gap, and passed into the richer soils of the Scion Kingdoms. A garrison of the League straddled the road at the transition, and they were pulled over and questioned. The soldiers were quick to let them through once they saw the ranger attire, and had spoken to Ochren.

From then on the foothills of the Scaffold Mountains crawled by on their left, while the rich farmland of the plains stretched away on their right. Somewhere out on the plains the Scion Kingdoms came to an end, and the rolling downs of the Marches took over, until at last the downs descended to cliffs that ran along the edge of the Trading Coast.

Despite their best efforts, Attica had still not appeared by the end of the day, and Senovila started to look around for a place to stop for the night. Ochren asked a few questions at one of the farmhouses, and they were directed to a walled compound off the road. It was a sprawling affair on top of a rise, and it dominated the farms below it. Ochren discovered he knew the owner, a retired ranger named Athren. Once that bond had been established the travellers were made welcome at the compound, and offered a meal and somewhere to sleep.

"Old habits die hard," confided Ochren to his travelling companions, pointing to the walls and fortifications about the top of the hill. The additions were obviously ranger work. "Good defensive position, see?" he added, and swept his arm across the commanding view. The others were quick to agree with him, except Mudge.

I'm not so sure, he thought. The dark things that were trying to find them wouldn't be put off by a 'good defensive position'. He thought of the winged creature again, and imagined it plucking one of them effortlessly off the hilltop and carrying them away. It would dismember its prey later, in the nearby Scaffold Mountains. In his opinion the travellers were going to stand out like a beacon here.

Nightfall followed, and Mudge could hear food being served in the workers' quarters. He didn't say anything to Ochren about his concerns, but he added himself to the list for night watch. After that he dumped his gear in one of the bunkhouses, and joined the others for the evening meal.

Ochren sent Mudge and Liam out on the first watch, and the two of them were in the central square of the compound when the sentries arrived for the changeover at midnight. Bear was one of the new sentries, but his presence didn't reassure Mudge. An uncomfortable feeling had come over him, and it wouldn't go away.

He turned in, but found he couldn't sleep. He calmed his breathing in preparation, and sent his spirit senses out over the farms on the plains. He went as far as the foothills of the mountains, then looped back until he was far out over the Marches.

He found nothing. No airborne life forms, no strange energy readings, nothing to indicate they were being hunted, or even watched. But something still felt terribly wrong.

Mudge wondered whether Ochren would appreciate him sharing his concerns about something he couldn't actually detect yet, but he could feel as a presence. He decided he was missing something, but what was it? Then the sensation got worse. The devil spawn take me if I'm wrong, he swore impatiently, and hurried outside to see Ochren. That simple act saved Bear's life, and possible the lives of all of them.

Ochren called out the other rangers immediately. They rose fully clothed and grabbed their weapons on the run, loosening swords and notching arrows as they came. Mudge and Ochren were looking up into the darkness when Mudge felt something appear above him, something dark and dangerous.

It was a spirit veil, though it was different to the ones he was familiar with. Moments later he felt it collapse upon itself, and then it was gone. Three of the winged creatures that had tracked them in The Wilderness dropped like stones toward the compound.

The first touched down briefly, and several dark shapes slid off its back. Then it sprang skyward again while a second creature landed, and unloaded more passengers.

Bear was on the far side of the square, alone. He met the dark shapes head on. They were smaller than him, but their teeth and claws were fast and deadly. One went down to a lightning-fast strike from Bear's sword. Then he spun round, driving his blade through another, but he didn't see the third winged creature as it landed behind him. Great, clawed talons fastened onto his shoulders, and it sprang skyward again, dragging Bear with it.

Ochren charged into the darting shapes, trying to follow Bear. Long heads and curved teeth snapped wickedly around him. Their bite was surely poisonous, and he concentrated on staying away from their jaws. Then Shyleen and Liam arrived together. Working as one they pulled back the powerful recurved ranger bows. Razor pointed arrows drove deep into the chest of the winged creature as it lifted into the air with Bear. It staggered, and its wings beat more wildly. Two more arrows followed, with deadly effect, and the unnatural demon collapsed out of the sky.

The compound's farmhands were now beginning to arrive, armed with pitchforks and quarterstaffs. They joined Colma and Mareet in a protective circle around Bear, while Mudge tore apart his shirt and tried to stop the bleeding.

Ochren, Shyleen and Liam pressed forward into the band of attackers, using their swords to kill several more of them. The strange creatures seemed uncertain against the greater numbers. Working shoulder to shoulder, the rangers pressed the attackers back. They were barely to shoulder height on the rangers, lean and otter-like, and the black and grey creatures seemed more at home on four legs than two. But they pulled themselves upright when they attacked, lunging forward with their snapping heads.

The rangers, though, had a longer reach with their swords, and as the battle turned it was clear the attackers would all soon be dead on the ground.

Colma called out a warning, and the crack of giant wing beats sounded from above. Ochren and the rangers fell back hurriedly. The remaining two winged horrors dropped to the ground, and the dark shapes scrambled to remount them. Then the giant beasts sprang into the air. With great parting beats of their wings, the unnatural monsters were gone.

As soon as it was safe the rangers worked their way across the square, moving among the corpses and making sure life was gone from each of their attackers. The farmhands joined them, looking down at the contorted bodies in amazement. They wouldn't go near the still twitching giant wings of the monster that the ranger arrows had brought down.

Arnima and Senovila arrived, and hurried to Bear's side. Mudge had stopped the worst of the bleeding, but it kept seeping through the cloth he was using. He was glad Arnima was there to take over.

Bear was now conscious, though he was grimacing as he bore the pain. Arnima had the farmhands bring him into one of the side rooms, while Mudge kept pressure over the wounds. She rummaged in one of her bags for the things she would need. Ochren's old friend Athren appeared, and Arnima gave him a list of things she didn't have. He sent a farmhand to the main house at a run.

Seeing Bear in good hands, Ochren returned to the square. There was no sign of further trouble, but he set double sentries this time. Then he motioned for the rest of the team to return to their rooms to get some rest before dawn, if they could after the excitement.

When she had finished with Bear, Arnima passed a hand lightly over his forehead, and he slumped against the pillows, sound asleep. Every line of pain had now vanished from his face.

"Tidy trick," said Mudge, who was helping her with the bindings around Bear's chest.

Arnima looked up. "I've given him healing dreams, and that's the best I can do. The mind has a very strong effect on the body, and healers have to use that to their advantage. He's at the limits of what a body can endure.

"The salves I've used will help him too," she continued.

She packed up the last of her things. Then she hesitated.

"What you see around me you keep to yourself, and what I see around you I keep to myself, understand?" she said abruptly, turning back to him.

Mudge nodded. It felt like he was being allowed into a secret. No, into a secret society. He was being included in a group of people who needed to keep part of their lives to themselves if they were to remain sane. He was pleased that she was including him.

"Spirit workers need friends," she went on. "Someone who understands. The things we do that are, mmm, different, we keep to ourselves. But with some people we can be lucky. These are people who have been through similar experiences."

Mudge saw the good sense in her words. He felt awkward being a spirit walker, as if he was on show, or on trial, it was hard to say which, and she was giving him a way to cope with that. He smiled broadly, and stepped over to wrap his arms around her in a big hug.

She looked up, a little surprised. Then returned his embrace.

"Thank you," he said warmly, "that's good advice."

He paused. "Life has got so complicated these last few days, it's a real treat for me to find something that makes sense."

She studied him thoughtfully. His father was coming out more strongly in him every day. Mudge would win the loyalty of those around him as the quest proceeded, and that was something his father would also have done. He would do it with his openness, and his appreciation of the efforts of others. Yet he was also different from his father. What would the prince become that the father was not?

She smiled at him. "Talk to me any time," she said gently, and gathered up her healer's kit. Then she headed back to her rough pallet in the common room. Senovila was already asleep, making peculiar whistling noises through his nostrils.

The bodies in the centre of the compound were badly decayed by the time morning came. Ochren kicked one, and it collapsed on itself, becoming a spreading, boneless bag of jelly.

"*Qin-ji*," said Mudge, standing beside him. "A summonsed creature. At least that tells us there aren't whole colonies of these things somewhere in our world. So there are no large numbers the enemy can send against us."

Ochren lifted an eyebrow, wanting to know more. Mudge wondered how he would explain this. He searched his memory for scraps of knowledge from his years at the Priatic School of Mysteries.

"These are made creatures," he said, "and now they're reverting to the stuff that gave them life. If they're coming from Xaan, then Ottar Bey's got some pretty nasty characters working for him."

He was about to add more, but stopped himself. Ochren didn't need to know that making such creatures was beyond any human agency. He would see what they were up against for himself when they got to Xianak. Doing this was also beyond any sense of morality. It meant capturing souls from the recently dead to animate the creatures, and that meant the travellers were up against something evil. Something that had no conscience, and no sense of the pain it caused others.

"How did they know we were here?" said Ochren.

That was a good question. Mudge worried for a moment that they were homing in on his spirit senses, but that didn't stand up to rigorous examination. The winged creature had found them in The Wilderness by chance. It had been searching for them for a day or two before it discovered where they were. Its kills on the hilltops proved that.

In the same way, the compound on the hill was an obvious landmark in the direction they were travelling. Mudge relaxed. He didn't need to invent supernatural causes for explainable events. He put all this to Ochren, who nodded in agreement.

"Athren says there have been some shady characters hanging around Attica lately," he said quietly. He stopped for a moment, planning their journey in his mind.

"I'm thinking of bypassing the place. We can stock up on provisions here if we have to. It might be a lot safer."

Mudge kicked himself. This was something he should have thought of. Attica wasn't that far away, and he could search the place with his spirit senses. He nodded, and said he'd take a look at Attica for the rangers.

He found a quiet place on the windward side of the compound, and prepared himself. Slowly, his mind began to settle. Then he heard the jingling sounds of a harness in the distance. The others were hitching the horses to the cart. He didn't have long to do this.

Mudge extended his spirit senses toward the town, and picked up the tell-tale spirit traces of people going about their every day lives. At first it was too much for him. There were so many people, the life signs mixed with animal traces, and the occasional brighter point of somebody with untrained spirit abilities.

Then he began to see a larger pattern. His vantage point rose, exactly as it did in his dreams. He could see the shape of Attica by the flickers of life that ran along each street, particularly where people were grouped together in houses, and the workers in merchant shops that were about to open.

Then he tried to catalogue the spirit traces. He was able to discern young from old, and the bright from the dull, and among them were some who flared with high spirit energies. He had almost completed his sweep of the town when he came across what had to be Xaanian agents.

The spirit traces he saw were muted, a dull red against the clear yellows and whites of the rest of the population. Did that mean they weren't human? Or did it mean something was possessing them, controlling their minds?

Two of the dull red traces appeared to be hiding in a storage room, and quick, jerky movements told him they weren't human. Another one, though, moved at normal speed along the streets. It seemed to be mixing with Attica's human population without any problems.

The dull red trace turned into a large building on the edge of town. Mudge realized it was a garrison for the Karnatic Defence

Force. He could clearly see the disciplined minds within the building.

Mudge felt his blood run cold. It appeared the Xaanian agents had infiltrated the garrison itself. Whether this one was passing itself off as a soldier, or had a firm control over the commander of the garrison by some means, he didn't know. Either way, it would be a very good idea to bypass Attica.

Mudge withdrew his spirit senses from the place, and returned to his body. He felt disoriented for a moment, and then he was looking about the walled compound. He stood with some effort, and shook the numbness out of his legs. Ochren turned his head as Mudge came up beside him, and waited for Mudge to tell him what he had learned.

"There's a Xaanian agent in the garrison," said Mudge quietly, "and two more in the town itself."

Ochren said nothing for a moment. The Legatus' boy seemed so young, so awkward, to be a spirit walker. It didn't feel right for Ochren to be sending him out to gather information like this, but he needed Mudge's skills, and the League would in the battles to come. Then he smiled. The boy had done well.

"One in the garrison?" he said, pursing his lips. That was not good. The Xaanians would know who was coming and going along the Trade Routes, and which League troops were being sent where.

Mudge nodded.

"If that's the case we'll get our supplies here, I think," said Ochren. "My ranger friend has already offered to supply us. It will take at least two days to cross the mountains, and we'll need to allow more for emergencies."

"The mountains?" said Mudge, surprised.

"The keep's pretty much opposite us, on the other side of the Scaffold Mountains," said Ochren. "I'd rather take the traditional route, the High Pass on the other side of Attica," he continued.

"Then we could travel back along the edge of the desert to the keep. But cutting through the mountains makes more sense if we don't want to be seen on the Trade Routes by Xaanian agents."

Mudge hesitated, and Ochren waited for the boy to speak.

"Why are we going to Tashigot Keep?" he said at last.

Ochren sighed. He had been expecting this question. The keep was on their way to Xaan, but there was more to it than that. It had been surprising no one else had asked him this question. The rangers, well, they knew Ochren would brief them when they got closer to the keep, and they were happy just to keep their minds on day-to-day survival.

"There's a little business there that we have to take care of," he said at last.

Mudge waited patiently.

Ochren sighed. This was going to be awkward. How much should he tell the boy? He decided that he might as well say something about the history of the place. There could be no harm in that.

"The keep was built where it is for a reason, Mudge," he said. "Yes, it marks the southern boundary of Xaan, and the place where the desert and the mountains meet. It's an obvious place to put an outpost. Right there at the foot of the mountains with a good view in all directions, but there are other places just as good."

Ochren paused, and looked at his young companion.

"The keep is built on that spot because something is buried under it," he said finally. "Something that is very old. Older than all the recorded history of Xaan, and certainly older than the brief years of the Karnatic League."

Ochren snorted at the long reach of history in this part of the world. Ultrich had pulled the League together in one short lifetime, and that was a great achievement, but it would take generations of great leaders to make the federation of kingdoms last.

"The Legatus wants us to check on what's lying under the keep," he said. "Make sure it's still there. The Xaanian spirit mages are using increasing amounts of spirit power, and it has to be coming from somewhere. It's up to us to see that the Keeper Stone is safe."

"The Keeper Stone?" said Mudge, a little startled. He had never heard of it.

"We'll be there soon," said Ochren, "and you'll see what I mean." Then he turned away, and it looked like that was as much of an explanation as Mudge was going to get.

"To get to the keep we have to do some hard hiking in the mountains," said Ochren, a few minutes later. "The others are ready to move out, and a guide should be here soon. Let's get this mad scramble under way!"

Mudge nodded. He looked from the compound toward the dark wall of the peaks. They were streaked with late winter snow in the valleys, and he shivered. He hoped the guide knew a way through the mountains rather than over the tops. Up there you froze at night, and one slip could be your last.

He wondered for a moment how his father's preparations for war were going. Senovila had mentioned the mobilization of the Defence League. In a way he wished he was there, doing something to help. What could be so useful about a side trip to Tashigot Keep? Weren't they just wasting time?

Still, the Legatus had decreed it. Just like everything else in his life, he thought bitterly, so there was no point in fighting it. Mudge hurried to Senovila's cart, and the small group of travellers made its way out of the compound in the early light. They followed the track down off the hill and onto the plains.

The guide pointed to a spot at the foot of the mountains, and they set off in that direction. A rough farm track ran between fields of just-planted crops. It was pleasant walking, and their backs were warmed by the early morning sun.

SEVEN

A sudden squall drove down the length of Taire Valley. Soldiers cursed as they ran to tie down tent flaps, while others launched themselves onto items in danger of blowing away. There was a small thunderclap, associated by most with the dark clouds racing overhead, and Sergeos, Cinnabar and the Legatus stepped out from behind a stores tent.

Cinnabar was the only other spirit walker capable of this sort of spirit transportation. Using her help, Ultrich was able to recover quickly from the prodigious feat he had just accomplished. Still, however you looked at it, transporting three people from Karnassus to Beltainia in an instant was quite a feat.

They strode toward Yeltar's command tent, clearly marked in the royal crimson and gold of the Beltainian nobility.

"Tell me again how you fix an arrival point with such accuracy when you haven't been to this place before," said Sergeos. He was ever the Mysteries teacher, keen to learn more about spirit walker abilities.

Ultrich smiled. "I didn't tell you," he said, and Sergeos looked a bit put out. Ultrich clasped his friend's shoulder.

"Never stop asking questions, Sergeos, we'd be worried if you did," he said, laughing. Cinnabar smiled too. It had taken her a long time to get used to Sergeos' inquisitiveness. But she had come to realize the Legatus was surrounded by officials and diplomats most of the time, 'yes men' in many ways. He treasured his friend's blunt questions.

"I did a flyover the day before," he said briskly.

"What, you flew over the valley in person?" said Sergeos, unable to contain his curiosity. The sort of power needed to overcome gravity for any length of time was enormous. Spirit transportation from place to place was difficult enough, but this . . .

Ultrich laughed outright.

"No, not that sort of 'flyover,'" he said, cutting Sergeos off. "Think of something like farsight at a much great distance."

Sergeos fell silent, trying to figure out how that might work.

The command tent was straight ahead. The Legatus would be given a guard of honour if the sentries recognized him, although he would still need to know the password. If they weren't recognized, and they didn't have the password, they would be trussed up and thrown into a tent until someone decided what to do with them. Yeltar ran a well-trained army. With a Xaanian invasion force just over the border, the three of them were extremely grateful for that.

"Legatus!" snapped the first of the sentries, standing so straight he was almost rigid.

"At ease," said Ultrich, though this seemed to have little effect on the sentry.

"Our Guardian is being informed you are here, Legatus," said the sentry, bowing deeply. His respect for Yeltar and Ultrich alike was obvious. His people revered Yeltar as an almost godlike figure, mostly for the way he had brought order to Beltainia, and then improved the living conditions of the people.

"If we may show you to the reception room?" continued the sentry. Ultrich nodded. The three spirit walkers found themselves flanked by soldiers as they made their way inside the vast tent. It had so many partitions they would have been lost by themselves.

"If you will wait here, Legatus?" queried the sentry, and Ultrich nodded again.

They were in a room about three paces by four. The earth floor had been beaten smooth and covered with a heavy mat. There were a number of low stools in the traditional manner, which allowed guests to sit with legs folded under them. Two of the camp staff glided reverentially in and placed a low table before the guests. The table was piled high with food and drink. Once they had finished their work the staff bowed deeply and left.

Ultrich wished Porteous was with them. The army commander from Middle March might be grey-headed, but he had lost none of his planning abilities. When it came to matters of war, Ultrich couldn't think of anyone better to trade ideas with about the Xaanian invasion than Yeltar, and Porteous would have brought a lot to the conversation.

Unfortunately, transporting anyone without spirit abilities was impossible. Ultrich wasn't sure the practical nature of the army man would survive the experience either. He didn't want his top strategist unhinged by the experience!

His thoughts were interrupted as Yeltar came striding in. The Beltainian commander hoisted Ultrich to his feet.

"Damn sentries should have brought you straight to me. How can you see what we're doing if you can't see the situation board?"

Ultrich grabbed Yeltar's free hand in both of his, and shook it vigorously.

"Good to see you too, you old ham actor!" he said, grinning broadly. He found Yeltar's impassioned speeches at court quite moving, but he still gave the Beltainian ruler a hard time about it.

"Don't start that again!" said Yeltar, raising a warning finger. Then he led the three of them out of the room and down a corridor of hanging cloth. They emerged into a large room in the middle of the tent.

At one end of the room stood a large flat table on trestles. This was the 'situation board', and a map of the area had been drawn on it, with Taire Valley taking the central position. Carved wooden figures in Yeltar's crimson and gold showed the positions of the Beltainian troops.

To the east, where the endless Xaanian desert began, a cluster of black and red discs had been lined up on the Desert Trade Route. At this stage the exact position of the Xaanian forces was unknown, but they would be at the border soon.

The two rulers fell to discussing manoeuvres for the battle. Yeltar intended to draw the attacking force into Taire Valley, so he could deal with it on a battlefield of his own making.

"I don't believe there are too many trees in the desert," he said archly, "so that's something the Xaanians are not used to. The firm ground here should give our cavalry an edge, too."

"The longer you can make their supply lines the better," said Ultrich, looking over the plan. "Have you thought of using the cover of the forest to circle round behind them once the fighting has started. You could attack their baggage train and reserve troops that way."

Yeltar nodded. Then his look grew serious.

"If I have enough troops for that, Legatus."

He looked up at the man who was his greatest ally, as well as his friend.

"Any help you can give me, and the people of Beltainia, would be greatly appreciated."

Ultrich closed his eyes. He didn't want to let his friend down, but there was little he could do. Cinnabar stepped in and told the Guardian about the outpouring of Xaanian troops along all three trade routes.

"If the League doesn't stop the south-marching army at Rotor Valley Pass, we'll lose control of the Scion Kingdoms, and the mines they contain," said Ultrich.

"We'll also have thousands of villagers displaced into the Marches. Our stores of food are going to be stretched supplying our troops, without extra mouths to feed."

He paused, wondering how the situation could be put in a nutshell. "We can't be of much use to Beltainia until we've secured our own borders," he finished bluntly.

Yeltar was silent. He hadn't been expecting this answer. Then he steeled himself. If you couldn't reshape your plans as circumstances changed, you didn't deserve to be a ruler.

"It can't be helped, my friend," he said softly.

"How long before the other Independent Kingdoms can assemble their forces?" said Ultrich.

Yeltar grimaced. "That's the problem. They've relied on Beltainia to keep the peace for so long now that their armies are largely hereditary, and untrained. They're armies in name only.

"Beltainia is by far the largest of the Kingdoms," he continued, "so I can't expect as many troops from the others. Wensh backs onto The Wilderness, so it has a battle-hardened force along the border to control brigands and the like, and they are already on their way here.

"Wensh's island colony Thyrox has a strong navy, because of the pirate threat along the coast. In the north Martilees maintains companies of skirmishers to keep the Wild Men of the Northern Waste at bay.

"I can count on experienced troops from some of those areas," he continued, "but anything else would be an untrained rabble. Willing enough, but little more than lambs to the slaughter."

Ultrich nodded. It was a familiar problem. A war on such a large scale needed a lot of preparation. There was training, arming and supply lines, let alone the support functions like healers and tents. He faced the same problems running the Karnatic League.

"What do you need most?" said Ultrich.

"Columns of armoured horses," said Yeltar, without hesitation.

Ultrich saw what he meant. The Xaanian mounted archers were well trained and highly mobile. Their horses were light, and manoeuvrable. The archers were the greatest threat Beltainia faced. The metal cladding on the armoured horse columns of the southern lands more than outweighed this.

It was unfortunate the contours of the Independent Kingdoms produced very little metal for an extravagance like armour.

"I'll send you what I can," said Ultrich, "but it may be some time away yet."

Yeltar nodded.

"I'll hold them as long as I can," he said. "Then I'll fall back to a position on the border with Glocks. The available troops from the other Kingdoms will be sailing soon for Thebes. They can march from the port to meet us there."

Ultrich approved of the plan. Yeltar would make the Xaanian forces pay dearly at Taire Valley, then fall back to a new position. Once there he would pick up reinforcements and rest his troops. He would be buying time at Taire Valley for the rest of the Independent Kingdoms to mobilise their forces.

"You can expect a little help from me when the battle is at its height," said Ultrich enigmatically. "Do you still have quantities of firecake available?"

The hard black cake was produced occasionally by the region's alchemists in their endless investigations into the nature of matter, and it flared brightly when it was ignited.

Yeltar had already put it to use as a means of sending a signal. A succession of flashes from hilltop to hilltop at night could send a simple message across Beltainia very quickly.

Yeltar looked sideways at him, and Ultrich smiled. "I want to show you a little trick with that stuff," he said. The two rulers huddled together over a sheet of paper as Ultrich sketched diagrams. These were the items he wanted Yeltar's alchemists to produce, and Yeltar nodded his understanding.

It ended up being a very useful meeting. The armies under both rulers would be better prepared due to the discussions that had taken place, and the spirit walkers would return to Karnassus confident of the support that would come from the Independent Kingdoms.

Many kingdoms away the rangers and those they were protecting walked or rode the cart toward the Scaffold Mountains in the distance. The day was already bright and sunny, and one or two villagers in the fields looked up as the cart went by and waved. The journey wasn't easy for Bear, though. He was lying flat on the deck of woven branches at the back of the cart, though his friends had made him as comfortable as they could.

At least the bleeding from the deep cuts to his shoulder and chest had stopped. A night of healing sleep and Arnima's skills at binding his wounds had helped enormously, but he was still weak.

There was little jolting from the cart while they were on a reasonably flat surface, but it wouldn't stay like that for long. Mudge could imagine the track becoming much worse when they reached the mountains.

"Isn't there some way we can help Bear," he said to Arnima, as they trudged along behind the cart. "At least make it easier for him while we cross the mountains."

She looked at him for a moment.

"No," she said at last. "Nothing beyond helping his body repair itself, which we're already doing."

Any hope Mudge had that she would miraculously heal Bear, like she had Senovila, evaporated. He guessed that she would have her reasons for not offering that skill. Perhaps it was only possible for her to do such a thing for someone she was bound closely to.

The travellers came to the foothills in the late morning, and followed a narrow plain beside a winding river. Then the track led into a gorge. They made reasonable time until the river veered off into an impassable defile it had cut through a rocky hillside. The path turned a different way, and zigzagged up a steep slope.

Senovila took one look at the climb and decided it was time for a midday meal while they thought through their options. The rangers unpacked the metal cones and got some food under way.

Senovila and Ochren dismantled the cart, and packed the parts onto the horses, while Colma transformed the woven branches from the deck of the tray into a stretcher to carry Bear.

When the meal was over they filled the water bottles from a nearby trickle of water and prepared for the climb. Colma and Mudge transferred Bear to the stretcher, and wrapped him tightly onto it with a blanket. He would be going up head first, carried by two of them, one at either end of the improvised stretcher.

The trip to the top was arduous. The afternoon sun blazed down on their heads, and the horses, with their heavy loads, needed constant encouragement on the narrow path. The travellers took the packs of the stretcher-bearers along with their own, and struggled on. Bear was awake for a while, and assured them he was more comfortable now than he had been on the cart. Arnima repacked Bear's wounds when they rested halfway up the track. The packing had been badly stained over the wound, but it was the clear weeping of something healing.

They'd all had enough of the winding track by the time they reached the top of the ridge and it was some time before Mudge's breathing had eased. Then he noticed the glorious views. The river they had left behind was a tiny trickle in the valley, far below. The compound where they had stayed the night was a toy fort in the distance. It was even possible to see the coast and the Trading Seas, far away on the other side of the Marches.

Mudge pulled his long greatcoat more tightly around him, and turned to look toward the remaining mountains. He saw a higher range of peaks looming over them, and his heart sank. That was where the rock and scree really began. The peaks were still heavy with winter snows, even this far into spring. The passes between the mountains were deep in shadow, and they would be frozen, inhospitable places. Any journey through them wasn't going to be easy.

Then Arnima called him over. He noticed for the first time Bear's pale colour, and the sweat on his brow. He had thought his friend was merely asleep, but now he saw how deeply unconscious Bear was.

"One of his lungs has started filling with fluid," said Arnima with concern. "A talon must have punctured it."

"What can we do?' said Mudge. It was distressing to hear his friend's laboured breathing.

"Not much while we're on the move," said Arnima bluntly, "but don't worry, he's young and strong. There's plenty of life left in him yet."

They followed the ridge for the rest of the afternoon, before descending into a dry, sheltered valley. They were still well above the tree line, with little shelter, but it wasn't long before it was time to make camp for the night. Senovila unpacked the horses, and turned them out to make the best of the dry grasses.

Mudge had been sensing something malevolent tracking them since the top of the ridge. Now he had the chance to find out what it was. While the others made camp, he sat with his back against a boulder and made himself comfortable. Then he closed his eyes, and sent his spirit senses out over the hills and mountains.

Two of the winged creatures were working their way along the tops of the mountain range, and he sensed them immediately. They would have been dots against the highest peaks if seen by human eyes. And they were hidden from view by a dark spirit veil, something Mudge saw as a grey fog moving against the mountains.

He travelled out on his farsight, effortlessly covering the distance to the high mountain peaks. Then he drew alongside one of the creatures, and examined the cloak around it more closely. The fabric of the dark spirit veil was different, unlike anything the Priatic Order of Mysteries taught. It was a strange thing, built of raw emotion. There was nothing of the natural patterns of the world in it. Greed drove the creature, or drove the thing that made it, and there were traces of anger, and rage, in the fabric of the veil.

Mudge teased cautiously at the spirit veil with his mind. The brooding, instinctive creature within the veil didn't respond. It flew on, scanning the mountains below, unaware of his presence. He pushed the spirit veil this way and that until he saw how it was constructed, and how it could be undone. He worked at it until he was sure he could unravel any spirit veil that was built like this if he needed to. Pleased with his efforts, he turned away from the giant flying lizard, and returned across the long, chilly distance to his body.

It took a while until he felt he was himself again, but then he could feel the rock against his back and the wind across his face. After a while he rose, and went in search of Ochren, and explained what he had seen to the senior ranger.

Ochren understood immediately how exposed they were to the creatures that were hunting them, and called for the half made camp to be dismantled. Mudge and his companions packed up quickly and hurried down into the valley. With any luck there would be some cover further down.

They made good time, even slowed by the need to stretcher Bear along, but it was growing dark as they headed down the last slope to the valley floor. Then Mudge felt a presence, and twisted one arm upwards until he was pointing straight at the disturbance. Then he unravelled the spirit veil in the skies above them with his mind.

There was a screech of rage, and two of the flying creatures appeared above them. They caught the last rays of the sun as they wheeled lower and lower, and the horses reared, jerking at the lines they were being led by. The travellers increased their speed down the slope, but the trees at the bottom of the valley were still too far away, while the creatures above them were gaining rapidly.

Ochren shouted a command, and the group veered across the slope toward a group of large boulders. Colma and Liam were the last to reach them, and they carried Bear into safety as the first of the creatures soared low overhead. It hissed its frustration as they ducked out of reach.

The horses were the worst of their problems for the next few moments. Senovila finally got the two war stallions backed into the deepest of the recesses among the boulders, out of the way. Then he blinkered their eyes. It seemed like a stand-off. Then Mudge felt the presence of another of the creatures as it landed further down the slope, and its sudden arrival cut the party off from the forest on the valley floor.

Mudge sensed the otter-like creatures on its back, and called a warning to Ochren. It was getting dark, and the rangers hurried to find flare torches in their packs. It wasn't long before the area was bathed in flickering light.

The rangers were just in time. A number of dark shapes bounded out of the darkness, and into the torchlight around the boulders. Several of them fell, pierced by ranger arrows, and that forced them back to the edge of the torchlight. More of the winged creatures circled above their position, looking for signs of weakness they might exploit.

Mudge edged over to Ochren.

"How long will the torches last?" he whispered.

"Not that long," said the ranger. "We've got two in reserve, but we can't keep this up for ever."

"We need every bow if we're going to make a run for the pine forest," said Mudge, "but the stretcher will take two of us out of action."

"Well, that's the only way out of this that we've got," said the ranger, "unless you can think of something, and think of it fast."

Mudge knew he had to find an answer to their predicament using his spirit walker skills, but how? He had been thinking of ways to make their progress over the mountains easier, and he wondered if he could use one of those ideas now.

He left the others to keep back the attackers, and found a place where two of the boulders formed a long passageway. He seated himself at the head of it, with the other end pointing down into the forest below. When he had focused his mind he reached out into the valley, sending a spirit call.

He waited a moment, and thought he detected a reply from the forest below, followed by another. He called again, and a scuffle of tiny feet flicked loose stones aside as something headed straight for Mudge. It stopped in front of him, and another presence scampered across a boulder on his left, then brushed passed him to disappear into an old animal hole under one of the boulders.

Mudge crooked his fingers, and a thought form tightened around the presence in front of him. It coalesced into a ball of pale fire. After a brief battle of wills, the sprite appeared to him in its true form, and Mudge was surprised. The sprites here were taller, and looked more intelligent, if that was ever a word to describe a sprite. They were dressed in clothing made from a woven fibre, which was unusual, though that was probably just another spritely illusion.

"We acknowledge you as master," said the sprite grudgingly.

That was new as well. The sprites around Shaker's Hope would never have made such a statement. They wouldn't have spoken to him unless they were commanded to do so.

There was the sharp crack of giant wings as several of the flying creatures descended above the boulders, while the otter creatures on the ground made a concerted rush.

Mudge could hear Ochren yelling commands, and the sharp hiss and thump as arrows struck home. There was more harsh screeching from above them, and then the creatures were gone, disappearing back into the night.

Mudge explained to the sprite what he wanted it to do.

A look of cunning came over the sprite.

"Does the young master ask for a boon?" it said in a silky voice.

Mudge hesitated. He could command them to do his bidding, because he was more powerful than they were. On the other hand he didn't like to think of himself as a dictator, even with such unthinking elementals as forest sprites.

"And if I ask for a boon?" he said warily. The sprite looked uneasy, and Mudge had to tighten the thought form around it to get the truth.

"Then sprites can ask an equivalent boon at some time in the future," it offered reproachfully, as if it were terribly unfair of Mudge to want to know the rules of the agreement.

"And what else?" said Mudge, tightening the thought form further. He had the impression there was more. The sprite twisted round inside its clothing, and keened consolingly to itself.

"Sprites must help master with all their powers, and are bound to do more than master asks of them."

Mudge was surprised at this. The Priatic Mysteries held that sprites were unable to think for themselves, but the detail and intent in this agreement showed the little creatures were much more complex than that.

"Torches are about had it," called Ochren from behind him. "We can make it to the pine forest before they give out, but we've got to go now!" That made the decision easy for Mudge. He released the sprite from the thought form, then told it what he wanted.

"Get us to safety in the pine forest down there," he said, pointing carefully in the direction he wanted to go. There was no telling how literally the sprites might be taking his words.

"Take all of us there, including the one on the stretcher – the bed," he added, "Go as fast as you can, and keep the torches burning. We need something to light our way."

The sprite was nodding and bowing so fast Mudge hoped it didn't hit its head on a boulder and hurt itself. Then it sent a message down into the valley. Mudge couldn't hear it with his ears, but it registered on his spirit senses.

At the same time the sprite hidden under the boulder popped out in front of him. It brushed its rough-spun clothing down and muttered noisily to itself.

Mudge just had time to explain to Ochren that he had enlisted help before the night was filled with the patter of tiny feet and the clink of dislodged stones in the grass. Arnima yelped as something brushed past her. Bear groaned as his stretcher levitated itself off the ground.

"Show yourselves!" commanded Mudge. None of the group wanted to trip over the sprites in the dash for the forest. There were gasps of astonishment as child-sized creatures in roughly woven clothes appeared among them. They were about the same in number as the group of travellers. One of the torches sputtered, and started to go out. Ochren cursed, and ran over with another one, but it wouldn't catch.

"We need more light," said Mudge sharply. One of the sprites nodded, and they all began to glow softly. Radiance streamed from them like the brightest moonlight.

"Everybody ready?" called Mudge. "We're going now!"

With the others behind him, and four of the sprites carrying Bear on the stretcher, Mudge left the boulders at a run. He started angling down the slope toward the densest part of the pine forest below.

"This way," said the sprite leader, tugging at his greatcoat as it veered toward some scrub against a bluff at the head of the valley. Mudge hesitated for a moment, then followed. Behind him he heard the twang of bows at work, and the thump of arrows striking home.

Overhead one of the winged creatures screeched its rage, and dived toward them.

A concentrated volley of arrows dropped the attacker out of the sky, and the little party covered the remaining ground as fast as they could. The bluff was coming up fast, while the dark shapes at the edge of the light seemed reluctant to press their attack. Mudge prayed the situation would stay that way.

Then he looked back, and saw the guide Athren had provided falling behind, until he was taken by one of the flying creatures. Arrows slammed home into its body, but the man disappeared into the darkness above them and Mudge could guess his fate. How were they going to find their way across the mountains now?

"Where can we hide?" he hissed at the sprite leader, running beside him, as the blank face of the bluff and the openness of the scrub became apparent.

"Master said take you to safety," said the sprite, unconcerned. Its legs were a blur as it ran beside him. Mudge couldn't see anywhere safe, but the sprite suddenly turned left and vanished into the rock wall of the bluff. He skidded to a halt, and a child-sized arm reached out and tugged at his greatcoat.

"Master come. Master find safety," said the sprite, from within the stone. Steeling his nerves, Mudge stepped into the bluff.

He passed through into a large cave with a sandy floor. He could see by the radiant light of the sprite that it was large enough to easily hold them all. He stepped back outside, and started guiding the others toward the rock face.

Ochren and Senovila arrived together, leading the horses on short halters. Once he realized where they were going, Senovila unstrapped most of the bundles on the backs of the horses and pulled them to the ground. That left just the bones of the portable cart. Ochren slapped the horses on the rump, and they galloped into the darkness. They were heading for the denser forest further down, looking for their own safe place. Once the horses were gone the two men dragged the bundles inside the cave.

"The horses can look after themselves," said Senovila as he passed Mudge. He was probably right, thought Mudge, remembering the fiery temperament he had seen in the warhorses.

The others arrived in a bunch, and disappeared into the stone wall after a little encouragement. At last Mudge followed them. He found them all looking around in amazement at this new world inside the bluff.

Then they dropped against the walls of the cave, breathing heavily after the long run. There was one sprite left now, the one Mudge had made the deal with, and everything was bathed in the soft moon glow of its radiance.

Mudge turned his face toward the non-existent cave mouth, then back to the sprite, and lifted an eyebrow. The sprite seemed to understood that he was asking a question. It smiled happily, enjoying its part in frustrating the creatures outside.

"Illusion," it said. "Cave is real, bluff is not."

Mudge nodded. The sprites had certainly fulfilled their part of the bargain, but Mudge still felt a little uneasy, what might they want in return?

Ochren set some of the rangers to make an evening meal, though it would be cold since the smoke from a fire might give them away. Shyleen burrowed her arms into the sand, and smoothed out a shallow depression.

"This will make a great bed," she offered, and the others nodded. She was right, and they all slept very well that night.

EIGHT

The next morning Mudge thought about their position inside the cave and decided it wasn't as good an option as he had first thought. The creatures hunting them knew where they were, and it was likely their refuge would turn into a prison.

"Master wait until enemies are gone," said the sprite, when he questioned it, and it seemed sprites had little idea of how important time was for the big people. The travellers still had a lot of ground to cover to get to the other side of the mountains, and all of it was out in the open.

He decided to try a little word game with the sprite. It had tried to keep some of the rules of the boon system from him when the deal was struck, so it didn't seem unfair to bend the rules a little himself. He had said the sprites were to get the travellers to the pine forest, but he had also said to get them to safety.

"Travellers are not safe yet," he said to the sprite leader. The sprite looked alarmed.

"While the flying creatures remain, travellers are not safe in the mountains," he continued. The sprite nodded in guarded agreement.

"The beasts are flying the length of the mountains. I saw them over the high peaks this afternoon," he added, and the sprite looked at him in disbelief.

"Spirit walker look," said Mudge, pointing to his eyes and away. "Farsight."

The sprites muttered among themselves, and the leader twisted and turned its body inside its roughly spun clothes. Eventually it cast its eyes down, which Mudge took to mean it acknowledged the point.

"Travellers will be safe when they reach Tashigot Keep," said Mudge, hoping this wouldn't be too big an ask for the little creatures.

The sprite looked like it was going to have a fit. Then it turned abruptly away and gave a spirit call of its own. A dozen or more of the creatures appeared out of the walls and gathered around it. There was a lot of animated discussion, and one of the sprites looked away from the group to give Mudge a baleful look. He smiled pleasantly back.

A thought struck him. This must be what it was like for his father, trying to negotiate with the kingdoms of the League. It was an uncomfortable realization, since he didn't want to ever have to take on his father's job. Still, it gave him a framework for dealing with the sprites.

What had he heard the Legatus tell his emissaries about diplomatic missions? He had said stay focused, work out one agreement at a time, and act as if the other side was worthy of respect, even when they weren't. He'd also said avoid strong drink and rich food when you needed your wits about you.

Well, there wasn't much strong drink and rich food along on this journey, thought Mudge wryly. The tedium of the grains and gathered greens in their diet was only lifted when the rangers caught something, but the rest of his father's advice applied rather well to his current situation.

The sprite leader left the group and came back to him.

"Take you all the way to Tashigot Keep is possible," it said guardedly. Mudge nodded.

"But two boons!" said the sprite triumphantly, barely able to contain its delight at its own cleverness. It jigged around for a moment, gloating over what it thought were its superior negotiating skills.

Mudge worked hard to suppress a smile.

"One boon," he said, holding up a finger. "One special boon. Spirit walker boon." Then he hesitated.

"Legatus boon," he said at last.

The sprite stepped back, obviously surprised.

Mudge didn't elaborate. He let the sprite think he had the resources of the League behind him. The sprite would have heard of the Legatus from the sprites in the Marches. What one sprite knew, they all knew.

This triggered another round of animated discussion. At last the sprite stepped forward once more.

"Legatus boon accepted," it said gravely.

Mudge wasn't sure what was required to cement the deal, but he knelt down and took the sprite's rough little hand in his own, small as it was. He placed his other hand on top of it. The sprite laid its remaining hand on top again, and they shook hands in that position.

Without further discussion he turned away to make himself a bed in the soft sand. The sprites gathered round an alcove in the far wall, and they seemed to be planning something. The last thing Mudge remembered as he fell asleep was the light from the sprites dimming. Then he was fast asleep, and dreaming.

He saw the whole of the world as he knew it, but from a great height. Tiny figures, and the small gyrating spires of spirit walker energies, as they populated the landscape. But there were other energies too, spires of a darker hue. They were fading in and out as he looked at them. What was he seeing?

This was important, he knew that. Yet he also knew he wouldn't remember it in the morning. He needed Luce and Jago to help him remember, as they had helped him before, but he couldn't find them anywhere. Something was keeping them from him. The same thing, he realized, that was suppressing his memories this time.

It was too difficult for him, too hard to remember, and he slipped into a dreamless sleep. Then it felt like it must be morning, but it was still pitch black. It took a while for Mudge to remember that he was in a cave, and he rolled over sleepily.

"Preparations are complete," said a sprite's voice behind him. He opened his eyes, and found he was looking at a stone wall, so he rolled the other way and saw the sprite leader. A dim light was emanating from its body.

Mudge grunted, then sighed. There was a moment's indecision when he tried to figure out how he could justify a few more minute's sleep, then he kicked the greatcoat off his legs. The sprite leader must have taken his actions as a signal to get the others up, and it nodded to other sprites, clustered round an alcove in the wall. They began to shine with the moon glow they had radiated the previous evening.

"Close the goddammit shutters," said Senovila in a sleepy voice. and stopped with a grunt as Arnima drove an elbow into him. Ochren was the first to his feet, and he roused the other rangers. It wasn't long before the whole party was up.

"I don't remember that doorway being there," said Ochren, walking over to take a better look, and the others crowded around too. An alcove in the far wall now framed a rough-fashioned stone doorway, one that led away into darkness.

"I hope this isn't a reverse illusion, and it's really a stone wall," said Mudge to the sprite. He was smiling as he said it, but the sprite looked at him enquiringly.

So, no sense of humour then, thought Mudge. He filed the information away with the rest of his knowledge of sprites.

"This way," said the sprite, and led him under the low doorway. A short tunnel opened out into a large cavern. It was impossible to see the size of it by the pale glow of the sprite's radiance.

"This will take us to Tashigot Keep?" enquired Mudge.

"Tashigot Keep," affirmed the sprite. It pointed along a dry, sandy stream bed to its right.

Mudge trudged back through the tunnel to the cave, and conferred briefly with Ochren. In the meantime, Liam and Mareet took digging blades from their packs and retraced Mudge's steps into the cavern. They scraped simple latrines against the walls in the adjacent cavern.

The sprites opened the cave entrance to the outside once again, and there was no sign of the flying creatures of the previous night. Colma and Mudge took the opportunity to gather dry twigs for the ranger cones and returned to the cave. Breakfast followed soon after.

Bear was an ongoing concern. He had been hard to rouse that morning, and didn't seem to have benefited from the night's sleep. Arnima changed the packing under his bandages, and checked his vital signs. Mudge lifted an eyebrow enquiringly, and she shook her head. He was no better, but at least he was no worse. Then she gave her patient something to ease his breathing, and settled him back on the stretcher again.

It wasn't long after that when they were ready to go. Four of the sprites carried Bear on his stretcher, as before, and the travellers formed up in the adjacent cavern.

Mudge and the sprite leader led the way, with the other sprites mixed through the party. The sprite radiance gave them enough light to see where they were putting their feet, but when they looked up everything else was lost in an impenetrable darkness.

Still, they were making progress, reflected Mudge. The sprite leader was explaining how the cave systems linked up, and would take them all the way to Tashigot Keep. Or to a place directly under Tashigot Keep it seemed.

The long, glowing line, sprite and human, made good time along the stream bed. To start with they found themselves descending. Then they were reduced to a cramped single file for a while as the walls closed in.

The passageway levelled off after a while and they entered a vast network of caverns, all connected through long passageways. It was like a giant honeycomb under the mountain, and water appeared for the first time.

There were a number of deep, clear pools that dotted their path. When Mudge tossed a stone into one of them, it rolled back the way they had come. It seemed the pools were connected by their own subterranean passages.

The travellers began to hear the musical trickle of running water, and passed a number of streams busy carving new galleries into the stone. Ahead of them the sound of a waterfall grew steadily louder, until at last they entered an enormous open space. Their only way forward was along a narrow ledge clinging to one side of the great cavern.

A river frothed along the bottom far below, and it burst out of the cavern wall as an enormous waterfall ahead of them. They were buffeted by spray as they made their way forward, and the path grew slippery. As they drew near the waterfall Mudge looked up into the heights above him, but there was nothing except darkness there.

The travellers eventually eased past the torrent and entered a more open gallery. The noise of the waterfall slowly diminished, and over time it died away altogether.

This gallery opened out into another cavern, fed by a number of gentle streams. Water spread out over the floor, linking together in a web of shallow lakes, before disappearing down a sink hole in the middle. A fierce draft from the sink hole blew some of the water back as spray, and they found themselves soaked yet again as they skirted the cavern, hugging the walls. Once they had reached the far end, the sprites led them into an entirely new cave system of long tunnels and narrow chambers. It was this they followed for the rest of the morning, and for the first time they were starting to climb.

It seemed about midday when Ochren called a halt. They had dried off as they walked, and were all looking forward to a meal after the activity of the morning. Mudge figured they must have left the foothills behind them, and were somewhere under the high peaks of the Scaffold Mountains.

He knew they would have been lost without the help they were getting from the sprites, and Mudge was glad he had taken such an interest in them during his days at Shaker's Hope. To most spirit walkers they were an insignificant part of the spirit world, but Mudge had already proved that idea wrong.

Bear groaned as he tossed on his stretcher, and Mudge saw Arnima tending to him. He went to help, but Arnima waved him away. He took his pack off, along with the others, and noticed a line of holes running across the floor of the cave. There was something about them that didn't seem right, something too regular.

The one nearest him had the remains of a post in it, and he kicked the stump with his foot, cursing as his toes hit a solid surface. He had expected the post to be rotten, but a closer examination showed it to be made of rock that looked like wood.

Mudge was familiar with the phenomena. There was a forest of stone trunks not far from Prias on the Middle March coast. But this post looked too regular to be a tree trunk. Surely it hadn't been shaped, and fitted into a hole cut in the cave floor?

"Work of the Sarn," said the sprite leader dismissively, and Mudge looked up.

"Old workings like this all through mountains," it managed, before lapsing into silence.

"When?" said Mudge, prompting it for more information.

"Before," said the sprite. Mudge raised both eyebrows.

"Before Builders come," said the sprite, and Mudge understood. The sprites called his people Builders. Sprites never lived above ground, and the need that humans had to construct dwellings out in the open was incomprehensible to them. The history of people in this land, as far as Mudge knew, went back a little over a thousand years.

So, the Sarn were here before that. How long they had been here before the arrival of his people he had no idea.

"Sarn build Tashigot Keep," offered the sprite. Mudge, in the middle of lowering himself onto the rocky floor, sat down with a thump.

That was something he did not know. He had been taught the keep was an outpost of the Xaanian Empire, something that had been built at the height of its power, around 300 years ago.

Ochren's enigmatic words about the Keeper Stone, that it rested under the keep, came back to him. The ranger had also said that the travellers' job was to check on it for the Legatus, but what exactly did that entail?

Then Arnima came to sit beside him. Keeping her voice low, she said, "Bear needs to be somewhere he can rest without being carried around. If I had known his lungs were going to fill with fluid, I would have said to leave him with the healers in Attica."

She looked pensive.

"I'm going to need to draw in some healing power for him, too. I'll need your help with that." She looked apologetic.

"I don't have everything I need with me. A place like the smithy, where I've lived for years, has a lot of power stored in it. I don't have that power to draw on here."

Mudge understood.

"When we get to Tashigot Keep?" he said, leaving the decision up to her.

She nodded.

"And the sooner that happens, the better for Bear," she said firmly.

Then she rose to help Liam prepare the midday meal in a more open part of the gallery. It was going to be something cold and quick since they had nothing to make a fire with under the mountain.

Tashigot Keep was closer than either of them thought, but it wasn't going to be easy to get there. By mid-afternoon they had reached the highest point of the cave system.

"This is the only way through?" said Mudge. He looked doubtfully at the crumbling, narrow gallery before them.

"Only way," said the sprite.

They had climbed some distance since midday, and the cave system had narrowed. The last trace of water had vanished long ago. They were following the slope of the mountain up, even though they were deep inside its rocky flanks.

This was the sort of country that the big mountain cats liked, remembered Mudge, the creatures taken as the emblem for the Karnatic League. The big cats might be the symbol for the League, he muttered, but that didn't make them any more friendly if the travellers came across one.

He pushed at some rotten rock protruding from the wall, and bits crumbled off where he touched it. It was unstable stuff, and he didn't like travelling through it. The granite bones of the mountain had been left behind them, and the smooth galleries that had been their main means of progress had disappeared. Mudge wasn't sure what this stuff was, but it was treacherous underfoot, and the passage they were following bent and twisted all over the place.

"Old mine workings," said Ochren, who had come up beside him.

Mudge nodded. Any mark left by tools had crumbled away long ago, but the passageway hadn't been made by water, that was for sure. Something flickered for a moment at a turning up ahead, and Mudge saw the sprite leader freeze in mid-step.

"Bar-sarn!" it hissed urgently, then vanished. The other sprites flickered out as well, leaving the passageway in darkness. There was a brief cry from Arnima, which Senovila quickly hushed, and they were left in total silence.

Mudge sent out his spirit senses. He detected the faint sparks of sprite minds around him, and the lighthouses of human consciousness. Then he flowed out ahead of them. He saw a flash in the far darkness, a flickering that came and went. Then another behind it. Both of them were tinged with the darker hues he had seen in his dream. The forgotten dream!

Suddenly the dream came flooding back, and he saw the overall plan of the giant red and black figure that had taken root in Xaan. He saw every contingent of troops it had at its disposal, and every agent it had sent out to spy on the Karnatic League and the Independent Kingdoms.

The same dark marks of red and black sullied the simple minds of the creatures ahead. Creatures the sprite leader had called Bar-sarn. Mudge searched for the sprite leader, and found the faint spark of its presence beside him. He touched its mind, very lightly, and felt it shy away.

"Tell me about the Bar-sarn," he said gently, sending his words into its mind.

The sprite leader recognized him, and calmed a little. Then it told him what it knew. It grew in confidence as it realized it could talk to Mudge mind-to-mind, the same way it talked to the other sprites.

"Bar-sarn servants of the Sarn, long ago, but few now remain. Bar-sarn exist only in the high places."

Mudge could feel it hesitating. It was trying to tell him about things it didn't fully understand itself.

"More and more they are changing. Before, we always have safe passage through the high places. Now, we do not trust them."

That made sense to Mudge. The Bar-sarn had the darker hues he associated with the evil emanating from Xaan. Willingly or not, that was the power they now served. He was about to ask something else when a high-pitched squeal erupted from the passageway ahead, quickly cut short.

Mudge sensed the distress of a sprite at the head of the column. Then, with his spirit sense, he felt the sprite leader reach out with its mind and converge on the affected sprite. The others did the same. It was the oddest sensation. One central point of fire grew ahead of him while a dozen empty shells remained, scattered along the passageway.

Then the sprite at the head of the column blazed like molten metal. It was a dazzling light that made Mudge turn his head away. Before he did, he saw indistinct shapes scuttle back into the darkness. They seemed ungainly, somehow badly assembled, as if they might drop onto all fours at any time.

Sprites, as Mudge knew, had become more people-like over the centuries. Their shape had changed during their association with the new settlers across their land. He wondered what it was that had degraded the appearance of the Bar-sarn so much.

He searched a long way ahead with his spirit sense, looking for more of the dark-hued creatures, and he found them scattered throughout the top of the mountain. They were few in number, as the sprite had said, and there were just four of them ahead of the travellers' current position.

Gathering up the minds of the Bar-sarn ahead of them, he soothed the primitive creatures into a state of sleep. Then he sent out his spirit senses further, in the direction of Tashigot Keep, but he sensed nothing else on the path ahead of them. That, at least, was something positive.

He pulled himself back to his body, and saw with his spirit sense that the sprites had returned to their bodies. He touched the mind of the sprite leader.

"Good trick," said Mudge, showing the sprite a mental picture of the dazzling light he had witnessed.

"Sprite warning," rustled the papery sprite voice inside his head.

Mudge nodded, then realized this action couldn't be seen in the darkness.

"Bar-sarn will not bother us again," he said reassuringly, sending a picture of them sleeping. "We can continue to Tashigot Keep safely."

The sprite leader made the mental equivalent of a nod. Its moon glow radiance returned, lighting up the section of passageway around it. The others followed its lead, and the column continued on its way, though Mudge was kept busy for a while explaining to the rangers what had actually happened.

The sprites guided them through a number of forks in the passage, and then the last of the crumbly, brown rock was behind them. They began to descend, and it wasn't long before they entered one of the familiar granite galleries they had travelled through on the way up. They were glad of the better surface underfoot.

"About time!" said Arnima imperiously, brushing brown grit off her overalls. It didn't help that they were several sizes too big for her with her loss of weight. She had taken several tumbles in the crumbling mine workings too, pulling Senovila down with her on one occasion. It was clear her pride was hurt, along with the odd bruise and graze.

Mudge smiled to himself. Whether it was regaining her fitness and losing weight, or getting closer to her Xaanian homeland, Arnima was sounding more regal by the day. She must have spent many years leading an aristocratic life when she first married Senovila. Something that had been buried under her existence in Shaker's Hope was now working its way to the surface. There was a new fieriness asserting itself in response to the challenges they were facing. Mudge doubted the new Arnima would lose her practical skills and generous nature, but the changes were amusing to watch.

The trip down the other side of the mountain passed quickly. Mudge estimated it was late in the evening when they entered a long cavern on the Xaanian side of the mountains. It felt to him like the end of a long day, and it didn't help that his pack had been growing heavier for some time.

"I would say it's nightfall outside," said Ochren. "Days seem longer underground. I don't know why that is, but I've learned to knock a few hours off my estimate of times."

Mudge nodded. He wondered where Ochren had learned things like that. Maybe he had spent time in the mines of the Scion Kingdoms. Whatever the time was outside, he was hoping for a rest soon, and his stomach was aching for something to be put into it.

Then Colma and Liam called a halt from the front of the column, and Mudge and Ochren moved up to join them. The two scouts were excited by something at the far end of the long cavern.

"That has to be a tunnel carved out of the rock," said Colma, and Liam agreed. It was a hard thing to make out in the soft light radiating from the sprites all the same.

Ochren motioned them forward to find out. It wasn't long before they came to steps at the foot of the tunnel, and next to it a low wall. It had been built to funnel seepage into a raised pool.

"Water for the keep," said Ochren. As a ranger he was keenly aware of military necessities.

"So the keep is just above us," said Colma, surprised, and Ochren nodded.

"Might as well climb the stairs and set up camp on the ground floor," said the ranger. "That way, we get to see the morning light."

Mudge suddenly realized how uncomfortable the long hours of dimly-lit darkness had been, and his spirits rose at the thought of sunlight. It was good to imagine a more normal day tomorrow.

"That means we can start doing something for Bear," said Arnima, who was now at Mudge's elbow. Mudge was thinking the same. It had been too long since Bear's encounter with the winged nightmare. His friend's slow slide into unconsciousness continued to haunt him.

As they climbed the steps he thought how odd it felt to be using an entrance made by thinking creatures. Had the Xaanians added the tunnel later, or were the Sarn responsible?

One by one the travellers entered the basement under the keep, and looked around them. The stairs continued up the inside wall, but their attention was taken by a raised plinth in the middle of the open space. On it an ornately carved disc supported a miniature dome.

"The Keeper Stone," guessed Mudge. He was surprised to see its resting place so openly revealed.

Ochren nodded. Ultrich had told him how to remove the dome and reveal the Stone itself, but that wouldn't happen until Mudge was ready. And when the boy was finally ready, only the two of them would be present.

"Let's have a look at the rest of the keep," said Senovila. He led the way up the stairs to the first floor of the massive structure. Stone walls separated the area into large rooms, crowned by massive beams that held up the floor above.

Mudge could see the arched stone entrance to the keep on one side, and a band of red through the doorway that signalled the last of the sunset. Ochren barked orders, and two of the rangers hurried to find fuel for the metal cones, while the rest of the company unpacked.

The senior ranger than set aside one of the central rooms for a small fire. He thought it was sufficiently screened from outside observers to not draw attention. A short while later the travellers were resting around the walls, bowls of food in hand, talking about the wonders they had seen under the mountain. Then Mudge called the sprite leader over.

"Sprites have proved themselves friends and allies," he said gravely. "They have earned the boon promised to them. Prince Rossi Monhoven swears by the Legatus that this promise will be honoured," and the sprite bowed so low Mudge was worried it would topple over.

"Sprites are honoured to assist the League," it said.

Mudge nodded, and was silent for a while. He wanted to show the little creature he appreciated its noble words.

"Sprites are free to go," he said at last, smiling and nodding.

The sprite leader skipped happily, and Mudge could hear the paper-rustling mind-to-mind sprite talk as it called the others to it. With a last round of bowing and nodding, the group faded out of existence altogether It made the room seem much bigger.

"You get used to the little ratbags," said Ochren quietly, and the others agreed, with some laughter. But Mudge didn't hear him. He was concentrating on his spirit senses, and they had taken him a long way away.

When he remembered the forgotten dream, under the mountain, he had also found himself able to sense the movements of the Xaanian armies, and the response of the League.

Now he detected a huge concentration of Xaanian troops marching across the High Steppes to the east of the keep. At the same time he sensed a rapidly growing League force in front of Rotor Valley Pass.

He wished he was with the League army in the High Steppes, preparing to defend his homeland.

NINE

Ultrich touched the mind of his mount lightly, urging it to keep pace with the horse beside it as companies of Lancers raced side by side across the High Steppes. Ultrich and Gosan, one of the young commanders from the Wild Marches, were at the head of the formation.

The Legatus rode bareback, as he always did. Part of his mind knew what his mount intended to do and he shifted his weight accordingly. He made it look effortless, but he knew he would ache all over later. Age was taking its toll. He really needed someone to take over the League, someone from his close family or one of his commander's sons. Anyone who could show themselves capable of the position.

So far, no one had come close. It was frustrating.

Ultrich scanned the empty wastes ahead of him. The High Steppes ran to the horizon, where the plateau descended to the Endless Desert, and the Great Salt Lake. Somewhere to his left a rough road cut through the edge of the Steppes on its way to the High Pass. He had known the Xaanian army wouldn't choose that way. They had headed straight for Rotor Valley Pass, with its good grazing and ample water.

The Xaanians had, however, shown a little greediness, and for that they were about to be punished. Somewhere ahead of the Lancers a whole wing of Xaanian horsemen and mounted archers was advancing along one of the shallow gulleys that were strung across the Steppes. They were hoping to fall upon the last of the hill tribes as they made their way to Rotor Pass and decimate them. The hill tribes were slow, burdened by herds and tents.

Ultrich knew the tactic well. A surprise attack was unsettling, and terror spread through unseasoned troops like wildfire if it wasn't checked. Drawing first blood would also boost Xaanian morale, but they weren't going to achieve those goals today.

The Legatus had been using his farsight to check the Xaanian advance since the middle of the previous day. He had seen the mounted troops ride ahead of the main body at first light this morning, and the Lancers behind him were his response to the threat.

The Xaanians thought themselves invisible in the gully, but that also meant they couldn't see the League forces approaching. At a command from Gosan, the horsemen lowered their lances and accelerated to a gallop. The thunder of so many hooves would take away the element of surprise, but by then it would be too late for a coordinated response from the enemy.

The edge of the shallow gully separated from the flat expanse of the Steppes ahead as the Lancers approached. A deep-throated roar went up from the riders as they saw it approaching. Then the Xaanian mounted archers boiled out of the gully, aware of the danger at last. They loosed a flight of arrows, followed almost as quickly by another.

Ultrich reached out and made some small changes to the laws of nature. The shafts grew heavy, and the fletching on the arrows unravelled, becoming a tangled clump. The arrows fell short in the dry pasture lands, and the Lancers hurtled over them, metal-clad hooves smashing the shafts underfoot.

Dismayed, the archers peeled away, but now the Xaanian cavalry poured out onto the Steppes. They stretched out to a gallop as they came to meet the challenge from the Lancers. There was barely time for the Xaanians to register the futility of charging lances with swords when the two lines struck, and almost every lance found its mark.

Dropping the long, metal-tipped poles the instant they smashed through their targets, the Lancers drew their sabres. They slashed through what was left of the Xaanian lines until they were clear, then wheeled their mounts about and prepared to charge a second time. They had been outnumbered two to one at the start, but the odds were already in their favour.

The Legatus urged his horse forward with the rest, and the Lancers picked up speed once more. The distance between the two forces closed rapidly, until at the last minute Ultrich reached into the minds of the Xaanian horses and took control of them. The legs of the mounts folded, pitching their riders forward, and bowling the horses along the ground. Then the Lancers were among them, cutting the riders to pieces.

Ultrich urged his mount through the fighting until he was clear, and brought it to a stop. Something wasn't right about the way the Xaanian troops were acting. They seemed to be under some sort of compulsion.

He followed his spirit senses in the direction of the mounted archers, where they had formed up on the other side of the gully. Ultrich walked his horse to the lip on the near side, challenging them.

Why didn't the archers turn and run? They were now heavily outnumbered, and they had seen their arrows fall out of the sky, useless. There was still time for them to make an escape.

Then the Xaanian captain barked an order, and dozens of arrows sped toward Ultrich in hard, flat trajectories. They parted at an invisible division in the air, passing on either side of him. The Legatus hardly even paused in his thinking for a party trick like that. Now he began to search among the archers for the source of the strange compulsion.

He found that the Xaanian captain wasn't the source of it, and continued on. Then Ultrich saw a movement among the mounted archers, and a strangely cloaked figure manoeuvred its horse out from behind the captain.

Ultrich smiled grimly. It was to be a challenge then.

A wave of unbearable worthlessness swept over him. He looked back over his life and saw the flaws in every decision he had ever made. He counted whatever gains he had made as nothing. Shame and guilt led him by the hand to the inexorable conclusion that the only way he could atone for his failings was to sacrifice himself to these, his enemies.

As he looked across the gully he saw how noble they looked, and how worthy. His life might at last be worth something if he just gave himself to their swords in penance. Despair ate at him, driving him forward. Despair and its cousin emptiness. And a profound isolation enveloped him.

All these emotions, and more, flooded over Ultrich in moments, but finding no purchase they rolled off his back and evaporated into the emptiness of the High Steppes.

He sat, unmoved, and thought about the challenge he had just defeated. Controlling the forces of nature was not that hard for spirit walkers, but controlling the devilry of the mind was a much greater challenge. That was why the best spirit walkers spent more time changing their 'human' nature than learning about the great magics within the world.

If there was no reaction to an event, nothing that was 'mine', nothing to live or die for. If the root causes of desire were cut off. If anger was overcome, and greed turned into an empty husk, then the human spirit could not be drawn into the world and manipulated by the ten thousand things it found there. It was this training that saved Ultrich from being sucked into his enemy's web of lies.

He shook himself, feeling vaguely begrimed by the assault, and considered his response. In the end, sadly, there was only one option. Like all the deadly sins of the human heart, such violence toward others needed to be met by itself. Only when those who caused pain and suffering felt the same suffering in themselves would they change.

The Legatus reached out with his mind and visited upon the cloaked figure the very things it had tried to inflict upon him.

The figure arched, a soundless, wordless scream. It slid off its horse. As it hit the ground Ultrich knew it was already deeply unconscious. He relaxed his grip on its mind, and the Xaanian horsemen roused themselves, as if from a long sleep.

They looked past Ultrich to where the Lancers had finished their grisly work dispatching the Xaanian cavalry. Now they were forming up into a line that would sweep down upon the gully. The archers turned and fled across the Steppes, back to the advancing Xaanian army.

Ultrich let them go. He walked his horse down the side of the gully and climbed an easy incline on the other side. Then he dismounted beside the fallen rider. A smell of marsh gases and freshwater lake wafted from the cloaked figure. It reminded Ultrich of rivers laden with silt. He dragged the cloak off its face with his foot, and exposed something reptilian, yet vaguely familiar. As if something human had evolved from different origins. Ultrich pursed his lips.

"Sarkosay," he said to himself. It was hard to believe.

They were creatures of legend, chameleon-like beings that could look like anything around them. They had the ability to control minds, to will others to do what they desired, and this one had been perfectly credible as a Xaanian commander.

He paused. What was the League up against? What power now controlled the ancient, and still potent, kingdom of Xaan? Whatever it was, these things would be perfect underlings for such an evil.

The figure twitched, and Ultrich felt its consciousness slip away. He wrapped his mind around it, following it into the netherworld. There were too many questions he wanted answered to let it go. He halted its journey, and started to guide its consciousness back to the land of the living.

Then he was ripped away from his prize, buffeted by the thoughts and emotions of an enormously powerful being. Steeling himself, he withdrew into his inner core, trying to survive the enormous energies whirling around him.

Traces of lesser minds came and went from the towering consciousness ahead of him in the netherworld. They were passing on information, and receiving new instructions. Ultrich saw the spirit trace of the Sarkosay pass into the centre of it all.

That same intelligence turned its attention toward him, and he fled for the world of the living. Before he could regain his body on the Steppes, he felt himself seized and lifted up. His mental shields gave way, and he was crushed by an overwhelming demand for answers.

He resisted, but the battering was too much. Barely conscious, he felt something snatch him from his tormentor. A great howl of rage was cut short behind him as he was ripped away. He remembered being returned to his body, and then he sank into oblivion.

"Legatus! Wake up! Dammit, someone get me some water," bellowed Gosan. He was unceremoniously slapping Ultrich's face with one hand. The Legatus was trying to reply when a whole canteen of cold water was poured over him. He sat up, spluttering, trying to push the Wild Marches commander away.

"All right, all right!" he managed at last. "Is there anyone who's actually survived your first aid?"

The men clustered around him roared with laughter. They were hugely relieved that their supreme commander had regained consciousness. Ultrich then got unsteadily to his feet, supported by Gosan. What in the name of all the hells had happened, he thought, trying to clear his head. Something had snatched him back from that thing in the netherworld, but what?

He calmed his mind, and tried to recall the event. What had the presence felt like? Who or what had helped him? He smelled an astringency in the air, and the faintest trace of cinnamon, and knew instantly what it meant.

It had been spirit walker work, and he knew of no one in the League with that sort of power. There was something familiar about the way it was done, however, and he tried to home in on it. Then the pieces fell into place.

Rossi! By all the gods, his son had saved his life!

"Are you all right?" asked Gosan, perplexed by the look of wonderment on Ultrich's face.

"Yes, yes I'm fine," said the Legatus, a moment later. He let go of the astonishing realization his son was capable of such things, and brought himself back to his role as supreme commander.

"I think we're finished here. Let's mount up and escort the last of the hill tribes into Rotor Pass."

Gosan nodded, and started barking orders. One of the Lancers brought Ultrich his horse, and helped him mount it. The horsemen formed up, and left the scene of the battle heading south-east at a steady pace. They were aiming for the dust clouds ahead of them. It was a marker that would lead them to the last of the hill tribes and their herds.

Ultrich was unsettled. His worst fears had been realized. Whatever that thing in the netherworld had been, it was more powerful than he was. Unless the League could find another champion, the evil in Xianak was going to be unstoppable.

Not that far away from the High Steppes, morning at the keep was a rather clammy affair. The mists that gathered round the mountain peaks most days were drifting off the tops and down into the valleys. Eventually they would roll out over the desert plains and evaporate, shrivelled up by the fierce desert heat.

Mudge woke to the sound of a fire sparking to life, and he saw that Ochren was piling more wood onto last night's embers. It felt like morning, but everything was still dull and grey. He shivered, and tightened his greatcoat around him.

"Time for the Keeper Stone, boy," said Ochren, nudging him with his foot.

"Breakfast first," said Mudge blearily, still half asleep.

"You won't want anything in your stomach for this," said Ochren. That woke Mudge up in a hurry.

They left Senovila and Arnima to rouse the others, with strict instructions that no one was to descend into the basement of the keep. Then they made their way down the steps that lined the outer wall of the basement. A patch of weak, grey light filtered down beside them, but once they were away from the steps it was hard to see anything. Mudge expected Ochren to light a pitch and brushwood torch, but he didn't.

They stumbled toward the raised plinth that housed the Keeper Stone, finding it mainly by touch. Ochren placed his hands on the dome at the top. Then he took a deep breath. Ultrich had told him what to do, but knowing the words didn't make it any easier.

He recited a line from an ancient language, and then the voice of the Legatus took over. It was coming out of the air all around them. Mudge figured it was a spirit trace that Ultrich had left to guard the Keeper Stone. He listened in fascination as the words rolled on, creating a spirit pattern.

This way of doing things had always been something he didn't understand. A spirit walker from the Priatic schools needed to see a pattern in the world before he or she could make changes. To Mudge the pattern was coincidental. He wondered why they didn't just reach into the heart of things, and do what needed to be done. That was what he did.

The voice of the Legatus finished its chanting, and the raised dome split down the middle, each half receding into the carved disc under it. The Keeper Stone blazed with revealed glory, lighting up the basement of the keep all around them.

Mudge looked away until his eyes adjusted. When he looked back he was surprised to see how small the stone was. He was looking at a rough-shaped piece of something like mineral ore. It was a piece that could easily fit in the palm of his hand.

"All yours, boy," said Ochren, pleased his part in proceedings was over.

Mudge looked at him enquiringly.

"Touch the damn thing," said Ochren, moving away from the raised plinth. "And make sure you've got your wits about you."

His words didn't inspire confidence in Mudge, but he wasn't going to back down in front of the head ranger. Ultrich seemed to think the Keeper Stone was important, and if Mudge could do something to help in the struggle against the invaders, he would do it. It was time to take a deep breath and get on with the task.

Tentatively, he laid a hand on the Stone, dimming its light. Mudge looked in surprise at his hand, made almost translucent by the light from the Stone beneath it. Then he felt something tapping at his spirit senses. He opened his awareness to meet it, and discovered the Keeper Stone was alive!

Mudge jerked his hand away. He hesitated for a moment, then cautiously resumed contact. He discovered that the Stone was more curious about him than anything else. It was wondering what he was, but rather idly so, as if the things of the physical world were of little interest to it.

Mudge thought about his father. He wondered how much the Legatus knew about the Keeper Stone. At that, the Stone's interest in him flared strongly. He could feel it searching him out, crowding around him. He forced himself to think about the keep, and his friends on the floor above. The Stone retreated. It was, once again, biding its time.

Mudge saw that the Stone responded to his thoughts, or perhaps the emotions that underlay them. There was so much he didn't know. How did the Keeper Stone work? What did it want?

Part of him wasn't ready to deal with this right now. Bear had been on his mind all night. He had thought Arnima would lead the two of them in a healing ritual for his ranger friend this morning, but instead he was here with the Keeper Stone, at his father's request. He was ambivalent about his father's part in this too, and now he was faced with a riddle that seemed as impossible as any ancient paradox.

Unwittingly, he thought of the moment the winged beast had seized Bear and carried him into the air. The image was emblazoned on his mind. He would never forget it. Moments later there was an abrupt scream from the floor above, and an anguished moan from Bear. It sounded torn out of him.

Mudge found himself in two places at once. Still with the Keeper Stone in the basement, yet witnessing what was happening on the ground floor of the keep. He saw Bear hanging in the air, apparently unsupported. He was in the same position as when he'd been dragged aloft by the winged monster.

The Keeper Stone! It was taking the picture out of his mind and re-enacting it. He saw Bear jerk spasmodically as the pain of being suspended by his wounded shoulders seared through him.

Mudge didn't hesitate. He just poured himself into the Stone, battering it back. He was struggling to control it, and stop it acting out his thoughts. It drew back, wondering at his actions. He felt the ease with which it could crush him, and the growing intensity of a question within it. Why would he risk his life?

Mudge didn't hesitate. His heart went out to his friend. He remembered the peace he had found at Shaker's Hope, but now two of his friends were dead, and he wouldn't let that happen to a third.

He launched himself at the Stone, reaching into places inside himself he had never been before. He gathered his energies to overcome the Stone, to take command of it and make it stop.

Then the Stone was gone from under his hand.

His fingers closed on emptiness, yet it was somehow still there. He could feel its presence, all around him and inside him. He tried to find something that was just the Stone, but it was impossible to separate what was the Stone, and what was himself. He pulled back, uncertain how to make it let go of Bear when he couldn't locate it. Then he began to understand.

The Stone approved. It understood the fact he would die for his friends, that he was someone who would die for the well-being of others. At the deepest level he cared about the state of the world, and the creatures that lived in it.

Mudge saw, in his strange, split state, that Bear was now back on his stretcher. He wanted to climb the stairs to check on him, but it was hard to move. Everything had changed, even the way he moved his limbs, as if he was back in his body in a new way.

Then he was scrambling awkwardly up the stairs, and stumbling to his friend's side. Arnima was trying to stop the new flow of blood that was seeping through the packing over his friend's wounds. It saturated the bandages around his upper body.

Kneeling beside her, he opened both his hands above Bear's recumbent form. He imagined Bear as he had seen him so many times before. Healthy, full of life, his capable frame undamaged once again.

Arnima snatched her hands away from the bandages, startled by the energies that suddenly surged through Bear's wounds. Mudge felt the Keeper Stone looking over his shoulder, guiding his intent, adding its energies to his own. He could feel muscle knitting together, and the delicate network of veins and arteries being restored. He felt the skin closing over the wounds.

When the healing was complete, Mudge let his hands fall to his sides. He nodded to Arnima. She looked back at Bear, then cut away the bandages. As she removed the packing, the others crowded round. There was a hum of amazement as they saw the faint lines on Bear's skin, all that was left of the deep cuts forced into his body by the monster. Then Bear opened his eyes.

"Where are we?" he asked weakly. Then he tried to sit up. Arnima hurried to support him.

"How did I get here?" he continued.

"That, you lucky streak of horse muck, is a long story!" said Senovila. They were all crowding around Bear now, overjoyed to see him well again. Mudge edged away, and signalled Ochren to join him.

"Keep them out of the basement until I'm ready to leave," he said softly. "Make breakfast, do a bit of hunting maybe. I have to sort out this Keeper Stone thing. I don't want anyone down the stairs until I'm done." Ochren nodded.

"Prince Rossi," he said quietly, and Mudge looked up. It was unusual for the ranger to use his formal title.

"I came here with your father, as part of my training, in the early days of the League. We came over the High Pass, and along the edges of the desert. There was a whole company of us. Ultrich tried to master the Stone then, too."

Mudge's eyes opened in surprise for a moment, but it made sense. The new Combat Prime would have sought to extend his spirit abilities as much as he could. Mudge was intrigued. He didn't know any stories about his father's adventures as a young man.

"The Stone damn near killed him," said Ochren. He looked Mudge in the eye. It had obviously affected him deeply. Mudge didn't know what to think. Then he realized the same thing could have happened to him.

"You let me touch the Stone, knowing it had the power to kill me!" he said, his face darkening, but Ochren seemed unperturbed.

"You aren't your father. If you were I wouldn't have let you anywhere near it."

Mudge's hands were shaking. The delayed shock of what he had been through this day was coming home to roost.

"No one said being heir to the Legatus was going to be easy," said Ochren mildly.

"I'm no one's heir!" said Mudge bitterly. "I'm just a kind of insurance policy in case the three ahead of me for the throne get struck down by lightning."

Ochren's expression didn't change, and Mudge recalled a similar conversation they'd had. Ochren had tried to tell him that the League was going to be his, and he needed to be ready when that time came.

"No!" he said, not wanting the job, and not feeling ready for it by a long shot. Ochren just nodded, and walked away.

Mudge wasn't sure how much time had passed. He was sitting on the edge of the plinth, deep in contemplation. He was beginning to feel a bit more relaxed about having the Keeper Stone always with him, always part of him. It was like a faithful if unpredictable wolfhound.

He felt its loyalty, but then he realized it wasn't loyal to him personally. It was loyal to the idea of selflessness, of being second after the needs of others, and, he thought, loyal to the beauty of creation itself.

He knew now that the Stone had been made in the beginning. Perhaps not even made, just formed out of nothing by some quirk of the energies that were at work then. It was, however, in some fundamental way moral. It had discovered an underlying order to the world, and allied itself immovably with that order.

Mudge smiled to himself. It was heart-warming to get such a confirmation of his own beliefs. He had always felt there was an underlying order to things, even if it didn't always appear to be so, and it made it easier to accept the fact he was probably joined to the Stone for the rest of his life.

He wondered what would happen when he died. Would it reappear in the keep? Once more sealed away inside the dome atop the raised plinth?

He could feel the Stone playing nearby, nosing around somewhere in the spirit world. Something unusual caught its attention, and its curiosity flared. It pushed against Mudge's spirit senses, bringing the matter for him to look at.

The world around Mudge faded as the Keeper Stone took him into the spirit realm. Then he realized he was outside the keep. A sudden sideways movement followed. It felt like he travelled a long way. Then he was over the heart of the High Steppes.

Mudge hovered above a gully as a strangely cloaked figure manoeuvred its horse out from behind a Xaanian captain. He saw it challenge his father. To his spirit sense they both blazed in unmistakeable power. The dull reds and blacks of the strange creature on one side and the pastel blues and faint smell of lightning round the Legatus.

He wondered why they couldn't see him, and concluded the Keeper Stone was shielding him. For that he was grateful. Then he felt a faint reflection of the emotional torment stirred up by the cloaked figure. His father, however, sat unmoved on his horse.

Mudge smiled. His father had pushed the value of detachment onto him all his life. For the first time, he understood why. He saw the Legatus reply to the challenge, and the gyrating pyre of red and black energies round the cloaked figure was snuffed out in an instant. He saw the soul of the creature leave its body, and his father's spirit energies follow it.

They entered the netherworld, the place of transition at the threshold of the dead. Mudge followed the pastel blue and faint cinnamon trace left by the Legatus. There he saw his father fall before a hurricane of red and black energies. Something that was allied to the evil that had risen in Xaan.

He couldn't remember exactly what happened next, but he cut through the energies holding his father motionless in one supreme act of will. He remembered the Keeper Stone singing a song of protection, throwing up an impenetrable wall around him.

He snatched up his father, and brought him back to the High Steppes in one tumultuous moment. Then he slammed the gateway to the netherworld shut. He saw his father's spirit essence re-enter his prone body. When he left the Steppes his father was unconscious, but alive.

The Stone showed him the good things they had done. How some futures for the League had closed, and other, much better ones, had opened. He felt the warmth of its satisfaction flow through him.

Far below him League troops gathered round the unconscious form of his father, and Mudge turned away, homing in on the keep. He felt oddly useful, vindicated perhaps, as if a hidden belief in himself had been recognized. On the other hand, the evil in the netherworld saw him and his father as nothing more than inconveniences. Minor opposition to its plan to spread its rule across the face of the known world.

Oddly, Mudge felt cheerful about the League's chances of proving the evil wrong, even if those odds were ten to one against. That's near enough to even odds for me, he grinned, as he descended toward the keep.

TEN

Krell had many titles of honour, but like Ultrich he avoided ostentation when he could. His full name, without the titles, was Krell parvan d'Hart. His daughter's name had been Direlli parvan d'Hart. When Ultrich married her, the Legatus had insisted his wife keep her hill tribes name, and Krell had honoured him for that.

Now Krell's daughter was dead, long dead in a hunting accident, but the bond between the high chief of the hill tribes and the son he had adopted into his family remained.

Ultrich swept into Krell's camp, his Lancer escort reining up beside him.

"You got to see some action," said Krell appraisingly. He was always able to tell if the men had been tested in battle that day.

Ultrich nodded, and slid off the back of his horse onto the ground. He gritted his teeth, and made a fair semblance of standing straight. It took a lot to ignore the burning sensation in his thighs and buttocks though. Krell laughed.

"Don't want to admit you're getting old, eh?" he chided. The Legatus looked rueful.

"Are the herds inside the pass yet?" continued Krell, and one of the riders snapped a salute.

"We passed the last of them on our way into camp, your Lordship," he volunteered. "The Steppes are now empty. Except for the Xaanian dogs half a day's ride out." It was Krell's turn to nod. Then he turned back to Ultrich.

"You must come inside," he said, and gestured toward his tent. Ultrich shuffled forward with what dignity he could muster, and the two men retired out of the heat of the sun.

"How ready are your cavalry?" asked the Legatus, once he had emptied a glass of the nomads' spice tea and started on another. Krell waggled one hand ambivalently.

Ultrich understood the problem. The hill tribes were superb riders, but they were not used to working together. Krell had been trying to instil some discipline into his people, but the idea of moving as one unit was unnatural to them.

"Don't worry about it," said the Legatus with a smile. "Just tell them to hold off until I give the word. We can rely on your chiefs to lead them into battle where they'll do the most good when the time comes. It will be a black day for those who get in their way!" he finished cheerfully, and Krell nodded his agreement.

Ultrich saw the bronze sketching Krell had commissioned of Direlli on their wedding day. It was hanging on one of the inner partitions, instead of its usual place beside the main entrance. He hadn't expected to see it there, and his heart leaped momentarily.

He had called her his heart. Even though 'Hart' in the hill tribes tongue meant something entirely different. Now he remembered how she had kept him human. Especially during the early days, when an extraordinary effort had been required to bring the League together.

Never a day went by when he didn't miss her, and he felt again the guilt that had haunted him since her death. She had been a superb horsewoman, like all her people. But on that hunt, on that day, the most unlikely of events had worked together to bring about her death. But regardless of how it had happened, he felt responsible.

Then the guards announced two more visitors, and one of Krell's nephews ushered Sergeos and Cinnabar into the tent.

"May your people fare well in your absence," said Krell. It was the traditional hill tribes greeting.

Sergeos and Cinnabar pressed their palms together and bowed. They were acknowledging the blessing, and accepting the promise of hospitality it implied.

"And may you travel safely when it is your turn," they replied, which was the traditional response. Sergeos turned to the Legatus.

"The Xaanians aren't far off now. Shouldn't we climb The Lion and get some idea of what we're up against?"

Rotor Valley Pass was guarded at its entrance by two imposing hills, The Lion and The Arrowhead. Further in it opened out into a wide, fertile bowl, but the entrance was narrow. The Lion was the taller of the two hills, and it was from this vantage point that Sergeos wanted to assess the Xaanian progress.

Ultrich smiled. He could feel Sergeos' nervousness, but he wasn't going to mention the spirit walker's lack of battle experience in front of the others.

"Plenty of time for that, my friend, plenty of time. Best thing to do before a battle is relax with your friends and family, and remind yourself what you're fighting for."

Sergeos made an effort to calm himself. Cinnabar, on the other hand, seemed to be always relaxed. It was partly her natural aloofness, he decided, and partly her guarded nature.

"Try some spice tea," offered Ultrich. "If I may?" he said, turning to Krell. He was asking for permission to offer hospitality in the chief's tent. Krell nodded, suppressing a smile at Sergeos' jitters. He had his own problems with commanders who had never seen action on such a scale before, and he liked Ultrich's relaxed approach to the problem.

Later, as it was approaching dusk, Ultrich finally indicated to Sergeos it was time to take a look at the Xaanian army. Once they had done that, they could think up ways of dealing with it.

"You're not going climbing now?" said Krell. "It will be dark by the time you get to the top."

Ultrich looked at him with a smile. Krell realized he meant to get there by doing things only spirit walkers could do, and he raised both hands to forestall any explanation.

"I don't want to know!" he barked. "Take yourselves outside before you start mucking about with the natural order of things. I don't want you to set the tent on fire!"

Ultrich laughed out loud. The hill tribes were the most superstitious of the peoples in the Karnatic League, and they had the most trouble with the idea of spirit walkers. He hadn't married Direlli to bring the tribes into the alliance, but it would have been difficult to get their trust any other way.

Krell was used to him by now, though he still had moments when Ultrich surprised him.

"Of course, your Lordship," said Ultrich, bowing as he did so.

"Don't 'your Lordship' me," growled Krell. Then he relented. "Come back from your little jaunt in one piece," he added, in a more kindly tone.

When the spirit walkers had gone, Krell turned to the bas-relief sketch of his daughter on the wall. He had noticed Ultrich's moment of silence, and guessed what lay behind it.

He wished there was something he could do for his adopted son, but such things were too complicated for him to understand. He wasn't much of an example either. Direlli's mother had died relatively young as well, and her place in his heart had never been replaced by the wives and concubines he'd accumulated over the years.

Sometimes he thought leaders without family commitments were better. They threw themselves into government, and defending the borders. Leaders who were happy at home seemed to have less time for those things, and they let the country get soft. Still, it didn't seem fair that both he and Ultrich had lost their great loves so early in life.

Not far out of camp, at the foot of the nearby hills, there was a discordant hiss. It sounded like a sheet of cloth being torn from top to bottom, and a moment later three figures appeared at the top of The Lion.

"No distraction this time?" asked Sergeos with a smile.

"No distraction," said the Legatus flatly. "I want the Xaanians to know we're here. I want to see what their response is, gauge what level of spirit activity we can expect when their army attacks tomorrow."

Sergeos looked around nervously. He hadn't realized the three of them were going to be used as bait. The Scaffold Mountains behind The Lion, however, were reassuringly familiar, and the Karnatic Defence Force had already taken up positions either side of the pass. Twilight was fast approaching, and it was then the farsight of spirit walkers was at its best.

All three of them reached out over the High Steppes, and homed in on the Xaanian army. It was a vast crescent of differing colours. Colours that seemed out of place on the dry Steppes. It looked as if fields of different crops had been sown in an odd pattern.

Ultrich had seen armies preparing for battle before, and it wasn't long before the blocks of moving colour began to make sense to him. The Xaanian mounted archers had set up camp on the flat plains to the right of the Pass. The right side of the battlefield would provide their horses with better footing, and that would suit their manoeuvrability.

The Xaanian infantry were still streaming in on his left, and the first of them had just started to erect shelters. They would be attacking over the rougher terrain to the left of the pass.

Ultrich's attention was drawn to the centre of the vast array. It was clear the bulk of the enemy cavalry would attack from that point. Behind the cavalry Ultrich could see rows of infantry in detailed uniforms, with standards on long poles. That meant elite troops. The personal bodyguards of the Xaanian aristocracy, along with hand picked fighters from the ranks.

In the middle of the elite troops were a number of wagons, and he could see that they were heavily guarded. The decks of the wagons were piled high with partially dismantled structures. They didn't make sense to Ultrich at first, but then he began to understand. They were war machines!

He understood the ideas behind such things, at least in theory. The right sort of machine could throw rocks long distances, or spew fire, or release many arrows at one time.

Where had the Xaanians learned how to make such things? Had Ottar Bey been scouring old archives for ideas? Or had the evil that put him on the throne in Xaan already known how to make these terrible machines? Ultrich picked the latter. Evil was timeless, and methods of destruction were never far from its mind.

His eyes narrowed at the thought. These machines could not be allowed to cause mayhem among the League troops when the Xaanian army attacked.

"Third quarter and high!" yelled Sergeos. Ultrich's eyes flicked up and to the right. Something was catching the dying rays of the sun, and it was coming in fast. Cinnabar lit it up, sending glowing skeins of light wreathing about it, sketching it in. Then they could all see the enormous wings, long neck and rows of serrated teeth.

"Chew on this," said the Legatus savagely, and gestured toward the nightmare shape. The gesture was a simple act that served to concentrate his mind, but the spirit power he cast was already doing its work. The winged creature began to arch in the air, even as it swooped closer.

It opened its long, jagged mouth in a rictus of pain, and one mighty downbeat of its wings lifted it over the three spirit walkers and into the air above the pass. Cinnabar and Sergeos put their efforts behind the spirit fire of the Legatus, and the creature burst into flames from the inside out.

A moment later it fell out of the sky a blazing wreck. Shepherds watched as they tended their animals inside the pass, and made signs to avert evil as the great, flaming carcass hurtled toward them. It burned out before it hit the valley floor, but they all felt the shuddering impact of what remained.

Sergeos saw it slumped on the floor of the pass, far below them, and breathed a sigh of relief. It was gone. Nothing could have survived that. But the Legatus was already looking back over the High Steppes, and he hoped there weren't going to be any more surprises. Dealing with this one had used up a big chunk of his reserves, and there was a long night ahead. Sometime before the attack tomorrow morning he would have to deal with the Xaanian war machines, and that wasn't going to be easy.

In the basement level of Tashigot Keep, Mudge stirred as he heard someone clattering down the stone steps from the floor above.

"What's been happening?" said Ochren anxiously, helping Mudge off the edge of the plinth. "I came down here after we had finished breakfast, and there was some sort of guardian standing over you. I couldn't see what it was, but if I tried to approach you I was pushed back. When I tried to force my way through it slammed me against the wall over there," he said, pointing to the exact spot.

Mudge realized his time in the spirit world had been longer than he thought, and the Keeper Stone had been protecting his body while his consciousness was out riding his spirit senses.

"The horses have found us!" called Senovila from the top of the stairs. He hurried down to join them, beaming happily, and it was clear his prize warhorses meant a lot to him.

"I don't know how they did it," he continued, "but they were waiting for me when I went outside to collect wood for the heating cones. They still had the pieces for the cart on their backs too!"

Mudge smiled. It must have been sprites that guided the horses to the keep. Once again they had done more than was necessary to fulfil the boon agreement, and the cart would make the journey along the edge of the desert easier. It was a wonder the skinny, creaking contraption worked at all, but work it did.

He stopped for a moment, puzzled. How had he known they were going to be following the edge of the desert north-west?

Then he worked it out. He knew where they were going because of the spirit map in his head. The one that told him where his enemies were. He could see the safest way to Xaan by looking at all the options, and it was along the edge of the Scaffold Mountains until they petered out in the Endless Desert.

Mudge followed Senovila up the steps of the basement to the first floor of the keep and found the others waiting for them. Bear was looking better, if still pale, and his friend came straight to him, hugging him fiercely.

"It seems I owe you my life," he said with a grin, once he had released Mudge.

The boy smiled. He knew Bear would have done the same for him. Anyway, it had been the Keeper Stone, more than himself, that had healed the ranger. He clapped Bear on the back and moved past him. Then he addressed everyone in the little party. "Time to move, people, we've got a long way to go before nightfall."

They looked at him blankly, so he told them about his plan to travel north-west along the Scaffold Mountains and out into the desert. From there they would find a way into Xaan itself.

Ochren looked disconcerted at the idea for a moment, and then he recovered his composure. He stepped forward to speak to them all, and it was clear he was speaking in his role as head ranger.

"We knew something like this might happen," he said. "The Legatus told us to help Prince Rossi in any way we can, and that means in any task he undertakes."

"I think this idea of his comes under those orders!"

He turned his head and whispered to Mudge in a voice all could hear, "Despite the fact it's the most hare-brained, poorly-prepared, badly thought out plan I have ever heard of in my life," and set them all laughing.

It did seem an outlandish plan, just to walk out into the desert, but then they had seen some pretty outlandish things on their journey already. These were extraordinary times, and they were caught up in forces far beyond their ability to understand. But it all came down to a choice between good and evil, and the survival of friends and families back home. With that at stake they knew they would carry on, whatever the odds.

The travellers dispersed to gather up their things while Ochren and Senovila set about putting the cart back together again. After that Senovila checked the horses over and harnessed them to the light-weight contraption.

"Cart's ready," he said. There was a general movement out of the keep to load belongings onto the tray of the cart, and it wasn't long before they were under way once again.

The procession wound down off the foothills, heading for the flat plain at the edge of the desert. Mudge scanned the high peaks carefully, but there was no sign of the winged creatures on this side of the mountains.

Then Colma came up beside him. He talked about the reappearance of the horses for a while. Then he hesitated.

"We really have to do this, Mudge," he said, "try to change things. That's my family back in Shaker's Hope. I'd much rather fight for them out here, and not have fighting devastate the village."

Mudge smiled. Colma had been thinking deeply about the situation, and come up with some answers. Then he realized this was probably how his father felt about the League. If people like Colma could give everything they had to protect their homes and loved ones, he had to do everything in his power not to waste that sacrifice. Then he closed his eyes for a moment. It was a responsibility he hadn't thought about before.

"I won't let you down," said Colma shyly. He strode ahead to walk beside Liam and Mareet, who were riding on the back of the cart, and Mudge was left with his thoughts. It wasn't long before the travellers turned left along the edge of the Scaffold Mountains.

Around mid-morning the wind changed direction. Cool breezes off the mountain were replaced by hot, dry winds off the desert, and it was a taste of what was to come. Ochren spent some time gathering every possible water container for use in the days ahead. There was still the occasional stream coming down off the mountains, but the way it disappeared into the desert sands was unsettling.

Mudge began to feel unnaturally tired. He wondered if it was the heat. He couldn't put his finger on it, but he felt like something wanted him to sleep. Bear, resting on the cart, noticed he was struggling to stay awake, and told Mudge to climb up beside him. It wasn't long before the gentle swaying of the cart slid Mudge into a gentle sleep. Then he began to dream.

Luce was there, chiding him for wearing her scarf under his shirt and out of sight. She gently teased it out and made it more conspicuous around his neck. Jago was holding Mudge's head between his hands and looking straight into his eyes. He was trying to tell him something, and Mudge understood at once. The tiredness he had felt had been Jago trying to put him into this trance state, so they could meet again.

"Ahead of you," Jago seemed to be saying. "The danger lies ahead of you." Mudge knew that. They were going into Xaan.

But that wasn't it. Jago kept shaking him, and Mudge checked with the map of his enemies that now ran continuously inside his head. There was nothing dangerous along the Scaffold Mountains, nothing that showed on the map, anyway. Then Luce was there, inside his head, pointing to things on the map.

"Sarkosay," she was saying, and pointing to a barren gorge up ahead. It split the mountains apart just before the range petered out in the desert. Mudge strained his spirit senses toward the gorge, and he began to detect the grey, foggy texture of a spirit veil.

This would be so much easier if I was awake, he thought. But he understood now. Something up ahead, of considerable power, didn't want its activities to be noticed. He tried to remember what he knew about the Sarkosay from his School of Mysteries days. He struggled with the name Sarkosay, but could only remember that they came from the most ancient of legends.

Was the gorge being set up as an ambush? Was it the sort of place the creatures naturally inhabited? Whichever it was, the travellers would be going past it at some point and he was feeling increasingly uneasy about that.

When Luce and Jago could see they had made their point, they relaxed. For a while they were happy just to be with him again, happy to look in on an old friend. Then Mudge went to say something to them and found himself back on the cart.

His tiredness had gone and he looked around, surprised at the time that had passed. Then he noticed how close the cart was to the gorge.

"Feeling better?" said Bear quietly, half asleep in the sun himself. Mudge laughed, overjoyed at meeting Jago and Luce once more. He jumped down, and called Ochren to him. The ranger listened quietly as Mudge told him about the gorge, and they scrutinised the landscape ahead. Ochren murmured something to Senovila, and the cart began to angle in towards the foothills.

"I see a likely place for water and pasture up ahead, boy," he said, "so we'll take a midday break there. What we do after that is up to you. I've no idea how effective ranger steel will be against these Sarkosay of yours."

Mudge nodded. This was going to take some thinking about.

The night on top of The Lion had drained Ultrich more than he realised. It felt as if he had just dozed off when he woke to Porteous shaking him by the shoulder. He sighed. It must be important if his commander-in-chief had come to get him in person. As he swung his feet to the floor he realized he was still dressed from last night's activities on top of The Lion.

Then he remembered why he was so tired. The spirit walkers had attempted to destroy the Xaanian war machines by burning them from the inside out, the same as they had when the winged creature had suddenly appeared. But there had been a number of those damned Sarkosay protecting the war machines, and the struggle had exhausted all of the spirit walkers.

There were more walkers coming from Prias, but they were still a day or two away. At least the war machines lay in ruins he reflected. Ultrich had hoped to leave them as no more than ashes, but some had escaped complete obliteration by the flames.

Porteous led him to the operations tent, and then to the situation board. It was set up to show the area in front of Rotor Valley Pass, and the distribution of the two opposing armies. There was also another board to one side, showing Yeltar's forces in Beltainia. The information on it was constantly updated, though its accuracy depended on when the last messenger came through.

"What are we, 450 paladia from Taire Valley?" said Ultrich.

Porteous nodded. "Almost two days by horseback under normal conditions, but a messenger has just come through who did it overnight."

Ultrich looked up, very surprised. He suspected the rider had untrained spirit walker abilities. It might be possible to do it in one day if fresh horses were waiting at each of the League garrisons along the trade route, but to do it overnight, even with a bright moon . . .

"Best messenger Yeltar's got," said Porteous. "She's being seen by the healers after an effort like that. She's in a bad way, but she passed on her messages before she let anyone do anything for her, and I've brought them straight to you."

Ultrich nodded. He stepped over to the smaller situation board showing Yeltar's forces, and saw the Xaanian army had formed a semicircle round the Beltainian troops.

"This was the situation last night," said Porteous. "Yeltar was expecting their army to attack at first light today, so the battle is probably underway. From what the messenger says, he seems to be expecting some sort of help from you."

Porteous' quizzical words reminded Ultrich of his promise. At first it seemed like he would have to be in two places at once to keep his word, but then he worked out a solution.

The Xaanian army in front of Rotor Valley Pass wouldn't be ready to attack until perhaps midday. Maybe that would give him enough time to get to Taire valley and help Yeltar. It was the best he could do with the time he had.

"Before I do that I need some more sleep," muttered Ultrich to himself. He left Porteous in the middle of the operations tent as he went back to his quarters. Porteous shrugged. The spirit walkers would be there to help his forces when he needed them, he trusted that. His more pressing concern was the placement of the League forces at the Pass, and there was still a lot of work to do.

Ultrich woke at mid-morning, prompted by an inner sense of the time. He felt better after the extra few hours of sleep, and he would need to be alert for the little show he intended to put on at Taire Valley.

Yeltar wouldn't be able to stop the Xaanian army at Taire, Ultrich knew that, but he wanted the first battle in Beltainia to cost the enemy dearly. Morale could win or lose a war, and he fully intended to bolster the morale of Yeltar's troops. It would also help if he made the invading army very, very nervous about advancing further.

For what he had in mind in Taire Valley he would be better off working alone. There had been no time to coordinate something with Sergeos or Cinnabar, and a lot of the spirit work he intended to do was complicated. It was better that the whole thing was on his head. With that in mind he set to work.

He sent his spirit senses half way across the continent, and touched Yeltar's mind lightly. From that he understood the situation in the Taire Valley. Battle had been joined. He felt the clamour and dust of war, the lines of combat that ebbed and flowed, but for now Yeltar's forces were holding their own. It was time for him to put in an appearance.

Ultrich outfitted himself in nondescript clothing and stout shoes. He needed these things to blend into the background amidst the chaos of war. A water bottle and a few essentials went onto his belt, and a simple leather cap with flaps disguised his face.

Then, prepared for what lay ahead, he made a small spirit jump to the foothills on the other side of The Arrowhead. None of the superstitious herdsmen in the valley behind it would have heard the passing crackle of his arrival.

Then he gathered himself into a ball of concentration for the feat ahead, and brought to mind the layout of Taire Valley. He transported himself over the Scaffold Mountains and the northern parts of Beltainia, reappearing on a wooded hill behind Yeltar's army.

The noise of his arrival was lost in the roar of the battle, but without Cinnabar to help him, the spirit transportation had been exhausting. He staggered, and sat down abruptly with his back against a tree. He needed to let his body rest.

His spirit senses searched for the black firecake devices he had asked Yeltar's alchemists to make for him. He found them, and breathed a sigh of relief. When he had forged the Marches into the solid foundation upon which the League would rest, his first task had been to seize the ports along the coast. That had meant vanquishing colonies of the Tengue Dynasty, the sprawling empire that ruled the lands across the sea to the south.

Fortunately the Tengue Dynasty had been struggling with troubles of its own at the time. It hadn't retaliated when Ultrich marched his troops into the seaports and simply took over. Now the League traded profitably with the Dynasty, among others, and the past was forgotten.

Most of the Tengue people in the Marches had been assimilated into the League since then, and many of the official documents at the ports at the time had fallen into Ultrich's hands. Among them had been a description of how to make a formidable weapon out of black firecake. Ultrich had filed it away for future use, and now he was glad he had done so. He only hoped the damned things worked the way they were described in the documents.

As his energy returned, he levered himself to his feet. He was thinking of ways to deliver the alchemists' devices into the middle of the Xaanian troops. They were rather heavy, and that was the first problem to be faced. The second problem was going to be harder to solve. If he wanted the element of surprise, he would need the devices to activate at the same time. He had no idea how he was going to do that, at least not by himself.

He started down the slope. His roguish appearance, intended to disguise him, made him unrecognizable as the Legatus. It took him some time to get access to Yeltar's operations tent.

"Finally arrived, have you?" said Yeltar brusquely as he entered.

Ultrich forgave him the discourtesy. The whole future of Beltainia and the Independent Kingdoms lay on his shoulders, and it was more than one man should have to bear.

"Of course, my friend," said Ultrich gently. He moved over to stand beside Yeltar at the situation board.

"Are the lines holding?" he said, examining the position of the pieces as they lay scattered about the board.

"Only just!" said Yeltar, his frustration showing. "It's those damned horse archers. They come in and pour arrows into one point along our line in a concerted attack. By the time we've massed enough cavalry to take them on, they're gone again!"

Ultrich considered this. Perhaps he could use that Xaanian trick when he brought the firecake devices into play.

"Can you set up a situation where the horse archers will feel compelled to attack?" he asked Yeltar.

"What, you mean like an ambush?" replied the Beltainian Guardian. "That wouldn't work, the large numbers of cavalry nearby would give the game away."

"Don't worry about that," said Ultrich, "I'm thinking of a different way of dealing with the problem."

Yeltar's eyes narrowed. He knew better than to question the Legatus on what he was about to do. He also knew he could trust him to get formidable results.

"I think I can set up something," said Yeltar. "They're attacking in fairly set patterns, and we can use that predictability against them."

"Good," said Ultrich. "Then here's what I want you to do."

Yeltar looked up questioningly.

"Make an attack along a wide front in the centre of the field, and then let the Xaanian counter-attack drive your troops back to their previous positions. It sounds simple, but that's all I want."

Yeltar raised his eyebrows. The Legatus was expecting a lot from his troops. On the other hand, knowing him as he did, it was probably going to be worth it.

"Will do," replied Yeltar crisply.

ELEVEN

At least the ground underfoot was drying out, reflected Ultrich. A scattering of showers in the preceding days had left it soft. On the plus side the soft earth had been slowing down the damned Xaanian horse archers. Now that the surface of the battlefield was improving, Yeltar's troops should be able to push the Xaanian front line back enough for Ultrich to lay the trap he had in mind.

At the moment he was overseeing the distribution of what looked like large river stones. They were being given to men who had been hand picked from Yeltar's infantry for their strength. The 'river stones' were heavy, but the burly men took the weight stoically.

Army clothiers fussed about each of them, adapting backpacks to solid, square shoulders. Each man was being set up so he could drop his unusual burden quickly and easily when the time was right.

The roughly spherical shapes gleamed like polished amber, and that description wasn't far from the truth. They were built up of many layers of cloth and hide, each layer coated with a resinous mixture that set as hard as stone. And each device contained as much of the black firecake as Yeltar's alchemists had been able to pack into it.

As he contemplated the spirit work ahead of him, Ultrich regretted not bringing Sergeos and Cinnabar along. He had never attempted the use of his powers on so many objects at once before, and he fervently hoped he could make the plan work!

"It's been a good, clear morning," said Yeltar. He was standing next to the situation board in the operations tent and Ultrich, and Yeltar's army commanders, nodded in agreement.

"As you know the Xaanians pulled back mid-morning, and we let them go. It was a chance for both sides to recover their wounded. But with the warm day and the wind, the battlefield's done a fair bit of drying out as well." Then he turned to one side and indicated Ultrich.

"The Legatus has explained what has to be done to the men we picked for him, and the ground is firm enough now for our cavalry. I think we should go ahead with his plan while we've got the chance.

"In the longer term we want to fall back to Thebes, and we want to do that with most of our army intact. Once we're there, and our reinforcements have arrived, it will be a more even contest. But I don't want to take the chance of being overrun as we fall back," he continued. "The sooner we bloody some Xaanian noses, the sooner we can make an orderly retreat in the confusion that follows.

"Any questions?"

There were a few questions, but the commanders were soon nodding over the details of the plan. Once they had done that it would be over to Ultrich to make things happen.

"I know most of you haven't worked with a spirit walker before," he said, though he knew in truth that none of them had. "However, the idea of bringing an enemy onto a prepared position is a military strategy you are all familiar with." He took a deep breath. The next bit was going to be difficult for them.

"The sudden eruption of the firecake devices will be new to your troops. I suspect it will be like thunder, only much, much worse," and the commanders looked apprehensive at that.

"You must impress upon your men that the enemy will be hit even harder, because they won't be expecting it. As soon as your troops hear a noise like a giant thunderstorm, we need them to fight their way forward like demons! Everything will depend on the next few moments, and we have to turn them and force them to flee."

The Legatus had to laugh inwardly. He was making an impassioned speech, just like Yeltar did. He was firing up the commanders, who would then go out and fire up the troops. It was the very thing he gave Yeltar such a hard time about.

"Every one of your men must charge the Xaanian lines as soon as the firecake devices explode, and I can promise you their army will fall like straw men!"

The commanders applauded when he said that, and Ultrich took heart. It told him they had some enthusiasm for the plan. The men didn't understand how, exactly, the devices were going to work, but they had come to trust the Legatus over the years. More than that, they trusted the fact that Yeltar believed in him.

A short walk later Ultrich was back under the tree where he had arrived in the valley, and the hill gave him a good vantage point. The first skirmishes of the late morning were already taking place.

The Xaanian mounted archers had cut into Yeltar's left flank, but had then been pushed back. The Beltainian infantry had taken the centre of the field a bit more rapidly than the Xaanian line had anticipated, and it was an advantage they were still clinging to despite fierce opposition.

Yeltar gave new orders, and war horns trumpeted a new message. Reserves hurried into the fray all along the line. For a while the sheer force of determined numbers pushed the Xaanian line back. Then, when he could see the forward momentum slowing, Ultrich signalled the operations tent. Moments later another message trumpeted across the valley.

The Beltainian line began to give ground, and Ultrich watched it nervously. Now came the hard part. Some sections of the line had advanced more quickly than others, and the infantry in the centre had hardly advanced at all against fierce opposition. But all sections had to fall back the same amount.

The firecake devices had been dropped to the ground at the 'fall back' signal, and Ultrich wanted the Beltainian troops well clear before he unleashed the forces within the devices.

Gingerly, making sure he had them all, he picked up the devices with his mind. Then he began to heat them from the inside out.

Splitting his mind into more than fifty trains of thought was an extraordinarily complex operation, and it was one he had never attempted before. He felt the sweat gather on his forehead as his concentration levels soared.

The war horns sounded again, which meant that the commanders of each section should by now have surrendered fifty paces to the advancing Xaanian army. Some sections slowed, fighting hard to maintain their positions, while others gave ground quickly to make up the distance they needed.

Sudden gaps appeared between the two lines for a moment. Open spaces that revealed a tangle of broken bodies, discarded weapons, and clumps of grass and blood. The detritus of war. Then the line held, steady along its entire length.

The firecake devices needed to reach a critical temperature, and that needed to happen soon. Already fresh troops on the Xaanian right flank were pushing the Beltainians back. He wasn't sure what, exactly, the firecake devices did, but he knew they wouldn't have much effect if they ignited behind the Xaanian lines.

Ultrich redoubled his efforts, and the centre of each device grew hotter. He realized it was different to working with living flesh, different to the winged creature on top of The Lion.

He scrambled to find ways to strengthen the spirit energy inside each of the devices, but his progress was slow – and Yeltar's right flank was being pressed even further back. Ultrich was beginning to despair of reaching the critical energy point the documents had said was necessary.

Then he heard more war horns. Through the sweat in his eyes, and the haze over the valley, he saw Yeltar's standard carried into the right flank. The shock wave of added troops moved the line forward again. It steadied itself somewhere near the place Ultrich wanted to be.

Yeltar's presence in the front line, risking his life to make the plan work, filled Ultrich with fresh anguish. There had been times when his decisions as the Legatus had cost him friends, and sometimes they had cost him commanders he had trained and promoted through the ranks himself.

Such deaths were especially painful for him, and he pushed himself beyond his limits to ignite the alchemists' devices. The valley receded as his vision narrowed, and everything turned into a blurry background.

He couldn't tell if the line still held, but it seemed to him it was taking too long for the eggs to reach that critical point, and every extra moment was agony. At the edge of his awareness he caught the cinnamon scent of another spirit walker. With a start, he recognized his son had somehow detected the mammoth task he was undertaking.

He almost laughed. Rossi was turning up every time he needed help lately, and he wondered if the boy would be needed. Then he returned with fresh energy to the task of igniting the devices from the inside out, and a moment later the first one caught fire.

The massive crump of its detonation stunned him with its savagery. He found his concentration weakening, then ground his teeth as he dragged himself back to the task in front of him. Another egg caught, and this time he ignored the visceral savagery of its detonation. He pressed on with those that were left.

The immense strain on him was easing now. With each one that caught fire there were fewer left, and there was more of his concentration to give to the threads of spirit energy that remained. He felt Rossi wish him well as he got the process under control, and leave him to it. Ultrich felt a moment's gratitude that his son had been there, just in case he was needed.

Two more of the devices went off in quick succession. Ultrich pressed the advantage home, building the energy levels in those remaining. There was a sudden and continuous roar, as a wave of detonations spread out from the centre of the battlefield. They rolled left and right in long fingers of fire.

Finally, only three or four of the devices remained, on the fringes of the battlefield. Ultrich stabbed savagely at them with his mind, and they followed the others in a simultaneous explosion that overshadowed the others, an exclamation mark to the rolling thunder that had preceded it. The echoes died away, and suddenly the battlefield was completely silent.

A ragged cheer went up from the Beltainian line, and it surged forward. The Xaanian soldiers, stunned by the force and savagery of the explosions, gave way. Their numbers had been decimated wherever the devices had exploded among them.

Knots of Xaanian resistance formed here and there, but they were soon overcome by Beltainian forces. The triumphant surge of a victorious army turned into an outright charge, and the Xaanian soldiers fled before it.

Ultrich watched as the Beltainian cavalry cleared the valley of stragglers. The Xaanian soldiers were run down and cut to pieces. It was the unarguable logic of war, whoever was spared today could take a friend's life tomorrow.

The war horns sounded again, and the cavalry turned back from the pursuit. All across Taire Valley the Beltainian army began to straggle back to its camp. They were headed for the rows of tents and cook houses that adorned the flat land below Ultrich.

The Legatus knew that the soldiers' day was far from over. Yeltar would march them all afternoon and long into the night, taking advantage of the Xaanian defeat to fall back to Thebes. Then they would be safe in the positions that had been prepared there. It was a good plan, and Ultrich felt a quiet satisfaction at his part of it. He had been able to help a friend.

Reluctantly, he heaved himself to his feet. He was exhausted, but that would have to wait. The battle for Rotor Valley Pass might already have started and he was needed there. He bowed his head, gathering his strength. Then the sound of cloth tearing emerged from among the trees at the top of the hills. The exhausted troops didn't bother to look up.

On the other side of the Scaffold Mountains, Mudge studied the terrain ahead while lunch was being prepared. Senovila and Colma looked after the horses and some of the rangers found twigs for the ranger cones. Ochren stood beside Mudge while they tried to unravel the tangle of ridges and valleys ahead.

"I think I see the start of the gorge," said Mudge, pointing to a drop off from a major plateau. The drop off was too sheer to be the start of another mountain pass.

Ochren nodded. He had fought in mountainous terrain often enough, and he could see the boy was right. But Mudge had been telling him they were unlikely to get past the gorge without a fight, and he was worried about that.

Rangers like themselves were at their best deep inside enemy territory with set, limited objectives. They weren't trained to face off against unknown 'Sarkosay', whatever in all the hells they were, and his instincts told him it was suicidal to go up against large numbers with a small party.

He had to admit there was one more thing as well. Rangers weren't trained to fight creatures with spirit powers, and Ochren wasn't happy about that at all. He considered his options. Perhaps they could go around the gorge, but that would mean a number of days in the desert, where the cart might get stuck in the sand. The heat of the sun would be a problem too.

He sighed. Being a head ranger often led to unpalatable choices like this. In the end he decided they would probably have to contend with whatever was in the gorge. He felt better about the decision when the rest of the travellers took the news calmly. Morale counted for everything when a team was on reconnaissance in strange lands.

The midday break provided its own surprises. Mudge and several of the others sat along an old log on one side of the rough camp site. In the middle of the meal there was a sudden, if delicate, cough from behind them. In the following split-second Ochren was already turning, his sword leaving its sheath, and Shyleen hesitated over an arrow she had notched and drawn. Mudge turned slowly to see what she was looking at.

"Master is busy?" said a voice from the shadows. Mudge squinted into the shade under the bushes. It wasn't easy to see what was there, with the sun high and directly in front of him. Then he saw something move in the shadows.

Mudge had rarely seen sprites during the middle of the day at Shaker's Hope, but the ones in the mountains, he reminded himself, were different. This one had taken up a position in the darkest shadows it could find, but Mudge could see nothing more than an outline.

"Master is not busy," he offered. He was uncertain if this was the sprite leader that had guided them through the mountains or not.

"Sprites request Legatus boon," said the sprite forthrightly. Mudge closed his eyes in exasperation. He hadn't expected this request to be made so soon.

There were enough unknowns in the gorge ahead without complications. Every day they were delayed might be vitally important to the survival of the Karnatic League. He sighed, it was some unholy law of events that problems turned up in groups, as if they enjoyed conspiring against people to throw lives into chaos.

He braced himself. Since this was the way of things, there was no point in wasting time and energy bemoaning it. Senovila smiled as he saw the look on Mudge's face. He had seen how unfair fate could be when he was a commander himself. Like his father, the prince was refusing to let these things unseat him, and Senovila was pleased with the boy's attitude.

"Prince Rossi acknowledges Legatus boon," said Mudge quietly. He lifted one foot over the log, and stepped toward the shadows in the undergrowth. Then he knelt down in front of the sprite, and noticed it was transparent even when he saw it close up.

He waited for it to tell him what it wanted. As he listened, the barest hint of a smile appeared on his face. Then it vanished, as he clamped down on his emotions – but this was good news, there was no doubt about that.

He had been unsure what to do about the Sarkosay in the gorge from the moment he had known they were there, and just getting past the gorge and surviving hadn't seemed enough. These things were agents of the evil that had risen in Xaan. His time with his father in the netherworld, chasing the twisted Sarkosay soul, had shown him that.

It felt like the best way to help the League was to clear the gorge of this nest of vipers. The fact the sprite had asked him to do the very same thing was a fortunate coincidence indeed.

"Spirit demons in gorge hold many sprite prisoners," continued the sprite in its strange, disembodied voice. It was a voice very much in keeping with its largely disembodied self at the moment.

"Sprites are forced to work for them. Many sparks of life return to sprite soul since demons come to this place. They come long ago, long time before Builders come."

Mudge wondered again if the sprites shared some sort of common soul. The way they all knew what one knew was uncanny. The long existence of the Sarkosay in the gorge was interesting too. If the sprites were to be believed, they had been there since before the arrival of people in the area. Yet there were no records of Sarkosay at this spot, at least according to the files at the Priatic School of Mystery.

How had they maintained such secrecy over such a long time? They must have kept a permanent spirit veil over the gorge since they first inhabited it. But the more immediate question was when should the travellers tackle the gorge. It was already mid afternoon, and the prospect of being trapped in the gorge at nightfall, if things went wrong, was not a pleasant one.

Mudge assured the head sprite he would do everything in his power to free the trapped sprites in the gorge. He didn't tell it he also intended to end the Sarkosay presence there though. The sprite bowed so low it seemed to be examining its toenails at very close range, and then it faded from view.

Mudge sat on the log again. He explained to the others about the sprite, and talked about his conviction that the best thing they could do was clear the gorge of Sarkosay. None of his companions looked happy at the prospect, but they were bound by oath to follow Mudge in whatever he did. It was Arnima who put the whole thing into perspective for them.

"This is at heart a spirit war," she explained, "and there's little we can do to help Mudge with that. What we can do is keep him alive while he does what he has to do.

"That's an achievable goal, and it's something rangers do very well. Let's concentrate on that, and leave the bigger picture to those who know it best."

Senovila was surprised. Arnima must have been listening when he had been a commander all those years ago in the Xaanian army. He had used her as a sounding board to work things out for his troops. And she was right. One person couldn't win a war, but if each person concentrated on doing their bit of it, the rest would take care of itself. He smiled. Though if one person could win a war on his own, this prince of the Monhoven line might just be the one.

Mudge nodded gratefully to Arnima for stepping in on his behalf. He had been talking to her more often lately, and the two of them were growing close. She had lost weight and got used to life on the trail, and taken to wearing the ranger green for camouflage, as had Colma. It was hard to tell her from the others these days.

The general consensus was that they should wait until first light the next morning to tackle the gorge. There was still a way to go to the entrance, and it would make sense to set up an evening camp further on. So they continued along the edge of the mountains, looking for a good defensive position for the night. Eventually they found one, and Ochren called a halt.

The rest of the afternoon was spent preparing the camp site in case of an unexpected attack. Ochren wanted a place to fall back on if things got too hot when they entered the gorge.

The travellers settled down to sleep later that evening. Ochren took the first watch. It wasn't easy to sleep under the bright stars of the mountain skies, especially when a moon that was almost full came up over the desert. Mudge tossed and turned under his greatcoat. He still had no clear idea what to do about the gorge on the following morning. Was leadership always like this? he wondered. Was it always more guesswork than knowing? He thought it might get easier in time, and this reassured him, until he finally drifted off into a troubled sleep.

The Keeper Stone was waiting for him. He saw it standing upright this time, as tall as himself. It was radiating a soft light that carved away pretension and revealed truth. He wondered if this was its true form in the spirit world, but decided it was a convenient shape he had given it in his dream.

There was a moment of joining, and he felt the Stone search through his memories for things that had happened since it was last with him. He realized it would always be looking over his shoulder like this, weighing his actions. Then he thought he detected a cautious note of approval.

He also realized that it had been busy on his behalf. He saw that it was now continuously aware of the Legatus. It had detected the strong emotional connection between Mudge and his father, uncomfortable though it sometimes was for the boy.

He saw too that the Stone had been ready to take him to Taire Valley to help his father, but it had not been necessary. Mudge watched pictures unfold in his mind of the firecake devices creating havoc in the Xaanian army. That was a neat trick, and he realized there was much about his father he didn't know.

The Stone showed him other things as well. It had worked out the strengths and weaknesses of the Sarkosay, and how he could break the control the evil in Xaan had over them. Then it wanted to show him something else, and he let it guide him through the gorge in his spirit form.

The Keeper Stone hid him from red and black spirit energies that glowed among simple dwellings carved out of the rock of the gorge. Mudge knew he would need to know this in the morning, when the travellers made their foray into the bedevilled place.

When Mudge woke at dawn, Colma had a hot drink ready for him. His friend's devotion to himself, and to their journey to Xaan, was clear to see. Colma hoped they could change the outcome of the war, and protect their homeland from invasion. These were the hopes and ideals that all the travellers were fighting for.

Mudge remembered his dream about the gorge, and recalled the information he would need to know. Then he realized he had the ghost of a plan, but it would depend upon the rangers buying him some time.

TWELVE

The camp prepared itself for the assault on the gorge in the cool of the pre-dawn. It was a time to move silently while they prepared themselves, mentally and emotionally, to risk their lives during the day ahead.

Mudge felt the comforting presence of the Keeper Stone. He was going to need it today, along with every bit of spirit skill that he had. The cart was soon loaded with the things they would be leaving behind, and hidden under branches in a stand of trees. While the last of the preparations were being made, Mudge went out over the gorge in his spirit form.

There were no sentries at the entrance to the enormous gash in the mountains, and no life yet stirred within it. The spirit veil over the gorge had served the Sarkosay so well, for so many centuries, they had become complacent. All the better for us, thought Mudge, as he returned to his body at the camp to rejoin the others.

There were the muted sounds of an argument behind him, and Ochren hurried across to shut it down. This was not the time for division.

"I will not stay behind with the cart," hissed Arnima, while Senovila rolled his eyes in frustration.

"I have been training," continued Arnima determinedly. She pulled a wicked-looking dagger from a sheath under her ranger-green top.

"And what do you think you're going to do with that!" snorted Senovila disparagingly. He unsheathed a sword that extended his reach by another arm's length. Arnima's eyes narrowed threateningly, and Shyleen stepped over to stand beside her.

"She's ready," said the ranger, looking Senovila squarely in the face. She was challenging him to contradict her, and Senovila looked to Ochren for support.

Ochren shrugged. It was up to each ranger to decide when a trainee was ready. There was nothing he could do about Shyleen's decision. Senovila threw his arms in the air and turned away.

"He's just worried about you," said Ochren quietly to Arnima. She nodded to show she understood. "Anyway, since when did you start training Arnima?" said Ochren, turning toward Shyleen.

"As soon as we left Shaker's Hope," said Shyleen. "Arnima knew Senovila wouldn't like the idea, so we kept it quiet. Women don't fight in Xaan. I guess it's hard for him to accept the possibility."

Ochren nodded. Her words made sense.

The cart was now loaded and hidden, and the horses were free to graze or make a run for it if danger threatened. The travellers were ready.

The company left the campsite in single file, led by Ochren. They descended from a small hill onto stony ground, and made their way toward the narrow entrance to the gorge. Mudge looked behind him briefly. His companions were all on edge, the usual nerves that came before a sortie into enemy territory. Bear had recovered quickly after his healing at Tashigot Keep. He was still a little weak from his lack of activity, but he was ready for some action.

Colma had been accepted by the rangers at Shaker's Hope because of his hunting experience and bush craft, and partly because they could see Mudge needed his friends about him. Then Liam and Mareet had taken Colma under their wing as they travelled north. They had provided him with some basics in sword work and infighting. His desire to stay alive, and the close eyes of the others if he got into trouble, would have to be enough.

The rangers moved lightly over the ground, and Mudge felt clumsy by comparison. He took more care where he placed his feet, and the travellers closed quietly on the gorge.

Then the high cliffs on either side of the entrance were just ahead. The desert on one side was already on fire with the first touch of sunrise. The gorge, though, was deep in shadow, with nothing visible in its inky blackness.

Mudge was tempted to scout the area again in his spirit form, but he knew that he was thinking more out of nerves than need. Nothing would have changed in the short time since he looked last. He called the Stone lightly and it responded, and he realized once more that the Stone would always be with him.

The company passed into the entrance of the gorge, and the tension increased. Ochren led them cautiously forward, and the blocky outlines of buildings appeared on their right. A tinge of grey was creeping into the sky, and details were becoming clearer.

Mudge wondered if the Sarkosay had cut these buildings out of the rock themselves, or were just living in something they had found. The odd, reptilian nature of the creatures didn't seem to go with buildings like these.

Then too, the doorways were all wrong. They were wider than they were tall, and they came barely a third of the way up the walls. Mudge hesitated for a moment. Maybe these buildings had belonged to the Sarn.

He thought the original inhabitants must have run on many legs, but stood upright when they were inside. The buildings were clustered in twos and threes on their right, as the company climbed steadily up the sandy bottom of the gorge.

Ochren made a hand signal toward Liam and Mareet. The two rangers crossed the gorge to examine one of the structures. They disappeared inside for a while before reappearing and climbing a path to enter another. Ochren motioned for the others to remain stationary until the scouts rejoined them.

When they did, Liam shook his head. He tapped his palm with two fingers, a hunter's sign that said the area had been long abandoned. Then the Keeper Stone nudged at Mudge's awareness.

A moment later, as he joined more fully with it, he saw what it was seeing.

Ahead of them a cloud of red and black energies swirled around a much larger building, one that was set apart from the others. It looked like a large storage barn of some kind.

Mudge touched Ochren on the shoulder, and pointed to the opening. Ochren nodded. As they drew nearer, a smell of marsh gases and rotting freshwater weed grew stronger. Water seeped from the opening, and it was clear the storage room was no longer fit for its original purpose.

Ochren sketched more hand signals, and the rangers spread out, taking up hiding places with bows trained on the entrance. Then Ochren continued up the floor of the gorge with Mudge. The thought of being used as bait to draw out the Sarkosay was unnerving, but Mudge had to trust the rangers to do their job.

Moments later the red and black spirit energies of the Sarkosay doubled in intensity. Mudge shouted a warning and reptilian figures, the same grey colour as the rock around them, boiled out of the storage room.

They scampered on all fours more than stood upright, and it was hard to find anything human in the way they moved. Mudge saw the sheen of mud and water on them, and understood then that they were somehow amphibian in nature.

The Sarkosay noticed the two humans on the floor of the gorge, and most of them reared upright where they stood. A shrill keening filled the air, and Mudge saw the flicker of red and black energies forming about himself and Ochren.

He felt the onslaught of despair as the energies thickened, and the will to fight drained away. Then the Keeper Stone reached out, shielding him. Mudge extended the shield until it covered Ochren, and then the others where they were hiding.

Liam and Mareet charged from their hiding places and attacked the creatures from the side. Liam sliced the heads off two of them in quick succession while Mareet fired arrows into those on either side of him. Then long claws raked Liam's left shoulder, and a savage kick knocked the sword from his right hand.

Gods above those things are fast, growled Bear to himself, as he cut his way to Liam's side. Shyleen was also picking off Sarkosay with arrows, reducing the numbers. The two men worked desperately then, side by side, trying to stay alive. Liam was keeping the creatures at bay with a pair of long knives, but his damaged left arm already felt like lead.

Bear ran his sword through a Sarkosay directly in front of him, but then he staggered as claws raked down his thigh. An arrow buried itself in the chest of the creature attacking him, and it fell. Bear recovered his footing, but he could feel blood running down inside his breeches.

The rangers needed all their skills as they retreated slowly toward the floor of the gorge. Mudge and Ochren were moving in their direction as well when more of the creatures exploded out of another entrance further along. They bounded across the floor of the gorge faster than Mudge had thought possible.

Senovila and Ochren cut down the first two, but then Senovila's sword stuck fast in the body of the next. Another one swarmed up its dead kin and slashed downward towards his face. Senovila lifted his free arm and blocked the blow, but another Sarkosay came in from the side.

Arnima was already there. She sliced the attacker's throat before it reached her mate, then slashed the outreached arm of another on the return swing. Senovila wrenched his sword free, and ran it through the Sarkosay about to strike above him.

"Thank you," he gasped, wishing he had put more time into getting fit. Either that or he was older than he realized.

"So I'm not as useless as you thought I was?" said Arnima pleasantly, far too pleasantly. Senovila was wise to the ways of women after years of marriage. He knew he was in a lot of trouble when this was over – if they lived that long.

Colma drove between them, impaling two of the creatures on a short stabbing spear. His attack sent the Sarkosay scattering, but it was clear the little group would soon be overwhelmed, despite the momentary advantage.

Mudge had to do something, and do it quickly. His mind whirled desperately, until he thought of something.

The Keeper Stone acted on his thoughts in an instant, and he heard the long, rolling waves of the Great Dance a moment later. It meant the Mesoans knew about his predicament, but would they come?

The floor of the gorge began to fill with wisps of light, and the Sarkosay quailed before them. The rangers looked around in wonder at the new arrivals. Then the reptilian creatures retreated toward their storeroom sanctuary, making more high-pitched, keening noises.

"Into one of the houses," snapped Mudge. He didn't know what was going to happen next, but he didn't want to be out in the open when it did.

Ochren led the way, making a run for a square building that sat low on their left, and the rest of the travellers were right behind him. They tumbled through the low, wide door into the gloom inside, and took cover away from the openings. The last of them hurtled through the door moments later.

"Close your eyes!" yelled Mudge. He screwed his eyes shut and placed his hands over them. Some followed his example, some buried their faces in their arms.

Then the music changed, becoming louder, and more charged. Even through his hands Mudge could see flashes of red light. He figured the Sarkosay were making a fight of it, but then the rock beneath their feet groaned ominously, and sharp booms shook the stone building.

Mudge had the sense of dark shapes marching past the low doorway, and he wondered what they were. The gorge grew darker, at least it seemed that way, and the noise grew deafening. He heard a number of wet, sickening thumps as something, once living, struck the walls of the building. Then there was silence. A deafening silence after the overpowering roar that had preceded it.

The Great Dance murmured around them, saddened somehow by what had happened. It seemed to Mudge it was disappointed in what the world had become since the days of creation. He opened his spirit senses cautiously, but he could find no trace of the Sarkosay.

What he could sense was the Mesoan homeland still passing through the gorge, though the dangerous undertones in the Great Dance had receded. He opened his eyes and looked around the room. He called softly to the others, and they did the same.

All around them a fine dust sparkled with its own inner light, and Mudge felt light-headed. He found himself smiling for no particular reason, and when he looked at the others he saw them smiling too. Coloured patterns of light expanded outward from his fingertips, from everyone's fingertips.

It felt like all things were possible. As if they were at the beginning of things, the starting point for all possibilities. Then the Mesoans were gone, and it felt like he had lost something. It was clear from the others' faces that they felt the loss as well, a sense of bereavement. Ochren pointed to the door, and Mudge nodded. With some apprehension, the travellers stepped outside.

The gorge had been changed forever. Giant fissures ran across the sandy floor now, and boulders from the slopes above had piled up along the sides, while most of the buildings had been reduced to rubble. It was odd to see the one they had taken shelter in still standing. Mudge wondered if it was the Mesoans or the Keeper Stone that had ensured that.

Of the Sarkosay there was no sign.

Then Mudge noticed that a red and black spirit power still remained. He realized it was a connection between the gorge and the power in Xaan, and it was beginning to unravel. He realized he had a rare opportunity to act, but he would have to do so quickly.

He didn't want to attract the attention of the evil in Xaan just yet, but they were running out of time. Battle was already joined at Beltainia and Rotor Valley Pass. He needed to know what the League was up against, and that meant using the spirit connection while he could.

He reached out with his spirit senses, and transported himself along the unravelling connection toward Xaan, though the spirit trail was fragmenting even as he rode it. Before he had time to find a safe destination, Mudge found himself at an unknown point somewhere in the capital city of Xianak.

"What is this?" snarled a rough voice in front of him. "A boy? Some shepherd drudge with a little spirit sense? He must have stumbled into the land of the Udjik, the fool." The voice seemed to consider the matter for a moment.

"Commander Uttan, kill him," it said dismissively.

Mudge finally recovered from his sudden relocation to Xianak, and looked around him. He was in a strange, high-ceilinged room, and from the opulence of the furnishings, he figured it must be the Royal Palace. The room certainly looked the part. It also seemed that in Xaan the Sarkosay were known as Udjik.

What worried him most was the fact his body had been transported along with his spirit senses. That meant the threat to kill him was a very real one. A solidly built soldier to his left, with grey in his hair and a regal bearing, drew his sword as he advanced on Mudge.

"Not here, you fool!" snapped the same commanding voice, coming from somewhere ahead of him. Mudge looked up and saw a group of people clustered round maps on a long table. One of them wore an ornate costume and headdress. He assumed the figure was Ottar Bey, the ruler of Xaan. Bey seemed a very average, sour-faced man, and rather slight. Mudge wondered why the others so obviously deferred to him.

Next to him stood one of the tallest women Mudge had ever seen. There was a hard-muscled bearing to her, despite being outfitted as a lady of the court, and she towered over the others. Her bearing also suggested that she was used to getting her own way.

"Of course, Empress Zilan," said the middle-aged commander. He now had a firm grip on Mudge's upper arm. Turning around, he steered his captive out of the impressive-looking hall at a trot.

The prince's mind was racing. He had known of Ottar Bey's ascension to the throne through murder and deception, but who was this woman? As they left the hall, through a large set of double doors, Mudge remembered Senovila's words about an evil rising in Xaan. Senovila had mentioned a black king, and Ottar Bey certainly fitted that description, but the Empress Zilan seemed to be the one wielding the power.

Uttan came to an abrupt halt, bringing Mudge to an equally sudden halt beside him. They were standing by the waste area for the kitchens, and Mudge realized the commander was going to kill him here, and throw his body on the nearby pile of refuse. He would eventually be taken out to the farms as compost.

He smiled. He rather liked the idea of being compost. He hoped his body would be of some use when he no longer needed it. But not today.

"Sorry about this, shepherd boy," said the burly soldier. He brought his sword round in a hard, flat arc as Mudge turned toward him. The commander didn't want his captive to suffer more than was necessary, and Mudge appreciated that. The old soldier wasn't a bad sort, though he had chosen to keep his status as a commander rather than oppose the Empress, even though his conscience must have told him she was a manifestation of evil.

For that reason, Mudge didn't kill him.

He snuffed out the commander's consciousness, and Uttan collapsed forward as the weight of the sword overbalanced him. The weapon fell from nerveless fingers, and clattered on the cobblestones next to him.

Mudge wove a small spirit trace around the commander to make sure he remained unconscious, and retreated to the back of some stables he found next to the kitchens. He opened a spirit connection to the gorge. It would be his way back when he needed it.

Now that he had an escape route, Mudge was free to investigate this 'Empress Zilan' more thoroughly. He sent his spirit senses drifting out over the hall he had just left, and then willed himself inside. Gentle as a wisp of smoke, he dropped below the high ceiling. He sank lower, taking in the activity round the long table.

Most of those present were what they seemed to be. Some shone with the bright, clear spirit light of a disciplined mind, army commanders and those used to leadership. A cloak of persuasive energies, calculated to bestow status and the right to command, swirled around Ottar Bey, yet he didn't seem to be a spirit mage.

His powers must come from someone else, decided Mudge, and that made him a puppet king, a pawn in someone else's game of power.

There were Sarkosay there as well. Short, grey creatures looking incongruous in a commander's cloak and walking awkwardly upright. Their chameleon-like spirit powers made them look like people to the others around the table.

Mudge looked for the Empress, but couldn't find her. He knew she was in the hall, but where? He sensed a powerful spirit veil swirling around the table, and realized she was hiding her presence. He let that pass for now. He would learn more about the Royal Palace first, and what was happening here. Information was always the key to winning a war, and he would challenge the Empress later.

Mudge ran his spirit senses out into the many rooms and galleries of the palace, and found nothing unusual. He searched beyond it, and detected something unusual in a large barracks close by. Strange, twisted energies lay coiled inside the dormitories, and Mudge gravitated toward the site.

At first he couldn't make out what the energies were, and then he saw they came from row upon row of soulless creatures, indistinct to his spirit senses. Each one was larger than a man, and each had been made, created out of inert components. He could sense the unnatural nature of them. They were inactive at the moment, but they wouldn't stay that way. Mudge had no doubt that they would rise and follow the will of the one who created them if they were called. But what were they?

Mudge felt a warning tap from the Keeper Stone, and felt himself drawn back to his body at the rear of the stables. He heard some excited shouting as a small group formed on the street out front. Someone must have found the commander, and raised the alarm.

Mudge berated himself for not hiding the unconscious soldier, knowing Ochren or Senovila would not have made such a mistake. Certainly not his father. It made him realize how little experience he had – but then he was learning.

Mudge had a decision to make. Did he want to tackle the Empress now, and find out what her strengths were, or should he and the Keeper Stone return to the gorge and the others?

He didn't like the answer, but he clenched his jaw tight in determination. The more he learned about the Empress, the better chance he would have to destroy her at some later stage. He was going to find out who, or what, she was, right now.

He sent his spirit form out into the hall, and searched for the veil he had detected earlier. The Keeper Stone formed its own protective shield about him, keeping him hidden. A hint of the spirit veil he had seen before came and went. It existed partly in the hall and partly in the netherworld, the entrance to the land of the dead.

Mudge knew that the Empress would be more powerful in the netherworld, much more powerful, as he had found when he pulled Ultrich from her grasp. But in this world, he and the Keeper Stone might have a chance. He managed to find a part of the spirit veil he was seeking, a 'loose end' that had escaped the Empress' control. She probably thought such a small thing was insignificant.

Mudge smiled. He knew all about the Empress' spirit veils. He had teased them apart when they cloaked her winged creatures over the Scaffold Mountains. Now, he dissolved this one, and the grey, fog-like material became clear where he touched it, quickly evaporating. The effect spread in all directions, and it soon revealed a sinuous black shape in constant motion, standing at the table and reaching almost to the ceiling in the cavernous hall.

Pandemonium reigned. Courtiers and attendants scattered in all directions, terrified of the monstrous shape revealed in their midst. The army commanders around the table stepped back a pace or two, but their discipline held. The soldiers on duty formed a tight group around Ottar Bey, and hustled him toward the back of the hall.

The Empress changed shape, and landed on all fours as a fearsome creature not of the natural world, its stocky body and reptilian head covered in a red and black pattern. Predatory eyes scoured the room intently, looking for the enemy that had forced it to reveal itself, an enemy it could not see.

Mudge felt the creature's intense searching for him, but the Keeper Stone kept him hidden. He felt a wave of relief, but he also knew he wouldn't stay undetected forever. He wondered whether he could control the creature, and reached out with his spirit strength to pin it to the ground. For a few seconds it roared savagely in impotent fury, and Mudge felt his confidence growing. Then the creature burst free, furious at its humiliation.

It changed back into its original form, and searched for him in the spirit world. This time it began to close in on where he was. Mudge felt power building, a blow destined to shatter the defences the Keeper Stone had built around him.

He returned hastily to his body in the stables, but the sense of building power followed him there too. He barely had time to throw himself along his escape route before an enormous blast incinerated the stables behind him.

Mudge landed in the dry gravel bed of the gorge much harder than he had intended. He cracked his arm on a rock, and planted his face in a patch of sand. His head came up slowly, his ears still ringing from the blast at the stables. For a few moments he lay there, wondering if anything had followed him along the spirit link, but all was quiet, and he felt the reassuring presence of the Keeper Stone nearby.

Then he heard a shout, and levered himself painfully to his feet. Ochren and Bear hurried over to greet him, followed by the rest of the travellers. Bear had the wound on his leg bandaged now, but he laughed it off as a scratch when Mudge asked him about it. Then he heard the hearty sound of other voices.

"Not long after you left," said Senovila cheerfully, arriving next, "some of your sprites arrived. They started looking for the ones of their kind that had been enslaved. At least, I think that's what they were doing. Pasty, see-through little beggars in the middle of the day, aren't they?"

Mudge smiled at the old smith. Senovila was really enjoying this. One last, great adventure before he retired with Arnima, something to tell his grandchildren. Then he remembered his promise to the sprites, and wondered if they had found their imprisoned kin. As if to answer his question, a sprite materialised nearby in the shadow of a cliff.

"Sprites have found lost ones," said the sprite, and Mudge assumed it was the sprite leader.

"Sprites have been badly treated," the leader continued. Its face showed a strange mixture of anguish and fear. "Sprites ask if Master will help."

Mudge nodded an agreement. The sprites hadn't tried to bargain with him this time, and the straightforward request was touching.

"Where are the lost ones?" said Mudge gently. The sprite took his sleeve and tugged him further up the gorge. Ochren and the rest of the company formed a ragged group behind them.

The sprite led him to a vertical gash in the rock. It was a little way beyond the last of the shattered buildings, and it led into a large cavern. On one side of the cavern they found a walled off compartment, probably an old storage room, and the imprisoned sprites were inside it.

"What is that thing?" said Bear, pointing to a low mound of bricks in the centre of the room.

"It's a soul stealer," said Mudge absently. He was more concerned with the dispirited sprites that sat around the walls. They had been chained in place, and were so lethargic they were barely able to lift their heads up.

"Looks like a pottery kiln," observed Senovila. He circled the machine warily looking for an entrance, but there was none.

"The Sarkosay that lived here took the spirit energies of others for their own purposes," said Mudge grimly. He remembered this much from his studies at the Priatic School of Mysteries. The idea of stealing life force from others held an abhorrence for him, and the swirl of dark energies he saw round the mound of bricks made him feel sick.

"Then we should destroy the evil damned thing," said Senovila, glowering, while Arnima nodded vigorously in agreement. Mudge looked up at Ochren, to see what he thought. Ochren nodded as well.

Much of dealing with the Sarkosay and their ways was new to Mudge, but with the help of the Keeper Stone he felt sure he could heal the sprites in the room and carefully dissipate the spirit energies that drove the soul machine. But after that the travellers needed to be on their way to Xaan. Time was growing ever shorter.

THIRTEEN

The Legatus arrived at the top of The Lion in the early afternoon to find Sergeos and Cinnabar were waiting for him. A short whump of compressed air announced his arrival, as he and a certain amount of atmosphere tried to occupy the same space.

"How did it go?" enquired Sergeos eagerly. Ultrich had taken longer in Taire Valley than the others had expected. He was reassured when the new arrival nodded his head, saying his efforts had been successful.

"Yeltar's forces will pull back now," said Ultrich. "By the time they get to their prepared positions at Thebes, reinforcements from the other Independent Kingdoms will have arrived."

Then he looked past Sergeos to his left. There were five new spirit walkers there. They were part of the force that had been making its way from Prias over the past few days. Ultrich acknowledged them with a curt bow. They made a more elaborate flourish in reply.

The problem with spirit walkers these days was they were so, so *learned*, thought Ultrich. It was frustrating that they had a limited amount of actual experience. They had the snow cat, the symbol of the Karnatic League, embroidered on the collars of their attire, but he wondered if it meant anything to them. Would these cats have any teeth?

He had tried to give Sergeos and Cinnabar some idea of what spirit warfare was like, taking them on a number of clandestine missions, but the rest of the spirit walkers might not be much use at all in this sort of fighting.

Cinnabar was more interested in what was happening on the battlefield below. She caught Ultrich's attention, and pointed downward.

"You're just in time for the first real engagement of the afternoon," she said, scanning the High Steppes below them with keen eyes.

Sergeos chipped in. "So far they've just been searching for weaknesses in our lines," he said. "Those damned Xaanian horse archers are very quick. They can dominate an area before we have time to bring up a response.

"However we did what you said, and kept the armoured cavalry behind the lines until the Xaanians committed themselves properly, and then we got in among them. At least the troops have been properly trained to overlap their shields and wait the archers out."

Ultrich nodded. He had no doubts about the training of the troops. Porteous was a stickler for doing things right, and the commanders under him were the best he could find.

"They made a determined effort with their infantry on the left flank about midday," continued Sergeos, "but we made them pay for that, and it didn't last long."

That pleased Ultrich. It had been his idea to split the Karnatic defence Force into mixed companies. Then the commander decided which of the squadrons of infantry, archers or cavalry would lead his company in, while the others took supporting roles. Traditional wisdom massed similar troops together, but Ultrich wanted his companies to be able to respond to changing situations faster than that.

"Now they're coming back for more," said Cinnabar. She pointed to the activity on the plains below them. The others didn't need Cinnabar's outstretched arm to tell them where the next skirmish was going to take place. The long standards of the Xaanian elite troops were moving briskly forward at the head of their columns. Behind them cavalry wheeled and turned in formation as they warmed up their horses.

Ultrich smiled grimly. A combination of infantry and cavalry probably meant they were about to launch the same well-rehearsed assault they had used several times at Taire Valley. If that was the case, they were in for a big surprise.

Ultrich conjured a spirit connection, and spoke rapidly to one of the Prias spirit walkers stationed outside Porteous' operations tent. He was silent for a while, listening to the reply. Then he spoke again, apparently answering questions. When he had finished he turned back to survey the plains below.

"Pray to the gods I've got this right," he said sharply. His words caused Sergeos and Cinnabar to exchange quizzical glances. Then the Xaanian elite troops hit the centre of the League's positions with all they had, pushing it back, until the advance slowed, and the line held.

The effect of the League's mixed units came into effect almost immediately. The archers fired over the shoulders of their own infantry at almost point-blank range. Squads of cavalry made brief sallies from the rear of the line as the troops opened up spaces for them to move up.

A war horn sounded, and the Xaanian troops re-formed into columns. Porteous' troops showed their discipline, and held their ground. Then the Xaanian cavalry poured into the avenues between the columns. They picked up speed as they headed for the League lines, but the League companies scattered when the cavalry were about to hit, leaving holes in their lines.

The Xaanian cavalry thundered through the gaps, and soon found themselves behind enemy lines. As they turned to attack the rear of the League positions, more war horns sounded, but this time on the League side.

The ground shook as Porteous' armoured cavalry poured forth from between the tents a short distance away. The League infantry reformed behind the Xaanian cavalry, cutting off their retreat. For a moment chaos reigned, and the Xaanian horses snorted and wheeled as their riders tried to make sense of the situation.

At last the cavalry formed up to meet the armoured cavalry bearing down on them. It was better to take their chances against the heavier and better protected League cavalry. The infantry behind them were now sporting rows of the long pikes that were deadly to horses.

At first the Xaanian charge seemed successful. Clustering in groups, they were able to punch through the more scattered armoured cavalry lines. While the heavy League cavalry struggled to slow its momentum and turn after them, the Xaanian cavalry carried on into Rotor Valley Pass itself, and that was their undoing.

Porteous had kept the hill tribes horsemen in reserve. He had waited until their speed and agility could be used to its greatest effect, and that moment was now. The war horns sounded out a new pattern.

The hill tribes horsemen had been resting up near the entrance to the pass. The spreading herds of their people lay behind them, and their tents ranged along the bottom of the hills. Now, to their surprise, the enemy were coming to them.

In ones and twos, then in dozens, they boiled into the entrance of the pass to accept the challenge. Others came in from guarding the herds, and from sentry duty around the edges of the grasslands. They streamed forward, outdoing each other in a race to make the first kill.

Ducking and diving, they dropped to ride hanging off the side of their horses before springing onto the unsuspecting cavalrymen. They broke open the cavalry charge, slowing and confusing it. In the confusion of the fighting they were just too fast. Long knives found weak patches in leather armour, and gaps where helmets met breastplates. Bodies tumbled from enemy horses all over the battlefield.

It wasn't long before the Xaanian formation was reduced to scattered groups of horsemen, banded together in a last-ditch defence. The sharp twang of bowstrings and the harsh rip of leather jerkins pierced by long knives rippled across the grasslands. Again and again cavalrymen fell from their mounts. The enemy were quickly reduced to solitary ones and twos, and then the sounds of battle ceased altogether.

The Xaanian cavalry had been completely annihilated. Sergeos walked back to the front of The Lion, looking down on the greater battlefield. He shook his head.

"I didn't see one of them get away," he said. He sounded almost rueful. "I wouldn't like to have the hill tribes as an enemy, that's a certain truth."

Ultrich nodded absently. There was too much going on for him to examine his reactions to each part of the battle as it happened. He would laugh, or cry, or throw up, when it was all over.

Back on the plains of the High Steppes, the Xaanian troops withdrew from the League lines. There was a lull in the fighting, and it seemed to last an eternity for those who were waiting.

"Come on," said Sergeos impatiently, when it seemed the enemy would never return. "Let's get on with it!" But he knew what Porteous had been told down on the plains. He was to wait for the Xaanians to come to him, and he was doing that.

Partly it reinforced the idea of the Xaanians as aggressors, which they were, and that built up a sense of injustice along the League lines. Partly it was due to an old saying Ultrich had seen to be true over the years. From unarmed combat to nations at war, the side defending had the stronger position. They had less work to do, and were more able to turn a response to an advantage.

It was hard for the troops to wait in formation in the heat of the day. From their vantage point, the spirit walkers could see water carriers scurrying like ants to the waiting soldiers, one behind the other. They came and went as they kept up with the needs of the League forces.

"Here they come!" said Sergeos at last, pointing to the Xaanian lines. Ultrich frowned. It was too easy to see this as a spectator sport when they were watching from the sidelines, with good guys to cheer on and bad guys to vilify. But people were dying on the plains below them, people with friends and families. Ordinary people caught up in this war on both sides.

From the top of The Lion the spirit walkers could see the whole of the Xaanian line advancing. It seemed that this time the Xaanian commanders were ready to commit themselves to a decisive battle. It was what the League forces wanted, but Ultrich still tensed.

The outcome of the war would depend on what happened below him during this afternoon. The League forces, and those of the Independent Kingdoms, were heavily outnumbered, though he had done much on both fronts to reduce the imbalance.

Ultrich wanted to win today, but not decisively. He wanted Xianak to send reinforcements to its army at Rotor Valley Pass, hoping they could still win. In that way the League would keep drawing the Xaanian forces into the pass, and it was an ideal choke point. The League forces couldn't be bypassed, and their supply lines couldn't be cut off. Ultrich intended to grind the enemy down one engagement at a time. He hoped to bleed them dry.

On the plains below, the Xaanian line rolled toward the League forces. Their horse archers, supported by cavalry reserves, reached the League lines first on the right. The elite troops in the middle hit next, having the better ground, and the infantry reached the League lines last, struggling over uneven terrain on the left.

Ultrich was reminded of one small wave overtaking another at the seashore. He had noticed such things when he was a boy. The waves were hardly moving, but the point at which they overtook each other sped along the shore at astonishing speed. That's what it looked like from the top of The Lion. The point of contact between the two lines ran across his field of vision faster than a horse could gallop.

At first the two sides seemed to close in silence. Then the roar and clash of the two armies reached the hilltop.

Ultrich saw wagons being rolled forward in the centre of the Xaanian advance, and then the covers were thrown off them. He saw a number of the war machines he had thought destroyed the previous night.

Damn it all! They must have worked through the remainder of the night and this morning to piece these few machines together, and they must have used parts from those that hadn't burnt out completely. Engaging his spirit senses he saw the black and red swirl of demon energies around the wagons. Sarkosay! This wasn't going to be easy.

Ultrich looked quickly about him. He was going to need help to stop this threat. The Sarkosay hadn't been expecting him last time, and the darkness had helped. But this time it wouldn't be so easy. He would have to rely on the Prias spirit walkers, and that didn't fill him with confidence. He motioned for Sergeos, Cinnabar and the recent arrivals to join him. Then he explained what he wanted them to do. They nodded, and he launched himself from the top of The Lion.

It wasn't really flying. That was impossible, but a series of short spirit hops through the air was nearly as effective. He noticed with approval he could no longer see his hands, and then the rest of him disappeared. The spirit walkers on top of The Lion were binding a spirit veil about him, and that should keep him invisible from the Sarkosay. Below him the war machines were in the last stages of preparation. They would soon be hurling their deadly loads over the heads of the Xaanian forces, and into the League infantry.

Ultrich could see columns of armoured cavalry forming up opposite the war machines. He was gratified Porteous had seen the threat and was responding to it, but the heavy cavalry would take time to clear a path to their objective. That meant the deadly war machines could destroy whole companies of League troops before they were stopped. If they were stopped.

Ultrich increased his efforts, but the energy required for continuous short spirit hops was immense. He would have liked to make the jump to the plains in one go, but that would create an unmistakable arrival signature. He was hoping to arrive among the war machines with the element of surprise still intact.

The first of the machines released its deadly load of stones as Ultrich landed lightly beside it. Each stone was made of heavy iron ore, and it was about the size of a human head. Another machine flamed into life as bundles of sacking soaked in oil ignited before they were hurled into the air. The roar of the battle around him was tremendous, and Ultrich hoped it would cover the noise of his activities. At least until he had disabled the lethal machines.

There were four of them. Each had a contingent of guards, and one of the Xaanian 'commanders' that he knew were Sarkosay. The two machines nearest him had not yet started firing and he climbed quickly over them, cutting vital lines and jamming any working parts he found. The crews would be mystified how the damage had occurred when they went to use them.

He might not have much time left if the Sarkosay detected spirit energy at work, so he had disabled these two by more mundane means. Then he was between the stone thrower and the fire machine. They were making ready to hurl more devastation into the League lines. He reached out with his spirit senses, focusing his mind on what he needed to do. Then he burned the war machines from the inside out.

It took time, but both of them finally burst into flame. Ultrich kept to his task, wanting the fire to be unstoppable. At the same time he knew he was drawing attention to himself in the spirit world, and the Sarkosay would be working out exactly where he was.

Then one of the reptilian creatures appeared, leading a contingent of guards. It burst through the confusion of troops round the burning machines and headed straight for him. It stopped a dozen paces away and gestured with its hands. It couldn't break through the spirit veil around him, but it managed to outline the veil in a red glow. On its command the guards lifted their spears, and threw them at the illuminated ball.

Ultrich tried to accelerate the fires on the war machines, and increase the heaviness of the spears at the same time. Unfortunately for him, the spears were being cast wildly, the troops disconcerted by what they were seeing. One of the higher reaching spears didn't drop far enough as his spirit sense pulled them all down. He felt an abrupt shock as it struck him high in the leg, spinning him round and dropping him to the ground.

Ultrich poured all his energies into the blazing war machines for one last moment. He looked up, and saw that they were well ablaze. Only then did he force himself to grab the shaft of the spear with both hands, and pull the long blade out of his leg.

He knew he was near to passing out, and he tried to picture the The Lion in his mind, so he could transport himself back to the top of it. But the fuzziness in his mind told him he wasn't going to make it. He felt a sense of regret, that he wouldn't have more time to enjoy the peace and prosperity that he had created in the Karnatic League. Then he collapsed back onto the ground.

Something slammed into his side, forcing him out of the blessed peace and quiet of unconsciousness. He could hear a voice shouting over the din, and groaned. Then he opened his eyes in time to see a vivid flash of light, and a Sarkosay dropping to the ground. Dead, it was revealed as the strange half reptile, half manlike creature it was.

Then he recognized Cinnabar's voice. She was chanting in one of the old tongues, and Ultrich could feel energy concentrating in front of her. She was haloed for a moment in the red fire of a dissipating Sarkosay attack. Then she whirled and blasted another of the creatures, slamming it off its feet in the process. He vaguely heard her saying something to him.

"Get up," she hissed again, hauling on his arm. She wasn't strong enough to lift him bodily from his sprawled position, and part of his spirit sense followed her mind as it closed in on the hilltop. She was going to try and transport them both. That was when he understood. He couldn't make the jump himself, but if she could visualize the top of The Lion, he could add his energies to hers to get them there.

He pushed himself up on one knee, then almost fainted as white-hot pain stabbed through his other leg. She shielded them both from another Sarkosay attack, and then knelt in front of him. He collapsed forward across her back, managing to bring one arm awkwardly around her. Then she transported them both.

Ultrich could feel the strain she was under. She was the only other spirit walker he knew who could transport at all, but she wasn't used to lifting two people. He poured his energies into hers, trusting in her ability to get them to the hilltop. The battlefield vanished from around them, and then he was unconsciousness again.

When he came to he felt like he'd been run over by a team of horses, and several times by the wagon following them. He lay still, his eyes closed, and listened to what was happening.

"The binding on his leg is tight enough," said a high-pitched, musical voice, "and Riban has guided the arteries back together with his spirit senses."

"What's happening with the war machines?" said a gruffer, obviously male voice. It was slightly muffled, and Ultrich realized the speaker had his head turned away from him.

"Two of them are still burning," said another voice. This time Ultrich recognized Sergeos. "I don't think they'll be using them again."

"What about the other two?" continued Gruff Voice. The response was more non-committal. They certainly weren't in action at the moment, and hopefully they would stay that way. Then Ultrich opened his eyes.

Cinnabar was in the middle of making something for him to drink. It would help with the shock of the deep wound in his leg. She smiled down encouragingly at him. Then she lifted a small container from within her robes.

When she gave him the tonic he accepted it gratefully. The way she fussed around him would make you think he was about to die, thought Ultrich, and a smile came to his lips.

"Yes! Yes!" exulted Sergeos suddenly, dancing on the spot in his excitement. It was enough to make Ultrich raise his head from the simple pillow Cinnabar had made for him on the ground.

"The armoured cavalry's smashed through the centre of the line," reported Sergeos. "It's taking advantage of the confusion around the war machines. They've opened up a gap several furlongs wide already, and the infantry's pouring through!

"Now they're curling round to the right," he continued.

"I think it's Gosan leading them. Whoever it is he's driving the cavalry forward like a madman. Now I see what it is! They're trying to trap the Xaanian horse archers against the hills."

There was a moment's silence.

"Now the League units at the end of the line are surging forward to help." Then there was another delay in Sergeos' commentary.

"By the prophets! It's turning into a massacre.

"Wait. Some of the archers are trying to escape into the hills, but the League units have come round to cut them off. They're dropping off our own archers on the hills overlooking the Xaanian archers. That's a good idea!

"Now the hill tribesmen have arrived. They're herding the horse archers back into the spears of the armoured horses." There was another delay while he followed developments.

"My god, the horse archers have been decimated! There's less than a quarter of them left. No. Wait, the remainder are surrendering."

Ultrich wondered at that. All the Sarkosay commanders must have been killed. From his experience, the Sarkosay drove their troops on until they were dead, if that was needed.

Still, the League forces had achieved what he wanted them to achieve. The war machines had been destroyed, the Xaanian elite troops had taken a hammering as the armoured cavalry forced their way through the centre of the enemy lines, and now the horse archers had been taken out of the picture.

Doing that to the Xaanian army was much like drawing a lion's teeth. What was left was still dangerous, but it was now reduced to a 'slug it out' mentality. It was incapable of the sudden cut and thrust that could tear the League lines open, and change whole situations.

Ultrich closed his eyes again. That should do it. That should force Xianak to send another army to Rotor Valley Pass. Then, he thought tiredly, the League would be faced with the task of doing this all over again. Well, he decided, that could wait for another day. Enough had been done on this one.

Cinnabar pushed him gently back onto the makeshift pillow. She called some of the newly arrived spirit walkers over, and they began making a stretcher for him. She checked his pulse and looked at something in his eyes again. She smoothed a cool ointment onto a scrape on his arm, something he hadn't even noticed in the fighting.

Ultrich had little choice but to give in to Cinnabar's healing ministrations. When she insisted on giving him something to make him sleep, he resignedly accepted it. Now the shock of the wound had worn off, his leg was beginning to hurt like someone was heaping hot coals on it.

The potion she gave him would help the pain too. Sleep was probably the best thing for him now, he realised, he wasn't going to be of much use in the battle still raging below them. As he nodded off, he wondered why Cinnabar had taken such a risk to save him. She had plucked him from the clutches of the Sarkosay, and certain death. He was touched by her loyalty.

He found his spirit senses connecting to her mind, and then he was drowsily aware of the many emotions that resided there. He didn't normally intrude on others' thoughts, but something was drawing him to her.

He wondered what it was. Then he realized she was a much more complex person than he had thought. Her feelings for him seemed particularly strong. He was intrigued by how personal they were.

She was a spirit walker from one of the old, aristocratic houses, and he had thought she was a hard-headed woman. He hadn't suspected she felt anything for anyone much, but he saw that she admired him. No, more than that, she . . . adored him?

Cinnabar snapped her mind shut, and Ultrich slipped into unconsciousness.

FOURTEEN

The desert stretched to the horizon in every direction. The heat of the sands shimmered the air above it, even in early morning. To the left long dunes of soft sand made the way impassable, but ahead and to the right gravel plains looked more inviting. They were covered in skeletal shrubs that looked battered and bereft of life.

"How far to the Great Salt Lake?" said Mudge with a sigh.

"Two, maybe three, days march," said Ochren sombrely. He was finding the journey equally unappetizing.

"This isn't going to work!" said a cross voice over their shoulders. Then Arnima bounced across to stand in front of them. Mudge couldn't believe how much she'd changed from the little butterball that had left Shaker's Hope. Back then she'd been adamant Senovila wasn't going into danger without her at his side.

He had to admit her healing abilities had come in useful more than once, though she had not brought anyone back from the dead, as she'd done with her husband. He was still hardly able to believe that.

"That lot are not going to pass as slaves!" said Arnima dismissively. She was pointing at the rangers behind her, and Mudge had to agree. They had made some attempt to dress in rags, and rubbed a bit of dirt into their faces, but their disgustingly good health and upright bearing made it unlikely they were slaves.

"Someone's going up in the world," said Senovila good-humouredly as he came up beside them. "I didn't have this many slaves when I was an aristocrat in Xianak."

"You did too!" said Arnima, rounding on him. "You're forgetting the housemaids and the gardeners," but her heart wasn't in it. Mudge was pleased to see the rift between them, caused when Arnima had learned fighting skills, appeared to be closing.

"They weren't real slaves," said Senovila, lowering his head in submission. "They were more like family."

Arnima smiled. "Yes, they were, weren't they." Then she looked more sternly at Ochren. "However, the rangers do not look like slaves, no matter how much we dress them up!"

The travellers had a plan to pass unnoticed through the countryside on the way to Xianak. Senovila and Arnima would be aristocrats travelling with their 'man' Ochren who spoke Xaanian, though not fluently. This was fairly common. Many foreign servants had earned positions of trust with their Xaanian masters.

The others were all much younger, and they were to be passed off as recently-purchased slaves. These were generally pathetic creatures who had got into debt and been sold to meet their obligations.

"Well, I do have some ideas," said Arnima, stepping down from her antagonistic stance, "but they are not going to like it."

Mudge and Ochren looked at each other warily. What did she have in mind?

"Dab this on your teeth," said Arnima a little later. She had made up a mixture of charcoal and some viscous substance out of her healing kit. "Don't spread it evenly, or swill it round your mouth. Just dab it on in one or two spots and leave it there."

The 'slaves' did as they were told. The grey paste looked innocent enough, though it smelt rather badly.

"Now let me scratch this across your skin," said Arnima. "Arms and neck mostly."

The soon to be 'slaves' looked at each other in alarm, as she advanced on them with a piece of spotted lungwort.

"Doesn't that bring you out in an itchy rash?" said Shyleen apprehensively, knowing the forest better than most.

"Yes," said Arnima testily, "and then I'm going to rub a little bird fat into the rash to make it look like its permanently weeping. You want to look sickly don't you?"

The others nodded glumly. Arnima swished the lungwort at their necks and arms with vigour. She applied it to some more than others, so they would appear to be at different stages of the disease. Then she applied the fat. At least the fat diminished the itching, which had soon become a nuisance.

"What do you think?" said Arnima, stepping back. Ochren and Mudge surveyed her handiwork. They had to admit the slaves did look pretty bad after she'd dealt with them.

"Smile," said Arnima, and her charges grimaced obligingly. Where they had dabbed the grey paste it had set hard and gone black. It looked like their teeth were in an advanced state of decay.

Ochren and Mudge laughed so hard they had to sit down, and pounded each other on the back. Senovila, who was attending to the cart, came back to see what the noise was about. He, too, laughed until tears squeezed out of the corners of his eyes.

The slaves looked at each other uncomprehendingly. Then they discovered the joke.

"This better not be permanent!" said Shyleen, rubbing at her teeth worriedly. She was a little more attached to her looks than the others, and Arnima had to assure her it would wear off in time. Quite a long time, unfortunately. Neither Shyleen or Mareet seemed too happy about it, but they said nothing.

"Can you all stop standing so straight," said Senovila. "Try to limp, or at least act exhausted. If you can manage that, then with Arnima's little touches you might just pass as slaves."

"A more reprehensible, diseased, and worthless lot of swamp foxes than I've ever seen," he added under his breath. That set Mudge and Ochren laughing once more.

It felt good to laugh, reflected Mudge. They seemed to have stopped laughing days, or was it weeks, ago. Everything seemed to have become so serious lately, and it was serious, but it wouldn't help if they went around acting like problems were insurmountable. Then it was time to prepare themselves for the desert

That first day in the extreme heat was the worst. No matter how much water they drank, they still felt light-headed and vaguely nauseous. Ochren rationed them to a cup of water every quarter watch, and more for the horses. The little party had to force itself over the stifling and never-ending gravel plain.

At midday Senovila freed the horses from the cart and settled them down under a cloth shade to keep the worst of the sun off them. The travellers shared the shade under the cart, little though it was, and tried to sleep through the worst of the day.

Ochren roused them as evening approached, and the cooler temperatures revived aching bodies. Mudge crawled out from under the cart and stretched. A dull ache at the back of his head told him he had a touch of sunstroke, but he figured that would pass as the day cooled.

Once the horses were back in harness, the travellers made good time across the dusty plain. As the sun dipped below the horizon they found themselves at the top of a gentle rise. They were looking down on a vast shallow bowl, in the middle of a desert landscape of epic proportions.

"Mmm, closer than I thought," said Ochren. "Still a day's march away though."

"What are we looking at?" said Mudge, as he raised his hand against the last of the sun, low in the sky.

"See the workings on the far side of the depression?" said Ochren, pointing in the direction he meant. The lowest point in the bowl seemed to be on the side furtherest from them. Mudge could see the dirty white of the flat plain that surrounded it.

It had to be the Great Salt Lake, which had once been water but was now entirely a plain of salt. Following Ochren's prompting he could see ripples on the surface, long lines of salt that had been mined and laid out in oddly geometric patterns. That must be the workings the ranger was talking about. They had a long way to go then, and he nodded that he understood.

"Those are the salt workings that supply Xaan, and produce much of the country's trading goods," said Ochren. "There's quite a town there, though you can't see it. It's called Jik, and most of it is underground."

That surprised Mudge. He couldn't imagine living in rooms made of salt, and what would the people do when it rained? He guessed it never rained in the desert, and his travels had already shown him people could live in almost any conditions.

Then he was struck by the similarity of Jik with the name the Empress had used for the Sarkosay, Udjik. He asked Ochren what Jik meant in Xaanian. He wasn't surprised to learn it meant hopelessness. That probably described the feelings of the slaves at work at the salt mines quite well, and it also described what the Sarkosay did. Turning all good feelings into ones of despair.

Ochren halted the company some time before midnight. He wanted them to get a good rest before they trudged into the salt town on the morning of the following day. That was when they would have to start acting like slaves and masters, and none of them were looking forward to that.

The travellers made the best of the rest period, stopping the cart over a patch of sand that was holding the day's heat in the grey darkness. It was, indeed, comfortable to sleep on, though Mudge pulled his greatcoat more tightly around him as morning approached. He was glad of the warmth of the others, packed with him under the cart.

Ochren let them sleep until the sun was just over the horizon. Then the company ate the last of the provisions they had brought from Shaker's Hope, which left them with a little cold meat left over from Shyleen's hunting expeditions.

Colma brought Mudge his food, and the prince took it from him with a nod. When Colma first appointed himself to look after Mudge, it hadn't seemed right, but Colma insisted that it made him feel more useful. In the end Mudge had accepted that.

It was something he had learned from being around his father. People had a wide range of talents and skills, and it was up to them what they offered. The feelings that created relationships was a complex one, and it was not up to him to say what someone should offer.

Mudge made the most of the morning meal. From now on the 'slaves' would be lucky to get grains softened with cold water twice a day, and they would prepare it themselves. Senovila would buy something similar to animal feed when they got to Jik. It was standard slave fare.

Shortly after that they were angling down the gentle slope toward the salt plain. The new 'slaves' were suitably dishevelled, and tied by short leather cords from wrist to wrist. With their backs bent in submission, they almost looked the part.

Senovila and Arnima drove the cart, while Ochren marched his charges alongside. He prodded them along with a hunter's whip that more than tripled his reach. They had been warned that there would be times he would have to act the part of slave owner, and the whip would be used.

The cart ambled into the salt town just before midday. The travellers had been on the salt plain since mid-morning, and the combination of sun above and reflection below had been hard on all of them. Closer to Jik the long rows of stockpiled salt had cut back the glare, and they had been thankful for that.

The new 'slaves' tried to get a look at the town with occasional sidelong glances. Mostly they just shambled along, looking down. There were low, flat mounds on either side of the street of salt.

Occasional entrances dove down into these mounds on either side. It was all very odd.

Senovila shouted something in Xaanian to Ochren, who pushed the slaves roughly toward a sign that said 'stables' on their left. They trudged down a ramp that led into a large underground structure. Despite his cowed posture, Mudge was able to work out his surroundings.

Large chambers, at least eight paces long and three paces wide, had been dug out of the salt and connected to form an underground labyrinth. Poles had been laid over the chambers and topped with rushes before being overlaid with salt. He guessed it made the stables cooler, and used the minimum of building materials. Everything the town used had to be brought in from the plains around Xianak, and they were two days away.

Ochren started to speak in his broken Xaanian to the stable hand, a slight boy of around twelve years of age, but the stable owner appeared and pushed the boy aside. He grimaced when he saw the weeping discolouration on the wretches lashed to each other behind Ochren.

"Take your slaves to the salt workings," he growled, "and stop wasting my time. They've got doss houses for them there."

"I'm taking this lot back to Xaan," retorted Ochren, "and don't worry, I'll pay twice the standard rate for two of your stalls.

"Come on now, what's it to be," he snorted, when the man hesitated. "Do you want our business or not?"

He stared at the stable owner belligerently, and eventually the man dropped his eyes.

"All right then," conceded the owner. "Just the one night, like you said to the boy."

He looked at the slaves suspiciously, noticing the absence of salt sores and the colour still present in the ragged clothing. These people hadn't been outside working in the bright sun that faded clothes so quickly.

"Kitchen duty," said Ochren harshly, guessing what was troubling the owner.

"One comes out in a rash and then they've all got it," he said in disgust. "The supervisors made one hell of a stink about it. Now I've got to take them all to Xaan for treatment."

Ochren figured there had to be kitchens somewhere, serving up slops for the salt workers. He just hoped the stable owner wouldn't ask him questions about it. He leaned conspiratorially toward the other man.

"Should just take them into the mountains and cut their throats, eh? Got to feed them while they're off work, and the apothecarists know how to charge for medicines. Too damn right!"

The stable owner nodded his approval. Ochren had taken him for a cruel and self-centred man, and the words played to those qualities in him.

Ochren led the slaves into the chamber the stable boss indicated, and tied off the leather cords to wooden fittings in the wall. He wondered why the fittings weren't made of a more permanent material. Then he figured metal bolts wouldn't last long in salt. A quick check of the other chambers told him the stables were empty. He knew that was likely to change when travellers arrived at the end of the day.

He told his slave charges to get some rest until the midday heat was over, and pointed to the rough straw along one side of the chamber. He made his voice hard, sour with life, but he winked when his face was hidden from the stable owner. Then he climbed up the ramp to find Senovila and Arnima.

The stable owner yelled something at the boy, who took a wooden bucket over to a barrel of water near the entrance. He was filling it when two hunters came down the ramp. They lodged their horses in chambers further along the corridor. When they had sorted out a deal with the owner and climbed back up the ramp, the stables were quiet again.

"Hey, kid," whispered Bear to the boy, when he brought the bucket to them. "Where does Jik get its water from? There's none in the middle of the desert."

The boy looked fearfully along the main corridor, but the owner was nowhere to be seen.

"Big aqueduct," he whispered. "Comes all the way from reservoirs in the mountains behind Xianak. The aqueduct is covered with stone slabs in the desert to stop it drying out."

Bear was struggling to keep up with the boy in his poor Xaanian. Ochren had tried to teach him the language, and it was a requirement for senior rangers to know at least one other tongue. Unfortunately, there had been little time to study with all his other training, and having to keep his ranger identity secret in Shaker's Hope.

"Hey, thanks," said Bear warmly. He turned to take a ladle of water that Shyleen was passing along the line. The boy smiled, uplifted by what was perhaps his first civil conversation in months. He hurried off to clean out stalls down the corridor.

"Strange little tyke," said Bear thoughtfully. He was sipping the water slowly, so his stomach didn't rebel after the hot, dry morning. He checked the corridor to make sure no one could hear them speaking in the Karnatic tongue.

"Yeah, but what's he doing here?" chipped in Liam softly. He had been surprised by the boy's upright bearing, though he hadn't understood the conversation with Bear.

Bear said he hadn't asked him how he got to the stables. Then he went on to explain how the aqueduct brought water to the salt mines to the others.

"That boy's not used to work," said Mareet quietly. "Did you see his hands, soft and slender, and no callouses. Look at the cords on his ankles to limit his steps, someone doesn't want him to get far if he tries to escape."

"Not that he would have much of a chance," added Mudge. "This must be the perfect place to imprison somebody, in the middle of a dry salt lake."

"Well, he does seem a bit out of place here," concluded Liam.

By late afternoon, most of the party had managed to doze off on the straw. Then there was a commotion from down the corridor, and a tremendous crash. The rangers were on their feet almost before their eyes opened. It was a reflex that had been hammered into them during their training.

The travellers crowded to the front of the chamber, as far as the leather cords would allow. They watched as the stable boy tried to lead a stallion along the main corridor toward the ramp. The stable owner appeared from somewhere and ripped the lines out of the boy's hand. A quick glance showed him the boy had placed the bit badly in the horse's mouth.

He surveyed the broken stable door and the other horse that had been in the chamber. It was disappearing up a ramp onto the street. Then he grabbed the boy firmly by the shoulder, forestalling any attempt at escape.

"My father is Usef Bey!" squealed the boy, fearing the thrashing that was to come. "You wouldn't treat me like this if my father was here!"

The owner hitched the horse to the nearest wooden fitting. Then he backhanded the boy viciously, knocking him to the ground.

"Your father's dead, boy," he hissed as he hauled him to his feet. Then he raised his fist to hit him again.

Bear's iron grip stopped his fist as effectively as if it had been nailed to the wall. The owner looked behind him, and saw Bear at the end of the line of slaves. The leather cord that had tied him to the wall was dangling uselessly from his wrist.

The owner snarled and let go of the boy. He pulled a dagger from inside his jerkin before slicing at Bear's hand. Bear let go at the last moment. The owner froze as he felt the prick of sharp steel at the base of his throat.

"I'll discipline my slaves, if you don't mind," said Senovila coolly, pushing the tip of the dagger a little deeper to emphasise the point. The owner pulled his head back, away from the dagger point, and raised his hands in surrender. Senovila took some money from inside his cloth belt and poked it into one of the man's pockets.

"Triple rates, can't say fairer than that, can I," he said. Then he took his dagger away from the man's throat. The owner scowled at Bear before returning his own dagger to his jerkin.

Ochren stepped forward from behind Senovila and slashed Bear across the neck with his hunter's whip. He opened up a cut that immediately began to bleed. Then he pushed the slaves roughly back to their chamber and re-fastened the leather cord.

Ochren was standing guard over the slaves when Senovila and Arnima led the cart down the ramp and lodged it in the chamber next door. The items they had bought were lashed across the tray. Senovila unloaded a sack of mixed grains, mostly horse oats and flax seed. Then he set a few handfuls to soak in cold water.

When he was sure there was no one around, Ochren hurried over to Bear. Shyleen had already wiped away the blood, and Arnima was preparing a paste that would close the cut and stop the bleeding.

"You all right, boy?" said Ochren quietly, concerned for his son. Before he could tell Bear he had been forced to strike him to make it realistic, Bear held up his hand.

"I let us all down, *sensa*," he said. He was referring to a senior ranger, or ranger in charge. "I let my feelings of outrage become more important than our mission. What is my sense of right and wrong against the future of the Karnatic League, and a worthwhile future for all our families?"

Ochren sat back on his heels. Bear had chosen to make this a ranger matter, rather than a family one, and he was right to do so. Ochren smiled. He had been about to let his feelings for his son take precedence over their mission, a similar mistake.

"Understood," he said briskly, standing up. He touched his fingers together for a moment to make the shape of an arrowhead. In ranger sign language it meant the team was unbroken, perfectly functional. Bear nodded once to acknowledge the symbol.

Mudge understood something too. His father the Legatus had tried to train him to see that his feelings were only part of a larger picture, and that was making sense now. He wished he had trained harder, and been better at it.

Ochren let them sleep for a few more hours, and woke them late in the afternoon. It was still early for other travellers to arrive at the stables, but he had been thinking. Checking that the corridor was clear, he outlined a change of plan.

"I was planning to stay here overnight," he said quietly. "That way Senovila, Arnima and I could listen to the street talk, and find out what life is like in Xaan these days. It's always a good idea to get as much local information as possible, so we can blend in when we get to Xianak.

"But I don't think the stable owner is keeping quiet about us. Word will be spreading through Jik, and someone might get suspicious. I think we should leave as soon as it gets dark. Senovila has asked about the way to Xianak, and the road starts at the end of the street."

"What about the boy?" said Bear. He was loathe to see the youngster continue to be so badly treated by the stable owner. Senovila cleared his throat and looked thoughtful.

"There was a Xandar Usef in Xaan when I lived there," he said hesitantly. "He was about my age, or a bit younger. We all thought he would make a good governor one day.

"Since then I've heard bits of news about a Usef Bey, governor of one of the outer provinces. It sounds like the same man." Senovila sighed deeply.

"That was before the purges by Ottar Bey though. Xaan lost most of its best leaders while the black king was rising to power. It's quite possible this boy is Usef Bey's son. Once the council bodyguard got rid of the governor of each province, the rest of the family would be sold as slaves. They wouldn't be considered a political threat."

"But the boy's not our problem," said Ochren bluntly. "We can't reduce our own chances of success by helping him in some way, even though he's in a heartbreaking situation here."

"You may be right," said Mudge thoughtfully, "but I don't think we're looking far enough ahead." The others looked at him for an explanation, so he outlined what he was thinking.

"Who's going to replace the Xaanian Council when we've destroyed Ottar Bey's hold on power? There's going to be a power vacuum when we remove the evil that put him there." Though he spoke positively, none of them knew if they would even get that far.

"Who better to give the people of Xaan new heart and a new direction," he said at last, "than the son of a respected governor from the times before?"

Ochren looked at him with new respect. It was a point of view worthy of his father. No, it was worthy of any great leader. It seemed the boy was growing into his own destiny, despite his youthfulness. Still, how did they know this hobbled slave boy was the son of Xandar Usef?

"Leave that to me," said Bear quietly when it was brought up.

From there they worked out the details of their night time departure, followed by a cold meal of the mixed grains Senovila had purchased earlier.

"How long do we have to put up with this stuff?" growled Bear. Nonetheless, he pushed another spoonful of the shapeless, colourless, tasteless gruel into his mouth. They were going to need it on the road ahead. The others smiled. It wasn't that bad, and it was nourishing enough.

Senovila and Ochren checked and double checked the cart and the equipment the travellers were carrying, while the others dozed through the late afternoon. Then they stored everything back on the cart, ready for departure.

"The boy's story checks out," whispered Bear later, when darkness had fallen. The town had settled down for the night, and it was now safe to leave. Ochren freed them of the leather thongs tying them to the walls, and Shyleen checked that nothing was moving elsewhere in the stables. They were ready to leave Jik.

"His name is Onjed Usef," said Bear. "He talks about living in a big house in the country, with servants. Then some people came and took him and his family away. The intruders wore black. They didn't say anything, just bound and gagged the family and threw them onto carts.

"He was split from the rest of his family, and held in a big city for a long time. Weeks, if not months. Then he was put in a wagon and brought to Jik. He thinks he's been here almost a year now."

"It fits," said Senovila. "The bodyguard for the Xaanian Council wear black, and that sounds like one of their operations. The timing is right too. Ottar Bey has been First Elect for less then a year, and the purges leading up to his election took place just before that."

"So, do we take him with us or not?" demanded Bear tersely. It was clear that the decision mattered to him, and the others looked

toward Mudge. This was a political decision, and he was the prince.
It was up to him.

Mudge wondered if this sort of responsibility would ever feel
natural, but he didn't have time to think about his own problems
right now. He nodded. "We take him," he said firmly.

FIFTEEN

The moon was a pale crescent in the western sky, and it was about to dip below the horizon. The cart creaked and swayed in the night, and the steady plodding of the horses was the only sound accompanying its wayward rhythms. Temperatures continued to fall on the dry lake bed, but there was no wind.

The boy the little party had rescued finally fell silent, which pleased Senovila no end.

Once he discovered that only two of his rescuers spoke Xaanian fluently, Onjed had attached himself to Senovila like a hunting hawk to its master. Brief forays away to talk to the horses or look at something interesting always ended in a return to the old smith's side.

He thought Arnima might have been a better subject for the boy's devotions, but Senovila realized he had been made some sort of substitute father. It was almost certain that Usef Bey was dead now, and Senovila didn't have the heart to discourage the boy.

The first part of their journey, clearing Jik, had been the hardest. They had pulled the cart themselves, avoiding the ruts and easing it along as quietly as they could. They had also muffled the horse's hooves. Without the weight of the cart the horses placed their feet much more quietly.

At last Ochren had considered them far enough away from the salt-mining town to harness the horses once more. From then on Onjed had been barely able to contain his joy at his new freedom.

Mudge walked on the other side of the horses to Senovila. Both of them were alert for traffic coming the other way, though there was nowhere to hide on the salt plain. But they didn't want news of their whereabouts to spread. Senovila passed him the reins, and Mudge walked steadily on, keeping an eye on the horses' progress. No one was riding on the cart. The whole party needed to walk to keep the cold at bay.

The road was hard to see here too, a mere scratch in the vastness of the flat plain, but the salt seemed to gather and strengthen the pale light from the declining moon. It made the indistinct road easier to follow, though it was unlikely they would get lost. The road ran as if it had been ruled on a page, and it was right next to the aqueduct bringing water to Jik. The dark stone channel lying on the salt was hard to miss. Mudge could see it narrowing to a dot in the distance, somewhere near the edge of the Great Salt Lake. Then Arnima moved up to walk beside Mudge.

"What do you think about us stumbling on the son of the governor like that?" she said quietly.

Mudge trudged on. He drew his greatcoat around him, against the increasing chill of the night. He hadn't really thought about the appearance of the boy. Onjed's situation just seemed like it needed to be fixed. It had been more of a 'what to do' problem than a 'why did it happen' one.

"Nothing happens by chance," Arnima prompted him. "All things are connected. The task for us is to decide when to act on what we see, and when the right time hasn't yet come."

Mudge nodded. His father had talked about something similar. The Legatus had talked about a force outside of the things spirit walkers knew. A kind of universal force that acted behind the scenes.

Mudge had to admit finding the son of Usef Bey suggested such a force acted in their lives, though the odds must be phenomenally against it normally.

"We get help if our cause is just and our hearts believe in it?" he ventured.

Arnima laughed. "Near enough," she said. "It's always hard to put such things into words, but when the situation is at its most impossible, that's when the cards will fall in our favour."

Mudge nodded. He would remember that. The two of them walked on in companionable silence, while Mudge recalled examples of when impossible things had changed the course of events in his life.

A dark mass grew out of the night ahead, and Mudge thought it might be a garrison outpost. If that was the case it would be full of Xaanian troops, but the dark shape didn't seem to get any closer as they trudged on.

"The Teeth of Kormac," said Arnima beside him. "Just high enough to collect a little rain from the westerly winds and feed the springs Xianak relies on. The mountains must have been higher once, high enough to produce the river that ran out into the desert, and created the Great Salt Lake."

She paused. "The springs don't flow like that now."

Mudge remembered the old legend concerning the birth of Xaan. Kormac was a nomadic chieftain, who discovered mountains in the middle of the Endless Desert. The land around the mountains was a fertile place, and he eventually moved his people there.

Kormac and his people held the new land against all comers for centuries, and his people grew into the great trading nation of Xaan. Though that early prosperity had not continued, with the nation's fortunes declining in the last hundred years.

Then something clicked in Mudge's mind. He realized why Ottar Bey had risen to power, and why the Empress had been able to gain a hold in Xaan. The people wanted their old prominence in the world back. They wanted to be wealthy again, and they had decided to do whatever it took to live well again, like their ancestors. Or the way they imagined their ancestors had lived, since human desire usually twisted the facts.

Their desire for more had thrown their country into war with its neighbours, and it would destroy so many people, reflected Mudge sadly. Such was the nature of human greed, and ignorance.

The road become rougher underfoot, and began to climb. Then it veered away from the aqueduct. Mudge realized they had left the salt plain behind. Then the night grew dark as the moon set behind the Teeth of Kormac. It was now almost impossible to see the road at all, and Ochren drew them off the rough surface and into the scrub that cloaked the foothills of the Teeth. They stopped to sleep for a while when he found a hollow hidden among the hills.

Barely had they settled down when Mudge felt the presence of the Keeper Stone again. It had been a while since he sensed it, his mind on more mundane matters while they crossed the Great Salt Lake.

The Stone directed him to the map in his mind, the spirit reference that showed him the positions of all spirit beings, and all events of power as they occurred. In the foothills ahead of them, coming from Xaan, was a column of horse archers. It was led by a Sarkosay. Mudge couldn't miss the swirl of red and black energies that headed the column.

Someone at Jik had sent word to Xianak, by a carrier bird or more supernatural means, and not long after the travellers had arrived in the town considering the swiftness of the response. Ottar Bey must have spies everywhere. The question of how to enter Xianak unnoticed had just got a lot more difficult. In fact a lot of things were going to get more difficult as they worked their way deeper into enemy territory.

Mudge cast a spirit veil over the camp in the hollow. It wasn't long before the column of archers passed noisily by, their hoof beats echoing back to the hollow as they followed the road out over the Great Salt Lake. The Sarkosay at their head hadn't detected the hidden camp, and that reassured Mudge all the more about the power of the Keeper Stone to keep them hidden.

He slept restlessly during the night. Dreams of a giant red and black figure standing triumphantly over Xianak tore at his heart. It had taken on a different appearance now. He recognized the tall, smoky black shape of the Empress. This time, the malevolent figure was looking for him. It cast restlessly this way and that in its search. Sparks of red and black fire lit up across the countryside as its agents searched for him and his companions.

Mudge could feel, even in his dream, the Keeper Stone maintaining the spirit veil over the camp. He relaxed a little when he saw that. Still, the Empress knew him now. She would be better prepared for their next meeting. And so would he, thought Mudge grimly.

Then Luce and Jago were there, trying to tell him something. They were telling him he had to put his trust in others, especially his friends in the hollow. He had to stop trying to take the weight of the world on his shoulders. There was a reason for everything, even the appearance of the Empress, if he could but find it.

A little later in his dream the Keeper Stone was talking to Luce and Jago, and Mudge wondered where exactly he was now. Shifting images floated past, a boat on a lake, and then a room lit by a golden sun. The Keeper Stone took a human form briefly, but it flickered in and out of focus, as if this was not a natural state for it.

The morning came too quickly, and Mudge realized the broken sleep from his dreams and the night travelling were catching up with him. Breakfast was more of the slave gruel. It was all they had left from Jik. Once they had eaten, Ochren gathered them around the cart.

"We have to work out how to get into Xianak," he said, and they all nodded. That time wasn't far away now.

"The Empress knows there is a group of us, and she also knows we have this cart. On top of that the rash from the spotted lungwort is wearing off, though I'm sure Arnima could renew our disguises," he said, turning in her direction. "But the Xaanians are looking for a group of slaves now, so that disguise won't get us much further anyway.

"Anybody got any ideas?" he finished.

The resulting suggestions varied from moving at night, to disguising themselves as farmers and separating into twos and threes. Mudge found himself wrestling with his conscience throughout the discussion. He didn't want the others to keep risking their lives to help him.

"I would never have got this far without your help," he said at last, "but we're less than a day's march from Xianak now. I can find my way from here, and I'm not even sure what I'm supposed to do once I get there. Maybe it's best if I work my way inside the gates, and just see what happens.

"The rest of you are in a perfect position to spread out and gather information on Xaanian troop movements. That will be invaluable to the Legatus when you report back to him." The rest of the company looked at him like he was mad.

"So you suddenly speak Xaanian now?" said Senovila dismissively.

"And what if the thing you're supposed to do requires a backup team?" said Bear, in a more kindly tone.

"You're not going to get rid of us that easily," said Arnima with a smile. She understood at once that Mudge was just concerned for their safety. He wasn't saying the mission would go any better without them.

"Butha would help us!" said Onjed, sitting on the cart, and the others turned toward him. They had forgotten the boy was even there, and Ochren was about to ignore his suggestion when the boy rambled on.

"Butha was my nurse. She lives in a small village just outside Xianak, with her husband. It's on our way to the city, and they were very loyal to my father.

"They have no love for Ottar Bey, or the new order. Butha knows everything there is to know about Xianak. She would be able to tell you what to do."

Ochren paused. It wasn't a bad plan at that, at least in the short term – if the boy's assurances could be trusted. After a long discussion about the advantages and disadvantages, it was finally agreed that this would be the next step.

"Clean yourselves up as best you can," said Arnima. "See me for something to clear up the rash if any of it still remains."

"After that we'll gather some herbs and spices," said Senovila, nodding craftily. Arnima smiled at him. She could see what he was getting at immediately. The others looked blank.

So it was that by midday a group of herb and spice sellers, spread out so no two would be seen on the road at the same time, made their way from the foothills of the Teeth toward the produce markets in Xianak.

They didn't look that different from the day before. They looked a bit healthier now than slaves, but they had the ground-in dirt and shabby clothing of foragers. Senovila had impressed upon them the need to walk slowly and act tired, as if they were bowed down by long hours of work and little food.

There had been good supplies of wild herbs in the area around their camp. Senovila knew that the poorer soils near the salt plain produced them in abundance, and it wasn't long before each of them had a large bundle to carry. They had, however, abandoned the cart, much to Senovila's disappointment, and the horses had been set free to fend for themselves.

Mudge had tried to contact the sprites in this area, to ask them if they could take care of the horses, but the sprites here were completely different from any he had met before. A pair of pale shapes had hovered in the air in front of him, but he hadn't been able to get a word out of them.

It was now the middle of the afternoon on the long road in to the city, and Mudge trudged along slowly, raising dust in the hot sun. They had all drunk their fill of water before they set out, but they had none of the Xaanian gourds that were common in the region to carry. They had thought it best to leave their League water bottles behind, and Mudge was beginning to feel the effects of thirst.

He could hear a heavy wagon, and a team of six or eight horses, coming up behind him. It wasn't travelling much faster than he was and took a long time to catch up with him.

Mudge bent his back even further under his load, and the bundle of greenery rode higher. He tried to look absorbed in his own thoughts.

"*Shehan dai!*" called the wagon driver, as he came alongside Mudge.

Damn, a talker, thought Mudge in irritation. Senovila had given them two phrases to use in desperate situations. His first advice, though, had been to discourage all communication.

"*Shehan dai,*" he replied tonelessly, keeping his head down. Hopefully exchanging greetings would be enough for the man.

"*Purdon que asdallient pro combala?*" continued the wagon driver.

"*Mordam pialla,*" said Mudge. He hoped the equivalent of 'life has its ups and downs' would be enough.

The wagon driver launched into a torrent of Xaanian that meant absolutely nothing to Mudge. He waited until the flow dried up a little, and lifted his hand in a vaguely waggling motion. He hoped that had some meaning in the Xaanian culture.

The man seemed to be asking a question, and Mudge shook his head. That, according to Senovila, meant the same in Xaan as it did in the League kingdoms.

The wagon driver wasn't pleased about something, but the wagon had now moved on, and he had to look back to see Mudge.

He was carried on down the track on the wagon, still talking to himself.

Mudge hoped the exchange wouldn't get him reported to the guards at the gates of Xianak, but even if it was, he didn't think one lowly forager would arouse suspicion. They would think he was touched by the sun as much as anything, and he hoped the others were getting on better than he was.

By late afternoon, Mudge had a dry mouth and a growing headache. He turned wearily left at an imposing inn with its own stables. It sat opposite an ale house. This was the turn-off he had been told to look for.

He realized someone else from his group, Colma by the look of him, was resting a stone's throw ahead. Mudge trudged silently past. Neither made any sign of recognizing the other. It looked like Colma was having trouble with his footwear.

A little further on Mudge saw the whitewashed wall with a tiled top he was looking for. He waited until he was past the wall, then turned down an alleyway beyond. At the end of it a young man beckoned him through a narrow gate. Mudge dropped his bundle of herbs into a woodshed among some trees, and followed his guide into the back of a sprawling house.

This was a mansion compared to the simple farmers' houses dotted about the area, though Mudge suspected it was nothing like the brick and terracotta houses of the nobility in Xianak. Working for Usef Bey must have been well paid if this was Butha's house as he expected it was. When he was ushered into the kitchen area at the back, he found most of the others already there.

"You need to go on more forced marches, boy," said Ochren jovially. He was enjoying Mudge's tired and dishevelled state. Arnima scowled at her husband, and brought a damp cloth over so Mudge could wipe his face. She followed this with a jug of water.

"This is Butha," she said, when he had finished half the water, and pointed to a stout woman cooking over fires on the far side of the room. Mudge noticed Onjed helping her, attentive to her every request. She stroked the top of his head, and he smiled happily.

"And this is Andrian, her husband," said Arnima. She introduced a solid man with a ruddy complexion from years in the fields. He was wringing his hands nervously.

"Welcome to our humble dwelling, your highness," he said quickly. Then he bent at the knees in something that looked like a cross between a curtsy and a bow.

Mudge realized Ochren had told the poor man his guest was a prince of the Karnatic League, perhaps even that he was a Monhoven, and related to the Legatus. Ochren must have had his reasons for doing that, but Mudge wished he hadn't said anything. He stepped over and took the man by the hand.

"You can call me 'your highness' at one of those fancy royal balls that waste a lot of time and money," he said with a grin. "For now it's 'Mudge', and we're most grateful for your hospitality."

After his initial surprise at the greeting, Andrian returned Mudge's smile. Then he shook his hand vigorously. There was a knock on the door, and the young man who had waited by the side gate for Mudge brought Colma in. Shyleen gave him a cloth to wipe away the grime of travel, and then Ochren came over to talk to Mudge.

"The old nurse is quite happy to take over care of the boy," he said softly. Mudge nodded.

Then Ochren added in a louder voice, "Butha's been telling us how people in Xaan feel about the war, Mudge, and it's very interesting."

Butha set Onjed to stoking the fire, and handed a wooden stirrer to a young woman next to him. Whether she was a daughter or a servant was hard to tell. Then she came bustling over to join in the discussion.

"Your man here," she said briskly, indicating Ochren, "says you're interested in what's been going on in Xaan. Well, some people are getting carried away with the idea of the glorious empire of Xaan rising again. Idiots all of them, if you'll pardon me, and more sensible people figure the cost of 'rising again' isn't worth it.

"It's all parades and making money while the army builds itself up. Then it's funerals and families without husbands and sons! And for what? Slave nations bowing to Xaan? Is that what you or I would want for our families?"

She looked at Mudge intently. Then she changed the direction of her argument.

"Tell me where it's written for any country that winning a war is a certainty. It seems to me it's a huge risk for an undesirable reward." Then she hesitated. "I guess you can tell which side I'm on. There are too many rumours of the High Council bodyguard up to no good, and it's not right to have those damnable Gorlen tramping around our streets like they own the place."

"This bit about the Gorlen is especially interesting," interrupted Ochren.

"The First Elect says they're our secret weapon in this war," continued Butha, "but I want to know who controls them. I certainly don't trust Ottar Bey to use them wisely, and I'm sure he came to power by unpleasant means."

"Mark my words," she finished, "some nasty truths will come out before this whole stupid business is finished."

"Describe these Gorlen to me," said Mudge gently. He wanted to steer the flood of information in a more useful direction.

"Big damnable things," said Butha, glowering at the memory while she raised her hand over her head. Then she stood on tiptoe to increase her height. "They've got a funny, waxy shine to them. They look like men, and walk like men, but I don't think they're men.

"When a Gorlen patrol goes by they all swing their arms at the same time, and bend at the knee at the same time. It's all a bit too uncanny."

Mudge nodded. Spirit walkers in the League sometimes talked about bodies animated by slave spirits, though he knew the subject repelled them. He wondered if it could be true, and delved into his memories to dredge up what he knew about the animation process.

If these Gorlen were shapes the Empress had brought to life, then the bodies that held the slave spirits couldn't be far away from the animated bodies. What he remembered from his studies said the slave spirit was normally touching the body it animated.

He smiled ruefully. The only bits of his 'schooling' that had stuck in his memory were the gruesome bits. So far they had been the only bits he needed!

The prodigious strength of the Gorlen was going to be a problem for the League, and also the fact a normally fatal wound wouldn't stop them. They would need to be dismembered to bring the giants to a halt, and the League troops wouldn't have time for that in the chaos of battle. It was desperate stuff. There had to be another way to kill them.

"I think we've found a way of getting you inside the walls of Xianak," said Andrian. "All of you," he added, sweeping the room with is hand. His words brought Mudge's mind back to the present. He saw Ochren nearby, nodding. It looked like he knew the plan already, and it had his approval.

"You go in by the pilgrim gate," continued Andrian, "so you'll have to look the part. But if you go through in ones and twos, when the gate is at its busiest, the guards will only give you a quick once over."

"We're good at pretending to be something else by now," said Mareet, with a laugh.

"And we should be able to hide our weapons under our pilgrim robes," said Liam.

Mudge turned to them. "This isn't going to be that sort of fight," he said. "The Gorlen can't be stopped by weapons, at least not by so few of us.

"I need you with me, but not as a bodyguard. I need you to give me courage, and I need you to keep me alive by other means."

"You underestimate us, boy," said Ochren with a grin. "We have a few rather special weapons hidden about us."

Mudge nodded. It was true he didn't know the extent of the ranger armoury, but this would become more and more of a spirit war. He knew that for certain.

"I can help with the robes," said Butha quickly. "Any length of cloth will do, as long as it's white or white with yellow edging. It will have to cover the body modestly."

The travellers decided they would join the morning rush at the pilgrim gate on the following day, and Butha assured them the robes would be ready for them by then, though she and her daughter would have to work through the night.

Andrian told them there was always a large crowd when the gate first opened. Pilgrims who had been travelling for days rested up outside Xianak so they could be fresh for the morning. They came principally for a circuit of the great shrine of Maat. It housed the holy relics of their faith.

Later that evening the company sat down to a fine meal that Butha had prepared for them, and they were able to make up for the limited intake they had been forced to endure over the last few weeks. Mudge was quiet while he ate. He had no plan, and no real idea of what was waiting for them inside the city walls. He just knew they needed to keep going forward. First into Xaan, and now into Xianak.

He wondered how his father was getting on, with the Karnatic defence Forces at Rotor Valley Pass, and how the Independent Kingdom forces at Thebes were doing. He could have sent a spirit hawk to find out, but it might give away their position to the Empress and he had resisted the urge.

He could feel the strands of fate as they twisted tighter and tighter about him and his friends. It was almost unbearable.

SIXTEEN

The following day dawned beautifully clear, and all the days had started the same way since they left the Scaffold Mountains. Xaan must be a nice place to live, conceded Mudge, at least as far as the weather was concerned. Still, if he survived this madness, his first preference would be to settle in the Wild Marches again. Shaker's Hope appealed to him.

The travellers made their way to the pilgrim gate in the outer wall. Then they broke into ones and twos and lost themselves in the crowd. Andrian had been right. The guards took no notice of the pilgrims as they gathered in front of the small gate in the wall. Then, when a bell sounded from somewhere inside, they were ushered through with no more than a glance.

"When do you think we should separate from the crowd?" muttered Bear. He had joined Mudge and Ochren once they were safely through the gate.

"When we see a few of the other pilgrims turning off," said Ochren quietly. The river of white and yellow robes had turned left after the gate, and now flowed down a wide avenue. "No sense in drawing attention to ourselves."

"Over there!" hissed Bear, looking down so he wouldn't draw attention to himself. But his left hand rested against his waist, the thumb overlying curled fingers and pointing slightly left of the stream of pilgrims. Mudge glanced in the direction Bear was indicating, and saw a line of tall figures in military uniforms scrutinizing pilgrims as they streamed past.

"Gorlen," said Ochren, speaking softly by his ear, "has to be."

Mudge glanced further down the wide avenue, and saw the tall spires that indicated the great shrine of Maat. He had no intention of making a circuit round the shrine, and he was more interested in finding a way to get off the avenue as soon as possible.

He closed his eyes for a moment, and saw the swirling red and black energies of the Gorlen ahead of them. The energy signatures were like those around the Sarkosay. There was no doubting that the Gorlen, too, were the Empress' creatures.

A wagon pulled out of a warehouse ahead of them and turned in the same direction the pilgrims were heading. Something jammed the brake shut, and the driver jumped down off the wagon. He kicked the offending wheel and wooden block, cursing loudly as he did so. The pilgrims behind him were forced outward to pass him, and then several stopped to argue with him about his language, which jammed the flow of traffic even further.

Seeing his chance, Ochren slid in behind the wagon. He pretended he was inspecting one of the wheels. Bear and Mudge began to chant nonsense rhymes, swinging their arms over their heads at the same time. It was the signal to gather at that spot the travellers had agreed on. The pilgrims were from all over Xaan and beyond. Ochren figured they weren't going to object to the religious practices of another group of worshippers. One by one, the rest of the company made their way to the side of the avenue. They gathered quietly behind Ochren, like flotsam caught in the gentle swirl of a backwater.

Seizing the moment, Ochren ushered them into the warehouse beside the wagon. Looking like a man with a purpose, he pointed toward the loading docks in the back. Then he strode off in that direction, and the others followed. They stepped off the floor of the warehouse onto more of the loading docks, and then down into a quiet back street.

Mudge looked round, trying to get his bearings. He opened his spirit senses to see where the Empress was, and soon spotted her. She was still in the Royal Palace, but there were many swirling red and black points between him and his destination. Gorlen or Sarkosay, or something else, he didn't know.

A few minutes later he was torn from his review of the area by the sudden appearance of a troop of Gorlen that came round the corner from the next street at a trot, heading straight for the pretend 'pilgrims'. Mudge realized with a sinking feeling the Empress had been able to trace him when he used his spirit senses, and she had sent the nearest troop of Gorlen straight to him.

Bear pushed open a door next to the loading docks and dived through it, dragging two of the others with him. Galvanised into action, the rest followed. One of the Gorlen pushed its way in behind them, but then Bear slammed the door shut.

Pandemonium reigned. Bear and Liam dragged some heavy shelves in front of the door to keep it closed, and the Gorlen that were still outside attacked the entrance with every weapon they had. The creature trapped inside the room towered over them. It swept Colma aside as it drew its sword, throwing him into Mudge. Bear ripped his pilgrim robes off and drew his sword, and the others followed suit.

Knocked to the floor, Mudge was still able to see Ochren slice the Gorlen's belly open, but it didn't seem to slow the creature at all. There was no blood, just a grey, gaping wound. The Gorlen returned a blow that knocked Ochren aside like he was made of straw. Gods they're strong, thought Mudge, as he scrambled out of the way. He took up a position at the back of the room, which was a large structure that appeared to be a storeroom.

The Gorlen turned its attention to Bear, who made a deep cut across its shoulder, but that didn't slow the creature either. To Mudge it looked, incredibly, like the cut across its belly was beginning to heal. He wondered if the rangers could stop such an unnatural creature. Then Ochren sheathed his sword and lifted a glittering string out of the carry-all at his waist, wrapping his hands in a cloth first.

The storeroom had been built inside the larger area of the warehouse, and wasn't closed in overhead. Light from the loading bays was enough to show the many sparkling reflections on the string as Ochren twisted the bare ends round his hands. Picking his moment he stepped behind the Gorlen and flicked the string over its head. Then he sawed vigorously back and forth across its neck.

Mudge watched in fascination as the string worked its way through the creature's thick neck. Then a forward lunge at Bear dislodged its head completely. The rangers drew back, waiting for the creature to collapse on the floor, but losing its head had no effect on the Gorlen whatsoever.

The disfigured body struck out at its attackers again and again. They were immensely powerful strokes, though the Gorlen wasn't as fast as the rangers. Only the number of its assailants, constantly badgering it from all sides, kept it confined to one corner of the storeroom.

Mudge heard a crash from an outside wall, and saw one of the roughly adzed planks splinter between two of the uprights. It wouldn't be long before the rest of the Gorlen smashed a way in to help the one inside.

Mudge saw the creature dodge ponderously to one side to avoid a blow from Bear, and then he looked again. Something was bulging upwards between its shoulders. The damned thing was trying to grow a new head!

A number of broken lances were piled together in one corner of the room. Colma grabbed the long shaft of one, and called something to Bear, who ran to grab it with him. Together they drove the lance between Ochren and Liam, hitting the Gorlen low in the chest and driving it back.

The creature hit the wall behind it, and was held there while they drove the shaft right through its body, and into the wall. There was a crunching noise, and Mudge felt, more than saw, a blur of red and black energies flicker for a moment and disappear. As Bear wrenched the makeshift spear free the Gorlen toppled to the ground and didn't move. Ochren kicked at an outstretched leg. There was no response.

"Turn it over," said Mudge. "Quickly." Judging by the noise outside, the other Gorlen were close to breaking into the storeroom. He bent down and cut the rough fabric away from the middle of the creature's back. A large crushed shell, dripping gore, sat inside a hollow he found there.

"Slave spirit," said Mudge. He was pleased to see his guess about the Gorlen's driving power had been right. He had no idea what they were, but they weren't natural. The Empress must have brought them into this world with her. The slave spirits must be able to take in enough information through their spirit senses to make the Gorlen function in the real world. That was how they carried out the Empress' commands.

At least he knew how to stop the Gorlen now, but a crash of splintering wood announced the Empress' creations had breached the outside wall, and the first one entered the storeroom. When Mudge looked up from the Gorlen on the floor, several of the creatures were advancing in formation.

Ochren decided this was not the time to stand and fight. He signalled a retreat, and Bear opened a door into the main body of the warehouse for the others to hasten through. The travellers stopped outside the room they had just left as they saw a large circle of Xaanians who had come to see what the commotion was all about. But the ranger leader realized these people were simply curious. He led the travellers at a run through the warehouse and out onto the loading docks on the other side. They were soon out on the same back street as before.

They had all ditched their pilgrim robes for the fight, and their ranger clothing was going to be conspicuous, though here in Xaan it was unlikely anyone would know exactly what it meant. Ochren led them quickly through a number of streets in an effort to lose the Gorlen who were still pursuing them. He was looking for somewhere they could hole up and plan what to do next. He turned a corner and dodged into a small eating establishment that was not yet open.

"Bear and Liam, scout the back and bring anyone you find out here," he said tersely. "Senovila, organize the others to get those storm shutters up."

Mudge looked round. The shop was a basic food outlet. Rough tables were not yet covered with cloth for the day's customers, and simple stools leaned against the wall after last night's cleaning. Fire pits at the back of the room contained cold ash. Small openings in the mud-plastered wall facing the street were equipped with storm shutters, and Mudge figured sandstorms must occasionally blow in off the Endless Desert. Colma and Mareet already had most of them closed.

"This is all we could find," said Bear, ushering in two adults and two children. "A family I think, but my Xaanian isn't really up to it."

"*Sudenia que?*" he asked his captives.

"Not a family," said the girl earnestly in Xaanian. "I am betrothed to Mustaf. It is my duty to work for his father."

Ochren and Senovila exchanged glances. They understood what she was saying. In Xaan children were betrothed while very young, though the marriage did not take place for years. It was quite common for the girl to be taken in by the boy's family. Senovila got their names, and set the family to work making a meal for the travellers.

"Tell them we won't be here long," said Mudge. "Tell them we mean them no harm, and say they'll be paid for feeding us." Ochren nodded. It was what he had intended to do anyway.

Mudge retreated to one corner of the room to think. He had something of a dilemma to sort out. The Empress could trace him, at least this close, if he engaged his spirit senses. Yet what they had learned about the Gorlen had to be sent to his father as soon as possible.

Mudge had done the sums. There must have been close to three hundred Gorlen in the barracks when he first came to the Royal Palace. When he had checked his internal map earlier that morning, he had counted no more than fifty still in Xianak. The rest would have been sent to the front lines to fight against the League, or the Independent Kingdoms.

Mudge smiled. Sending the Gorlen to the front lines probably meant the war wasn't going so well for the Empress. He raised a silent cheer for his own side. Nevertheless, he was going to attract the Empress' attention the instant he sent a spirit hawk, and that would put the company in danger again. He needed to send the spirit hawk when he was alone, and if he was caught his friends could make it out of the city and back to the League lines. They deserved that.

Mudge beckoned Ochren over, and told him what needed to be done. He stated his intention bluntly, and thought he left no room for discussion. But Ochren raised his eyebrows and took a deep breath to dispute the point.

"That's an order, soldier," snapped Mudge. "Don't remind the others they're sworn to support me in my mission, then argue the point when I tell you what I need you to do!" Ochren subsided, though he was clearly not happy with Mudge's decision.

"Don't tell the others until I'm gone," said Mudge. "We haven't got time to sit around reaching agreement about this one."

Ochren nodded reluctantly. Then Mudge clasped the ranger's arm, and Ochren returned the salute. A little later Ochren called the others to one of the tables to talk about what they would do next. Mudge saw his opportunity and slipped out the door onto the street. Then he blended in with the citizens of Xianak.

He turned into two more back streets before he came across another warehouse. He ducked into a loading bay, and heard voices

laughing in a room at the back. He made his way into the main
storeroom and hid himself where the goods were piled highest.

Once he was well hidden, he relaxed, and stilled his mind. Then
he reached out with his spirit senses for his father. He intended to
send a spirit hawk, but as before he found himself looking through a
window that opened abruptly in front of him.

And the instant he did so, Mudge felt the presence of the
Empress. He felt the rage that drove her constantly on, and the
intensity of her search for him. Then the Keeper Stone closed about
him, shutting her out.

Mudge brought his attention back to the connection with his
father. He saw the startled look on the face of the man next to
Ultrich. Then he saw the faces of a number of hill tribes chiefs in the
background.

He recognized Krell, the high chief of the tribes. It took a
moment for him to realize Ultrich and Krell must be conducting a
meeting in Krell's tent. Then he remembered the superstition with
which the hill tribes regarded spirit walkers. His timing, as always,
was terrible. For a moment he was tempted to laugh bitterly,
thinking how well he was proving himself an inadequate prince all
over again.

"What is it, Rossi?" said the Legatus calmly. Mudge saw at once
the skill his father had as a leader. By reacting calmly to the sudden
intrusion he was setting a standard for the reaction he expected, and
the chiefs would not want to fall short of it.

"My apologies for the sudden intrusion," said Mudge humbly.
Then he outlined the threat he believed was marching on the League
positions, and possibly the Independent Kingdoms. When Ultrich
and Krell had grasped that, he explained how to kill the Gorlen.

Ultrich raised his eyebrows. This was pivotal information
indeed. Then a burst of scarlet energies tore at the shield the Keeper

Stone had built around Mudge. The Legatus stepped forward, immediately concerned.

"That feels wrong, even from here," he said quickly. "Is everything all right, Rossi?"

Mudge looked round him in the warehouse. The swirling energies of the Empress' attack had set stacks of cloth on fire. Startled shouts emerged from the men in the back room he had heard earlier. There was the sound of running feet, and he turned back to Ultrich.

"No, it's not all right," he said quietly, "but that's my problem. You're going to have enough on your plate with the Gorlen." He looked at his father with a touch of sadness, tinged with pride.

"If you really believe in those things you used to talk about, in that which created the world, put in a word for me," he said simply. Ultrich nodded, and Mudge closed the window.

A scarlet whirlwind pulsed and arced around him. The warehouse grew indistinct, and Mudge sensed a build-up of energies that would lead to a spirit jump. He thought for a minute of making himself immovable, fixed in space and time, but that would only put off the inevitable. The confrontation with the Empress must come sooner or later.

Then Luce and Jago were with him, holding his hands, dancing around him. They were laughing at the difficulty of the situation, and then the whirlwind of red and black energies constricted more tightly. Mudge pulled his friends close, making a centre of sanity in the storm. Wrapping the Keeper Stone tightly about them all, he finished the spirit jump the Empress had started. The three of them burst into the Royal Palace before an array of startled faces.

He saw at once that the Empress had taken Butha and Andrian prisoner, along with Butha's daughter, and the young man who had waited in the lane when they first came by. Onjed peered out in wonderment from behind them, and several of the black-clad bodyguards stood nearby.

Damn the Empress, thought Mudge angrily. Somehow she had tracked down an innocent family that had simply been hospitable to strangers. At least she hadn't found the rest of the travellers.

Then Mudge looked around him. He was in the same high-ceilinged room with its opulent furnishings as before. The long table was still there, laden with maps and documents, but the courtiers and attendants of the Royal Palace were absent. The atmosphere of the place had changed though, it was on a war footing now.

Commander Uttan was present. This time he presided over a full company of the council bodyguard. There was also a very noticeable squad of Gorlen. Mudge saw a flicker of movement at one end of the long hall, and recognized Ottar Bey. The First Elect was in his full leadership regalia, surrounded by a contingent of soldiers.

Mudge almost smiled. No one went to a showdown hampered by a costume like that. He had a moment of compassion for the puppet king. The man was too frightened to take an active part in the battle for his kingdom, and too uncertain of his position to stay away. His dream of power must have long since become a nightmare.

Mudge doubted Ottar Bey, or the Empress, had any idea that the boy they had sent to the salt mines was the son of Usef Bey, the governor who would have taken the position of First Elect in more normal times.

The tall, solid shape of the Empress was the first to recover from Mudge's sudden appearance. She hissed something in a language that the prince didn't recognize. It certainly wasn't Xaanian. It sounded much older, like one of the ancient languages of power. The consonants slipped and changed as he listened. They were indecipherable to the human ear, and Mudge didn't have time to force them to reveal their true meaning.

The Gorlen marched forward at the command, forming a line between Mudge and the Empress. He noticed how precisely they kept in step. Then the Empress hissed something else, and the black-clad guards around his new-found Xaanian friends stepped up and twisted their heads to one side, pointing long daggers at their throats.

So, thought Mudge. A threat to be overcome and a promise of death to the innocent. She's trying to panic me into making a rash move. He suddenly noticed how he was above it all, how calm he felt. Maybe Ultrich's training on staying centred was making sense to something inside him at last. He knew he couldn't afford to make decisions based upon his emotional response. Emotions were too easy for others to manipulate, and emotions always twisted the facts. He would go over his feelings about the situation later, when all this was over, but not now.

Luce and Jago left his side, drifting toward the bodyguards. Mudge could feel their outrage at the Empress' actions toward the innocent. Then two of the black-clad guards twitched, and their eyes glazed over. It was enough for the other guards to look nervously around. Mudge realized that he was the only one who could see the spirit shades of his friends taking control of the guards. It was a brave move, but it wasn't that sort of a fight.

Mudge reached out and took away the life energies from the bodyguards around Butha and her family, and they slumped to the ground unconscious. Then he did the same, though more gently, to his Xaanian friends. It was best that the Empress took no more interest in them. Jago and Luce drifted away, understanding that it was Mudge's fight now.

The Gorlen marched toward him, unsheathing their weapons. Mudge tried to gain control of the slave spirits that animated the creatures, but it proved a fruitless task. The Empress had shielded them from outside interference using a number of spirit wards, and Mudge didn't have time to unravel them.

He took control of one of the creatures, wresting it away from the slave spirit that animated it. He could control the Gorlen by force of will, but he couldn't disable the slave spirit, and that made controlling the cumbersome body difficult. Using all of his power, he made his new body turn in mid stride. Then he made it cut off the head of the creature to its left.

The wounded Gorlen stumbled, and Mudge drove his sword into its back, searching for the shell-like creature that controlled it. He stabbed again, and this time heard a satisfying crunch. The lifeless body fell to the floor.

Several Gorlen on the right of the creature he controlled grabbed its arms, and one to his left set about systematically dismembering it. Mudge relinquished control, and the creature fell to the floor. It tried to push itself upright on the stump of one arm. In time it would regrow its missing limbs, but for now that was two of them out of the fight.

Mudge realized his delaying tactics would only work for so long. He would have to retreat, but he didn't want to leave his Xaanian friends in the clutches of the Empress. He needed to remove the threat that the Gorlen posed, and nullify the remaining bodyguards. Only then could he think of engaging the Empress in a contest based on spirit power. He looked at the Gorlen again. There were too many of them, and there was only one of him.

Mudge felt the beat of the music before he heard it. He knew why he suddenly felt more optimistic. Then he heard the music itself. The strange rhythm quickened his step, and made him feel glad in his heart. A moment later there were Mesoans all around him. They had told him how difficult it was for them to exist outside their homeland, yet here they were.

As wisps of light materialised inside the Great Hall of the Royal Palace, the Empress gave up the pretence of being a Xaanian noblewoman. She reared upward, turning into the same smoky, black shape that Mudge had seen her take before. Then she coalesced into a towering daemon shape. Mudge recognized it from the old writings he had seen in his studies at the Priatic School.

This was *Esharla*, one of the three daemons of the cycle of destruction. The old writings had said she would destroy all life at the end of the world. Mudge eyed the gross and repellent thing suspiciously. It was likely the Empress was taking this form for her own ends at the moment, to rend and destroy.

One of the wisps of light touched Mudge on his arm, but it didn't turn into a copy of him this time. Perhaps it was easier for them to exist outside their homeland as light. Then he realized it had passed on knowledge to him. He understood the long history of enmity between the Mesoans and the Empress. Both had been there at the beginning of creation, but on opposite sides.

Some of the light beings present in the beginning had rebelled. They had wanted to make worlds of their own, but the others had known the rebels' understanding was too limited to accomplish such a task. They would only create a hell for themselves, and more importantly, for all the beings within their new creation.

In the end the rebellious ones had been imprisoned inside this world, buried deep within it, unable to influence the world above them directly. The Mesoans were one of the groups that had imprisoned them. They had chosen to stay on in the world, protecting it in case the prisoners ever managed to get free.

Mudge shook his head in wonder. It seemed incredible that the world had its own guardians. Was the Keeper Stone another one? But the Stone didn't answer his question. One thing, though, was clear. The Mesoans were sworn to undo everything the Empress intended. As Mudge realized this, the daemon *Esharla* screeched a challenge. The discordant sound conveyed its extreme hatred for the living, and the free.

The remaining Gorlen closed on Mudge, and he tightened the Keeper Stone's shield about him. He wondered if it would be enough. Numerous Mesoans now converged on him also, and the Gorlen drew back from the brightening columns of light among them. The Mesoans swarmed over the Gorlen, surrounding them with pulsing light, forcing the slave spirits inside the animated creatures to burst into flame.

Mudge saw the Gorlen split apart and collapse across the floor, one after the other. He saw them return to the simple clay and vegetable materials they had been constructed from. The bright Mesoan columns of light were left standing, undiminished by the destruction of the slave creatures. The people of the dance had done more than Mudge had expected of them. He knew that survival in his world was hard for their kind, and he wasn't surprised when they began to fade away, and the music of the dance faded with them.

The Gorlen had been cleared from the hall, but there would be more of them elsewhere in the palace, and the Empress would be calling them. The remaining bodyguards, and the soldiers around Ottar Bey, began to move forward. They were more scared of what the Empress might do to them than what Mudge might call up next, and Mudge decided his best strategy was to retreat from the hall. He turned, and restored the life energies he had taken from Butha and those around her. Then he hurried to help them to their feet.

"This way!" he urged, as they moved unsteadily to follow him. "Hurry, we have to run!" he called as he got ready to close the doors to the room behind him.

Butha was the first to regain full control of her body. She dragged Onjed toward the exit Mudge indicated, and shouted at the others. Seeing what was happening, the bodyguard broke into a run.

The prisoners made it through the door just in time. Mudge was delighted to see a heavy bar, and anchor points, on the back of the doors. He closed them and slammed the bar home, and turned to look behind him. A long corridor ran off into the distance, where it split left and right.

Was this all that was left to them, he wondered, as they hurried along the corridor. Running and hiding until they were caught?

SEVENTEEN

Ultrich looked out over the scarred battlefield from the top of The Lion. He recalled the events of the last few days with a considerable amount of satisfaction.

The League forces had made the High Steppes their own. They had cowed the Xaanian army sent against them, and completely obliterated the troublesome Xaanian horse archers. On top of that the victories of the League had forced Ottar Bey to send reinforcements.

He hoped this would take some of the pressure off Yeltar and the Independent Kingdoms. By now they would have left Taire valley and be entrenched behind their new positions at Thebes.

The Legatus considered the First Elect of the Xaanian Council more carefully in his mind. He had suspected for some time that Ottar Bey was a puppet leader, and now Rossi had confirmed it. His son was up against – what? A human power behind Ottar Bey, or something much worse?

The unknown Empress troubled him. Some things in the netherworld were best left alone. If they were awakened, whole civilizations could be destroyed. He hoped the 'Empress' that had arisen in Xaan wasn't a supernatural being of that order.

Then Sergeos pointed to a plume of dust on the horizon. The Xaanian reinforcements seemed to be never ending. The array drawn up in front of the pass was already as big as the first one the League had defeated.

On his other side, Cinnabar drew herself up to her full, aristocratic height. She snorted disdainfully at the new arrivals. Ultrich felt her awaken her farsight, and send it out toward the distant column.

She had been so different lately, he reflected. She seemed brittle around him, finding excuses to be elsewhere. He had accidentally discovered how she felt about him when he had been injured, but rather than bringing them closer it seemed to have opened an unbridgeable gulf between them.

Her feelings for him had come as a complete surprise to the Legatus, but he had to admit he didn't mind the idea of a relationship. Maybe it was time, finally, for someone to take the place of Rossi's mother. But how he would get past Cinnabar's considerable defences and make a case for her affections, would have to wait. The many problems facing the League needed to be resolved first.

"Legatus, you'll want to see this," snapped Cinnabar beside him. "There's something in the middle of that damned column and it doesn't look right to me. If I was pressed I'd say it wasn't human!"

One interesting side effect of her crustiness was the use of the occasional swear word. It made Ultrich smile. He engaged his own farsight, and got his first look at the advancing Gorlen.

Rossi had been right. There was more than a hundred of them. According to his son a smaller number would be on their way to fight Yeltar's forces at Thebes. Ultrich blew out a long breath. It was just his luck to get the larger share of the indestructible creatures. Almost indestructible, he reminded himself. Rossi had given them enough information to give the League a fighting chance.

He had always wanted the bulk of the Xaanian forces here at Rotor Valley Pass, and his wish had been fulfilled. The bottleneck in the mountains and the short supply lines back to the Marches made it an ideal place to grind down an enemy. But a hundred plus supernaturally empowered Gorlen had not been in his original plans.

He wondered what Yeltar would do when the Gorlen arrived at Thebes. Ultrich had sent the column of armoured horses he had promised at their earlier meeting, and they should arrive at Thebes before the Gorlen did, but it wouldn't be enough to turn the tide against overwhelming Xaanian forces.

He glanced at the battle lines on the plain below. The League still had some hours before the enemy launched an attack. The enemy reinforcements needed to be properly bedded in to their new positions, and that meant an attack was unlikely before late in the afternoon.

Ultrich had faced up to the fact his League forces might not be able to hold against the mix of Xaanian troops and Gorlen-led reinforcements, and adjusted his plans. He had ordered a last line of defence to be built at the furtherest end of Rotor Valley pass, where it narrowed the most. Past that point it dropped away into the Scion Kingdoms, and then the Marches.

The hill tribes were already moving their herds through the pass, and down off the mountains. Enough grass could be found for them in the lush lowlands of the Marches. He had told his governors to put their minds toward finding a solution.

His engineers had recruited the most experienced builders for the last line of defence he had in mind. Now they were piling up logs and rocks in a massive construction across the narrowest section of the pass. It would give the League the advantage of a higher position at the narrowest part of the valley, but would it be enough to stop the Gorlen?

Ultrich turned his mind toward preparing the troops for the coming battle. He drew Sergeos and Cinnabar to him in preparation, and lifted the three of them down to the plains below. There was a barely audible pop as they vanished from the top of The Lion, and a more audible crackle as they reappeared behind the tents below. A sentry scurried out to investigate the sound, and snapped to attention when he saw who it was.

"Find Porteous," said Ultrich as the three spirit walkers hurried past. "Tell him we'll be addressing the League forces as soon as he joins us at the flag."

The sentry saluted briskly and left at double time for the operations tent. Porteous and Gosan met the spirit walkers a few minutes later by the flag of the Karnatic League. It had been erected in the middle of the long crescent of League forces, ahead of the tents and behind the troop positions.

The federation flag was a simple map of the constituent territories. Fluttering to the left of it was the bold red flag of the Karnatic Defence Forces. Equally imposing on the right was the castled emblem of the Monhoven line, which was there in honour of the current holder of the Throne of Power. The many flags of the Marches, Scion Kingdoms and hill tribes stood behind these three.

Ultrich could already hear the commanders calling the companies to order, preparing their troops for inspection. Then there was one mighty cheer, rolling like a wave as it swept out along the ranks and reverberated off the foothills. The troops stamped the ground with their feet and beat weapons against shields and breastplates. The clash of metal on metal hit the spirit walkers as an almost physical blow. It built to a crescendo, before slowly dying away.

Ultrich extended his spirit senses along the League lines. The troops were getting used to his spirit speeches by now, though some still looked a little nervous. His voice rolled out of thin air, the same strong, cleat voice in front of each and every company.

"You are free men and women!" acknowledged Ultrich, his iron will very clear in his voice. "You have come with your friends and neighbours to defend your homes and families.

"No one commanded you to do this. Every one of you came for yourself and for your fellows. You came so that together we could defend what the League has built up, and what others want to tear down!"

He paused for breath, and decided his speech was going well. Perhaps he had gained something from listening to Yeltar's impassioned oratory. He smiled at the memory of his friend. Then the harshness of the struggle ahead of them all sobered him.

The Karnatic Defence Force would need all its courage to fight the Xaanian troops in the days to come. They would need to remember at every moment what they were fighting for, and the loyalty of the men and women they were proud to be fighting with.

Ultrich had no doubt the situation would become desperate, and many of the troops would lie dead on the battlefield before the battle was over. The chances of holding the pass, even at the fall-back position they had prepared, were probably less than half.

Regaining his momentum, he finished his speech in a few more sentences. He waited until the roar of approval died down, and retired with Porteous to the operations tent. There was still work to do on the League tactics. It was already well past noon, and Ultrich expected the Xaanian forces to attack soon.

He would have liked to be at Yeltar's side, helping him face the Gorlen at Thebes, but he was needed here. Everything he now knew about the animated creatures had been sent to his friend, and it was up to Yeltar to make the best of his situation.

It was late in the afternoon when the war horns sounded the first Xaanian charge. The attack followed the same pattern as the previous day. The spirit walkers on top of The Lion scoured the ebb and flow of troops with their farsight, relaying anything new to Porteous.

Ultrich noted the Xaanians were still woefully short of horse archers on the right flank. That pleased him greatly. The League forces on the left flank were already dug in with long pikes. It was unlikely the Xaanian cavalry on the left would commit themselves to a full charge against such a defence.

The centre of the enemy attack, however, posed more of a problem. At the front of each company of foot soldiers strode two waxen giants in extravagant armour. They were head and shoulders above the foot soldiers, and spikes coming from their shoulders and heads made them look much bigger again.

Ultrich understood the tactic. The Xaanian commanders were using the Gorlen as shock troops. They hoped to burst open the League lines and spread dismay, sapping the soldiers' will to fight.

Ultrich's resolve hardened. He knew the League forces were more than a match for such psychological warfare. He watched as hand-picked axe men took up positions in the front of the League lines. Each of them was protected by a champion on either side. Swordsmen whose job it was to keep the Xaanian troops at bay. If the axe men were given enough time, they would be able to inflict terrible damage on the Gorlen.

A small smile came to Ultrich's lips. The Gorlen were a good two paces in front of their supporting troops, and that would help his plan. There was such a thing as being too confident.

The Xaanian forces were approaching fast, and then the Gorlen smashed into the League troops. The Gorlen drove on through the League lines with the sheer weight and power of their attack, but they didn't notice the League forces flowing round them, letting them through, and isolating them from support. The League infantry pushed back the Xaanian troops following behind.

Ultrich used his farsight to watch one determined axe man go into battle. He was a veteran, judging by the first touches of grey in his hair. The man had sacrificed most of his armour for speed, and dodged smoothly under the great sweep of the opposing Gorlen's sword. He stepped sideways as he did so, placing himself behind the creature. The swordsmen on either side followed him, taking on the last of the Xaanian troops, and clearing an area for the axe man to work in.

Ultrich could see a lifetime of effort reflected in the axeman's broad shoulders and bulging biceps. Without pausing, the veteran placed his feet solidly, and began hewing away at the middle of the Gorlen's back.

The thick fabric that held the front and side leather armours in place gave way. The axe continued to move rhythmically, over and under. It was cutting through the waxy material of the Gorlen in the same way it would cut through the trunk of a tree. There was no blood.

The Gorlen seemed unconcerned for the first few strokes of the axe, and then it shuddered in protest. Stepping to one side it moved away from the irritation behind it, but the axe man moved smoothly with it, keeping to his task. At last the Gorlen turned, one massive arm driving an equally long sword toward the man.

One of the axeman's champions, a swordsman almost as impressively muscled himself, saw the movement and reacted. He whirled in one smooth movement, and drove the edge of his sword into the join between the plates of armour at the Gorlen's elbow. He cut the arm almost through in that one blow. The forearm and sword swung sideways toward another of the League swordsmen, to be cut off completely, and the veteran never paused in his grisly work.

Moments later, higher on the back of the creature than he had expected, his axe bit through the shell of the slave spirit that animated the creature. The Gorlen dropped, lifeless.

All along the front line, the same contest was decided in favour of an axe man or his opposing Gorlen. The giant creatures disappeared under the onslaught, or they bested the squads sent against them, and pushed deeper into the League lines.

The middle of the battlefield disintegrated into milling knots of fighters. The most successful League companies broke through the Xaanian lines, and turned to attack their enemies from behind. Where the Gorlen had survived, Xaanian forces were almost through to the tents and supply depots.

It was mayhem.

Porteous was down at the operations tent waiting for Ultrich to decide what they should do next. Sergeos and Cinnabar stood silently beside Ultrich on top of The Lion. Their anxiety showed clearly on their faces. They looked in the direction of the Legatus for instructions.

Ultrich made his choice. Of the three options he had discussed with Porteous, using the cavalry still looked the best. He called out a short code word, and the spirit walkers relayed it to the tent far below.

The war horns sounded briskly, and columns of armoured horses swept along behind the League lines. They turned and charged across the centre of the battlefield. The League troops tried to make passages for them, forewarned by the war horns. Then the armoured horses were riding hard at the Gorlen, smashing them down and trampling them underfoot.

Ultrich lowered his head. The armoured cavalry had done their best to avoid the League infantry, but there had been casualties on the League side. He heard a cheer, and lifted his head. The cavalry charge had cleared the centre of the battlefield, pushing the Xaanian forces back. It was then Porteous sent out his reserves of Lancers.

The trampled Gorlen rose eerily from the ground. Broken bodies straightened, and missing limbs regrew. But the Lancers rode them down. They skewered the Gorlen with their long spears, driving the weapons home until the Gorlen bristled with them. Occasionally a lance struck one of the slave spirits, and the League troops cheered as another Gorlen went down, and didn't rise again.

The Xaanian commanders must have felt their losses were enough for the day, and the loss of so many Gorlen more than they could accept. War horns sounded up and down the line, and the Xaanian forces began an orderly retreat.

Ultrich looked down on the plains as the battlefield cleared. He saw little space between the bodies, almost nothing of the sparse mountain grasses that grew on the High Steppes. He thought of dragging his own dead back to the tent lines, but didn't think the League would have time for that. The Xaanian commanders would be eager to push on to some sort of conclusion.

A short time later he was proved right. His heart sank as he saw the way the Xaanian lines advanced. This time the Gorlen came forward in one long line, shoulder to shoulder. Infantry ten deep marched close behind them. Every archer the enemy had sent shaft after shaft raining down on the League troops. The League infantry raised their shields for protection, and that opened them to the Gorlen attack.

Ultrich realized that the new Xaanian strategy was likely to push through the centre of his lines, and take control of the entrance to the pass. Once they had done that, the Xaanian forces would be able to block the retreat of the League flanks into the pass on either side. Many would be surrounded and killed, or dispersed across the plains. Much of the Defence League would be finished as a fighting force. He called out a new set of commands, and the spirit walkers relayed them to Porteous.

Moments later the League flanks began to fall back behind the League centre, retreating into the pass. The Xaanian forces howled and clashed their weapons, sensing victory.

Then the League forces in the centre charged the advancing Gorlen, trying to push back the attack. They were desperate to gain time for their comrades to retreat behind them, but the axe men and their champions found their tactics didn't work this time. Shoulder to shoulder, supported by troops, the animated creatures weren't easily overcome.

The defending forces were pushed back into the entrance of the pass, and the withdrawal behind them became more frantic. Cavalry ferried archers to the sides of the pass, where they scrambled up the hills to gain more advantage. Supply staff were desperately loading wagons and ferrying the contents back into the pass. Ultrich saw the operations tent being collapsed. Porteous and his staff were preparing to shift the command centre to a safer place inside the pass. But the League forces were still streaming into the pass from the flanks when the Xaanian attack closed off the entrance. The League troops in the centre had been pushed relentlessly back by the advancing Gorlen.

Ultrich couldn't think of a way to remedy the situation. It looked like much of the League army would be trapped outside the pass and destroyed, and he could think of nothing that might reverse the League fortunes.

"Is that Gosan down there?" called Cinnabar suddenly. She was using her farsight to understand why there was a growing concentration of cavalry just inside the entrance to the pass.

"I think so," said Ultrich, once he had found where she meant. He tightened his focus on a figure that seemed to be giving orders. An image of Gosan sprang up before him, so close he could have reached out and touched the League commander.

"That's him all right," he said. "The cavalry are forming up behind him, so they must have finished transferring archers to the hills inside the pass." There was a pause.

"I wonder what he's up to," said Cinnabar. Then the massed cavalry began to move forward at the canter.

The Xaanian line had closed off the right side of the entrance completely, though not until the bulk of the League forces on that side had slipped through, but the enemy were less well established on the left. There, the League infantry inside the pass were battering at them on one side while their comrades trapped outside the entrance were making equally desperate attempts to rejoin them.

"He's going to charge the blockade!" exclaimed Ultrich. He realized how dangerous the move was for the League troops in the way. He bypassed the normal chain of spirit walkers to talk directly to Porteous. His chief commander was deep inside the pass, and about to set up a new operations tent.

To his credit, the old soldier did no more than jerk upright in his saddle as a ghostly outline of Ultrich appeared before him. The apparition urged him in a booming voice to sound the 'disengage' signal on the left side of the pass. Once Porteous had got the message, the phantom apparition disappeared with an audible pop.

"I might have overdone that," said Ultrich. He was breathing hard as he sat heavily on a cloth-covered bench of sods the Prias spirit walkers had built nearby.

"You think so? I could hear you from here!" said Cinnabar, but she was smiling. That was an improvement over the icy aloofness of the last few days. Then the war horns sounded below, and the League forces inside the entrance scrambled out of the way. Moments later Gosan and his cavalry smashed into the Xaanian troops, pushing them aside like a plough turning a field.

The attack had the desired effect, punching a hole in the Xaanian lines. The League forces tore the hole wider, until they had secured a corridor against the hills. Then they kept it open, though many paid for their bravery with their lives, until at last all of the League troops had made it inside the pass.

The Xaanian forces hesitated. Their plan to break through the centre of the enemy lines with the Gorlen had failed, and they were unsure what to do next.

"That's what comes of being unprepared," snorted Ultrich. He quickly relayed instructions to Porteous below for an orderly retreat while holding the entrance to the pass. It was one of the many strategies they had rehearsed over and over again with his commanders.

The rest of the League withdrawal went like clockwork. The retreating infantry gave way to the Xaanians grudgingly, buying time for the cavalry and supply wagons to move deeper into the pass.

Finally they climbed past the wall of logs that was the last line of defence.

The makeshift road up the side of the palisade was cast down, leaving only a sheer wall of logs facing the invaders. Other preparations had also been made. The ground below the wall was studded with jagged stones to discourage cavalry and slow the attack.

The last of the League infantry scrambled up the steep sides of the pass. They joined the archers behind barricades that now ringed the hillsides. That left the grassy plain to the advancing Xaanian forces, but it was a hollow victory. The League army was still mostly intact, and the troops behind the barricades jeered derisively as the Xaanian forces set up new lines below them. The enemy soldiers were careful to stay well out of bow shot.

A short while later, Ultrich gathered with his senior commanders on a makeshift watchtower overlooking the pass. Dusk was falling. The short climb to the top had left some of them, and not always the older ones, out of breath. The Legatus diplomatically surveyed the League's defences while he waited for his commanders to catch their breath.

The palisade was disappointingly thin when seen from above. It rose well above the plain, but the walkway along the top could only hold two or three abreast, and that was not enough against a determined army. The long lines of barricades, twisting and turning along the sides of the pass, had been even more hastily erected. How long would it all hold together?

For the moment, however, Ultrich had some discouraging news for his commanders. He turned to them with a heavy heart.

"Yeltar held his fallback position around Thebes for as long as he could," he said. "He had fresh troops from Wensh and Martilees, and a column of our own armoured horses, but the cost of holding the Gorlen back was too high." His commanders looked from one to another, afraid to ask just how bad the situation was.

"He has retreated into Thebes itself," continued the Legatus. "His forces are attempting to hold the outskirts while every ship they can signal on the Trading Seas gathers in the harbour to take the bulk of his forces off. Wensh sent its troops in carriers, which has been a help with the evacuation, but it's in the lap of the gods whether enough ships will arrive in time."

There was a long silence. Every one of those present felt deeply for Yeltar and his troops. The thought that the Independent Kingdom forces may well be trapped and massacred at Thebes lay unspoken among them.

It also boded ill for the League. If the Independent Kingdoms fell, it wouldn't be long before a Xaanian army would be at The Gap to the west. From there they had easy access to the Wild Marches, and then the Scion Kingdoms. Ultrich couldn't imagine the League holding out on two fronts at the same time for long.

He tried to find something encouraging to say, but he didn't get the chance. The whistle of air being compressed over leathery wings grew louder. Ultrich knew immediately what it meant. He pulled Cinnabar to him and transported them both away, just as a giant winged creature landed heavily on the watchtower. It began clawing the structure apart, its long neck and serrated teeth stabbing at the commanders as they scrambled for safety.

Ultrich landed heavily on the walkway of the palisade below. Cinnabar sprawled awkwardly where she had landed beside him. He rolled over, and looked up at the watchtower. It give way under the extra weight of the creature. Then the watchtower toppled, as if in slow motion, down the hillside.

He reached for Cinnabar's hand, and lifted both their outstretched arms from the planking to point at the demon creature. It shrieked its frustration, and beat its enormous wings as it struggled its way into the air again.

He felt her body tense, as she understood what he wanted. He poured all their spirit fire into the winged creature, focusing on one point and building spirit energies there. He held the intent until it felt like he would burst. The nightmare vision veered out over the pass, and burst into flames from the inside out, falling like a meteor. Then Ultrich slumped back onto the planking, pulling Cinnabar back with him.

"I can sense another seven round the pass," he said tiredly, "and that's not all of them. It's going to be a long night."

She hesitated for a moment, then put a comforting arm around him.

"That's why we need to face them as a team," she said softly. Ultrich could feel her sending out a spirit call, bringing all the spirit walkers they had at the pass straight to them. He relaxed, just for a moment. It felt good to have her beside him, and he allowed himself a few moments of peace. Then he rose shakily, and prepared for a long and desperate vigil through the night.

EIGHTEEN

Mudge and his companions were somewhere in the Royal Palace, but it was hard to tell where. He surveyed the room they were using as a hiding place with trepidation. He was beginning to get frustrated with running away all the time.

Rough benches were stacked along one wall. Tables in a somewhat better condition were pushed together along the end furtherest from the door. There was no way out apart from the way they had come in, and that didn't please him either.

Andrian had found the room off a long corridor in the depths of the palace, and Mudge guessed they were somewhere in the servants' quarters. Regardless of where they were, Andrian had insisted they rest until Butha was able to catch her breath. At least they had lost their pursuers for the moment.

Mudge suddenly realized something, and kicked himself for being an idiot. Ochren had been right. The travellers should have entered the Royal Palace together. He had always thought of this journey as some sort of solitary quest, but it wasn't so.

The situation also helped him understand his father better. The Legatus was a man who worked with the nations around him. He had made alliances from the very beginning, and then forged the different countries and kingdoms into a team. That was why the League was such a peaceful, prosperous place today.

When he had taken on the Empress by himself, there had been only his strengths, and sometimes his strengths weren't enough. Jago and Luce, and the Mesoans, even Butha and her family, had tried to fill in the gaps where they could. In fact they had a better understanding of what friends were for than he did. It showed Mudge that some of his assumptions had been flawed from the beginning.

He thought how selfless the others had been, how they had been prepared to lay down their lives for the good of the Karnatic League if necessary. All that time, he had been thinking about his own journey. The realization hurt, but at least there was still time to change things.

The prince concentrated, sending out his spirit senses to locate Ochren and the others. Using his spirit senses would tell the Empress where he was, but that wasn't a bad thing. Once his companions were back beside him, the next step would be to confront the dark sorceress. He needed to bring this thing to an end, whichever way it played itself out.

Mudge smiled to himself as he looked at the map of the area in his head. Eight golden sparks of life stood out from the rest, their colours tinged by their close connection to him. They were moving in single file through the labyrinth of lanes and alleyways behind the Royal Palace. They hadn't left Xianak as he'd ordered, or tried to make their way back to the League lines. They had decided to follow him into the palace. Their loyalty was almost too much for him to bear right then, but he pushed the emotion aside. He would tell them what he owed them later – if they all survived.

Mudge reached deep into his spirit senses. It was an odd feeling, exploring the strange, otherworldly space inside himself. He realized he hadn't shown much interest in his abilities before because it might mean he was moved up the queue for the throne. Fourth in line had been a safe place, and much less threatening.

Now he saw that he had more talent than he admitted. Shifting an object from here to there across the face of the world was well within his grasp. He hoped shifting eight of them into the centre of the palace would be as easy.

Mudge traced a spirit path for each of the golden sparks in his mind. Then he reached inside himself to change the order of things in the world. With a chaotic whump of displaced air, his travelling companions appeared in the room beside him.

"Devil work!" shouted Ochren, dropping instinctively into a crouch. He drew his sword from inside his cloak. Then he recognized Mudge.

"Ah, all clear," he amended sheepishly, returning his sword to its sheath. The others followed his example.

"Thought you were that irritating damn sorceress," he said. Mudge knew it was an apology for waving his sword at the son of the Legatus. The rangers understood what spirit walkers could do, but they hadn't expected to be on the receiving end of spirit energy like this. Not in a normal lifetime anyway, but these weren't normal times.

"I hadn't thought of calling the Empress 'irritating'," said Mudge with a laugh, "but you're right. I'll have to think of her like that from now on."

The prince went on to explain his change of heart. How they would only succeed against the Empress if they confronted her as a group. It was an admission gruffly received by Ochren, and then the others. At least they managed to stop themselves saying 'I told you so'.

There was one other thing that bound them together. They were determined to take the fight to the Empress. Every one of them felt they had been hiding in the shadows for too long.

"We're going back into the main hall using spirit energies, the same way you arrived here," said Mudge, as he explained his plan. "I want the hall cleared of everyone but the Empress, and I need to find a way to secure the doors against intruders.

"When it comes to the final attack on that 'irritating damn sorceress'," he said, with a smile, "I don't want any reinforcements arriving from outside."

The travellers nodded. Butha and Andrian looked the most worried. The thought of being hurled through space to the main hall was completely new to them, though it didn't seem to have killed the recent arrivals. Ochren gave the householders a knife each when they said they wanted to help. They had no previous experience with swords.

The Keeper Stone made busy circuits about Mudge's consciousness, like a hound dog brushing against his legs. It was telling him it wanted to be of use too. He made it 'sit', if that was the right word. There were some things he wanted to do for himself, just to prove he could do them.

Then he sighed. He was doing it again, thinking about what he wanted and ignoring others. Now he was ignoring their shared goal again, an end to the intrusion of this evil into their lives. He called the Keeper Stone to him. It merged with him, and then it became him, an effortless extension of his own will.

After that they were ready.

The first contingent, those who were not rangers, appeared in the middle of the main hall with a thunderous roar. Mudge had orchestrated the noise to buy himself time. The rangers were to be sent next, and he needed to prepare their arrival well.

The company of council bodyguards was still present, under its commander Uttan. The Empress was at the long table, looking at the battle plan for Rotor Valley Pass. She looked up, startled by the noise. Ottar Bey was standing beside her, with his guard of honour at attention behind them. Both of them had thought the palace guard would have tracked down and destroyed the intruders by now.

At least the Empress hadn't ordered more Gorlen to the main hall, thought Mudge. Perhaps they were with the rest of the bodyguard, tearing the palace apart in their search for the intruders. Well, he and his companions were back, and she hadn't expected that.

"Kill them," hissed the Empress fiercely, "and this time don't make a mess of it!"

Uttan hurried to obey, hoping to redeem his previous failure. His company of bodyguards spread out in a line, shepherding their quarry into one corner of the huge room. Senovila, Colma, Butha and Andrian formed a defensive wall, with Mudge, the two younger people, and Onjed behind it.

They backed slowly away from the bodyguards. Then a number of the hindmost attackers jerked backward. They scrabbled at their necks as they tried to cry a warning, but their bodies stiffened, and they slid gracefully to the floor. A dozen were taken this way before the others noticed what was happening.

"Demons! Invisible demons!" shouted the captain of Ottar Bey's bodyguards. He was the first to understand what was happening to his soldiers. Uttan's men whirled around and backed away from the invisible assailants.

The Empress made a swirling motion with her hand. The ghostly outlines of the five rangers could be seen inside a crimson cloud of sparkling dust motes. As the remaining attackers turned, and rushed to engage them, Senovila and Colma led a charge against the bodyguard from behind.

Mudge conjured phantom shapes among the rangers, to more than double their number and make their true location uncertain. The bodyguard couldn't determine what was a real attacker and what was not. Their nerve broke, and they fled to join Ottar Bey's honour guard.

The Empress was furious.

Mudge heard the strange, distorted spirit call she sent out across the Royal Palace. Next the double doors at one end of the hall burst open. Then the side doors shattered their wooden locks. The Empress had opened the doorways for her forces, preparing for their arrival.

That was interesting, noted Mudge. The Empress doubted. She wasn't sure she could defeat this strange gathering of worldly and spirit abilities on her own. Mudge smiled. Perhaps they had a chance against her after all.

The Empress ordered the honour guard forward, and indicated imperiously that Ottar Bey should lead them. Mudge almost felt sorry for the man. He was more terrified of the Empress than the intruders, despite the fact it was a strange group of crimson wraiths, phantom shapes and peasantry that advanced across the hall. The honour guard moved nervously to intercept them.

As the fighters clashed, the Empress finally broke through Mudge's spirit veils. The rangers appeared in their true form, and the phantom shapes fighting among them vanished. Mudge cursed under his breath. Nothing he conjured against the Empress lasted for long.

The fighting proved more difficult this time round. The rangers were outnumbered, and they had some non-participants to protect. Mudge had been given a dagger by Senovila 'in case of emergencies', but he knew his greatest contribution would come from keeping his wits about him, and his spirit senses at the ready.

By sheer force of numbers the honour guard drove the League defenders back to one side of the main hall, and Mudge knew he and his companions couldn't allow themselves to be trapped there. More of the black clad council bodyguard, and some of the animated Gorlen, must be on their way by now.

The Empress seemed content to let the two sides fight on, and watched from her position by the table. Mudge knew he had to end the skirmish quickly before help arrived for her forces, and then he needed to seal the hall off.

What could he do to take the fight out of Ottar Bey's honour guard? The Keeper Stone nudged him, placing an idea in his mind.

He almost laughed at the outrageousness of it. Was it even possible? Then he decided to try it.

Reaching inside himself he changed the nature of light in the room. He bent it round himself and his companions. The honour guard stopped, uncertain. It was as if the defenders had ceased to exist. Bear and Shyleen took the opportunity to leap forward, dropping two of the attackers. To the honour guard the blades came and went from nowhere. The guard scattered, tripping over themselves in their haste to get away.

Mudge felt a tug at his side as Onjed leaped past him. He looked down to see that the dagger at his belt was gone. As he looked up the boy was already in front of Ottar Bey. The First Elect had been left behind as his honour guard deserted him. Onjed swung wildly at Ottar Bey's throat. This was the man who had killed his father.

The First Elect brought up his sword, mostly by reflex, and managed to parry the blow. He sliced through Onjed's sleeve, and cut into his forearm. The boy went deathly pale, a combination of determination and shock. He stepped back. Ottar Bey grinned. He had just realized that his attacker was only twelve summers old. He flicked his sword round in a two-handed sweep at Onjed's neck.

It never landed. The boy had seen the First Elect start his swing, and just as quickly had stepped inside it. Then he drove the knife under his enemy's ribs and up into his heart.

"You killed my father, and now I kill you!" he shouted into the face of the startled king. They were the last words Ottar Bey ever heard. Onjed used both hands to pull the knife down and out of the man's chest and the First Elect slumped forward, dead before he hit the floor.

Mudge was surprised. The boy was fast, much faster than he had thought possible. He noticed the Keeper Stone at the edge of his consciousness, and wondered if it had given the boy an edge. Then the honour guard turned, and in a sudden burst of loyalty scrambled back toward the rangers to avenge their king. Unfortunately, Onjed and Mudge were right in their way.

Mudge reached deep inside himself, and made changes. He needed to be immune to things like swords, and that's what his body became. He lurched upward, and changed shape. Then his eyes adjusted to his new perspective.

He was towering over the guards now. He swatted one flat with a giant paw, and cowed the others with a snarling roar. He had taken on the shape of a giant snow cat, the emblem of the Karnatic League. How fitting, he thought, as he launched himself forward.

The Empress answered the challenge with an inhuman shriek. She changed from the dark, smoky shape of her true nature to the reptilian predator he had seen before. In two quick bounds they closed the space between them, and slammed into one another with an impact that shook the floor throughout the hall.

Powerful fangs ripped into a red and black shoulder, while rows of jagged teeth scraped across the side of the great mountain cat's head. The honour guard scattered, retreating to the doors at the end of the hall. They hesitated in the doorway, then realized the battle here was lost. The guard fled into the long corridors of the palace.

The rangers moved away from the two giant creatures, joining Senovila and the others in one corner of the hall. It was the safest place as the giants rampaged back and forth across the floor.

Pushing down the pain of the Empress' claws and jagged teeth, Mudge glanced sideways. He saw that the bodyguard were gone, and his friends were safe, but he knew that wasn't enough. The doors weren't closed yet, which would keep the Empress' reinforcements out of the hall. As if in response to his thought, more black-clad bodyguards poured into the hall. A moment later the sound of heavy footfalls told him a company of Gorlen were on their way.

Opening his spirit senses, Mudge called on the spirit world to help him. What had his father said? That there was one underlying and fundamental cause, something that "might possibly be our ally in the terrible times to come"?

The Empress squalled another inhuman shriek, and broke off the struggle. Mudge realized the powerful sorceress was afraid, and he hadn't expected that. She understood what he had done, and she remembered. Something had imprisoned her, and all who rebelled at the beginning of time, in the netherworld. She feared it might happen again.

Mudge struck the dark sorceress hard, and then again, using the mountain cat's terrible strength. The Empress' moment of indecision was an opportunity for him. Before she could recover, he bound the dark creature using the Keeper Stone. It took all he had to keep the bonds around her from loosening, but for now he held her motionless.

By taking the form of the giant reptile the Empress had vastly increased her strength in this world, but it had weakened her in the spirit world. As long as the Keeper Stone could contain the Empress in her creature form, drawing off her energy, Mudge had achieved a kind of stalemate.

Then the prince noticed the double doors at either end of the hall slam shut. The timbers of the doors lengthened, twining their way in and out of the walls around them. The advancing Gorlen were shut out, though it was too late for one of them. Caught by the writhing timbers, it became part of the doors as they grew around it.

Mudge knew it was spirit work, but who had caused it? He noticed a smell of salt and earth, and searched his memories for when he had last experienced that. When the answer came to him he was astonished.

It was sprite work. He had not thought them capable of something like this. If they were the ones who had shut off the hall from the rest of the palace, then they wouldn't be far from their handiwork. Where were the cagey little creatures?

He sensed their presence, and finally understood. The ground under the palace was honeycombed with cellars for storing food, and he noticed several escape tunnels. It was perfect sprite territory.

Tell-tale spirit signs swirled through the earth beneath Mudge's feet. They were a different sort of sprite to the ones he had met in the mountains, but then the mountain sprites had been different to the ones at Shaker's Hope.

But the different tribes must be connected in the way all sprites were. These ones would know about the destruction of the Sarkosay at the gorge, and the imprisonment of their people, and their help couldn't have come at a better time.

The bodyguards that had just arrived were staring nervously at the giant figures in front of them, the Empress trapped inside a web of silver spirit ties. Then they looked behind them, and realized they were just as effectively trapped inside the hall. There was a moment's indecision, and then they drew their weapons and advanced along the wall toward Ochren and the rest of the company.

Once they could see that they outnumbered the League defenders two to one, the bodyguards began to advance more boldly. Ochren motioned for his people to spread out, and that forced the attackers to widen their line. Then the harsh clash of metal reverberated through the hall.

The rangers favoured one particular tactic against greater numbers. Bear managed to get a spare moment, and thrust sideways at the bodyguard on his right. The unexpected thrust sliced along the man's ribs, and it was enough to distract him. Shyleen pushed through his weakened guard, and delivered a deadly wound. The guard fell. The other rangers followed Bear's lead, stabbing sideways when they could, catching them unawares, and the bodyguard numbers were slowly reduced.

The attack faltered, and Mudge took his attention off the Empress long enough to close down the minds of the remaining bodyguards. They collapsed on the floor, a line of rag dolls in front of the defenders.

"You don't see that every day," said Shyleen, breathing hard. She prodded the nearest crumpled form to see if perhaps they were pretending.

"Pity, I was just getting the hang of this," said Bear.

Ochren jerked his thumb in the direction of the giant figures in the middle of the room.

"That'll be the prince helping us out," he growled. He wondered if the rangers could make any impression on the giant black and red reptile facing the equally huge snow cat. It didn't take him long to decide to stay out of that fight.

Not everything, however, was apparent to the League defenders in the hall. In the spirit realms the Empress shifted under the binding of the Keeper Stone, and began to work her way free. The prince added his power to that of the Keeper Stone, but still the sorceress grew in strength in the netherworld. Mudge knew that ultimately she would have to be defeated there, but that was where she was strongest, and the powers of Mudge's world the weakest.

Somehow that didn't matter. Until she was completely destroyed, the Empress would return to enslave the League, and all the kingdoms of this world. She would inflict misery and death upon the human population time and time again. Then the Empress worked her way free from the Keeper Stone, and vanished.

Mudge knew where she had gone. It only remained for him to decide whether he would follow her there or not. Stretching the big cat for a moment and enjoying its suppleness, he reverted to his human form.

Then the shades of Jago and Luce appeared on either side of him. Other shapes solidified from the air. There were many of them, all across the hall. Some he recognized, but many were so insubstantial he couldn't work out what they were.

There seemed to be sprites of different sorts, and other elemental creatures he didn't know. There were the shades of a number of rangers, wearing camouflage green. One or two Mesoans stood out as wavering lights, but not in the numbers Mudge had encountered in their homeland.

Several figures looked like spirit walkers from olden times. Their heavy, homespun clothing dated them by centuries. He presumed they were the shades of departed walkers. Then he saw them clustering together, gathering power for a summoning.

There was a burst of light, and Ultrich appeared. He looked surprised at his sudden relocation. There were several spirit walkers of the present day that Mudge recognized, but they too were present in a strangely insubstantial form.

"I think it's time, boy," said a voice at his elbow. Mudge turned to see Senovila beside him. The old smith waved offhandedly at the throng pressing around them.

"You can see them?" enquired Mudge, a little surprised.

Senovila nodded.

"Senovila's right," said Ultrich. The grey shade had come to stand by Mudge. "It's time to finish this."

"Why are you so . . . faded?" questioned Mudge.

"For the living to be here we have to be in two places at once," explained Ultrich. "It's a little confusing for me at the other end, where I'm helping Porteous defend Rotor Valley Pass against the Xaanians." He hesitated. "It's a constant battle to stop the two places from colliding inside my head."

I'll bet it is, thought Mudge, in wonder. He realized how much more experienced his father was in the ways of spirit walkers than he was.

"It's time for what?" said the prince to Senovila, though he more than half knew the answer.

"Time to finish this battle with the Empress," said the Legatus. "That's why the others are here. They heard the call."

"The call?" said Mudge in confusion.

"Your call, in part," said his father, "but also the signs. This confrontation between the two worlds has been coming for a long time, and the signs are noticeable everywhere now."

He seemed bemused at Mudge's confusion. "Signs from that which is unseen. Beyond the beyond. *Endata,* or primary cause, in our poor understanding of the ultimate purpose of this world."

Ultrich paused. "That's why we've gathered here. Every one of us is pledged to remove the Empress from this world, and make sure she doesn't come back."

Mudge was beginning to understood. The fact there were so many different entities here, ready to help, made a lot of sense.

"The Empress won't know what hit her," he said with a smile.

Ultrich looked at him quizzically.

"Not just the Empress, Rossi. There's a whole damn nest of the unborn in the netherworld."

Mudge's heart sank. Then a bright light burst open like a flower in the middle of the hall. Every member of that great throng disappeared from the Royal Palace, including Mudge. All that remained was a softly pulsing point of light. It was a Mesoan anchor. It marked the worldly end of the passage into the netherworld. When they came back, if they came back, the anchor would guide them to the land of the living.

Butha and Andrian looked around at the abandoned hall. For some reason, probably their lack of fighting experience, some of them had been left behind. There were the sounds of fists hammering on the outside of the doors. Or at least the spreading woven patches where the doors had once been. There were dozens of dead or unconscious Xaanian troops on the floor, and Butha shepherded the others toward an empty corner of the hall.

Kneeling, she drew Andrian down beside her. She motioned for the other two to do the same.

"Your excellency," she said, bowing to Onjed. "You will be First Elect when this is over. It is what your father would have wanted."

Onjed tried to convey a regal presence, but his body began to tremble. This loyalty was too much after the ordeals he had just been through. He ran to throw his arms around her.

NINETEEN

The floor of the main hall disappeared from under him, and Mudge landed with a jolt that sent a stab of pain up his leg. He grimaced, and balanced himself on one leg as he rotated the other, checking it for damage. The last thing he wanted right now was some damage that might slow him down. Beneath his feet, flagstones the size of dinner tables ran in all directions.

Deciding there was no serious damage to his leg, the prince pushed the dull ache in his ankle to the back of his mind. In the meantime the pressing throng of shades, supernatural beings and spirit walkers was beginning to thin a little, as they spread out to examine this new world. A sickly yellow hue came from an overcast sky and washed the colour out of everything. It would have been unnatural in any world.

The new arrivals appeared to have landed in an enormous street. The scale of the flagstones, and the width of the thoroughfare, gave them the impression they were dwarves in a giant world.

Looking up, Mudge saw buildings of stone. The whole street soared into the sky above him. The buildings were only two or three stories high, but they were built on such a scale that their height was multiplied by a factor of ten.

Following his League friends, he headed for a giant doorway on one side of the street. He looked up at the metal fastening on the door, and saw it was well above his head. It had been sandblasted through aeons ago, and he had seen the same damage when he arrived in Xianak, due to the occasional desert storms.

When the company went inside, they encountered a picture of desolation. Powerful winds had scoured the furniture until it lay sagging and broken in the corners. Stone edges around doors and windows had been sandblasted until they were curved and smooth. The changes must have taken an unimaginable length of time.

The entourage kicked their way through drifts of sand and piles of debris. Eventually they came to a stop in the middle of the room.

"It's been abandoned for centuries," said Ochren. He shrugged, and slid his sword back into its sheath.

"*Idiosa*, the folly of the underworld," said Ultrich. He looked around in amazement. "I thought it was just a tale from the School of Mysteries."

Mudge started at the voice. He had not heard his father's footsteps joining the group. Then he looked down. The Legatus' feet drifted slightly above the ground.

"I rather like being a double, it's better than walking," said his father with a smile.

"Why is this a folly?" continued Mudge. He was confounded by the vast, abandoned city that must have been built for giants.

"Ah, yes," said Ultrich. "You didn't make it past your second year at the School of Mysteries, before I sent you off to Shaker's Hope."

His voice was gentle, carrying no recrimination.

"Best thing I ever did, sending you there," he continued reflectively. Then he turned to face his son.

"When there was rebellion at the beginning of time, some of the rebel spirits came here, and built a great and terrible city in the underworld. They built it to show how powerful they were, and how marvellous their talents. They peopled it with soulless, self-seeking minor spirits, beings like themselves they incarnated into giant bodies.

"It was meant to rival the greatest cities men and women would ever build in our world, through all the millennia to come."

He paused. "But it was missing essential things, like our love of the land, and of each other. There was no sense of purpose in the city, no heights to aim for. There was no chance for them to progress beyond their own selfishness and greed.

"Left to themselves, the giants took to fighting for power. It was the only thing they understood. Life in the great city degenerated until it was no more than a brutal struggle for survival. It wasn't long before the buildings were abandoned, and it has lain here in the desert winds for all the long ages since.

"That's why it's called *Idiosa,* the foolish choice."

Mudge nodded, he understood now. He and the others walked slowly back to the enormously wide street, and joined the throng there. Then they noticed the colour of the sky had darkened. It was a more ominous shade of purple now.

"Does that mean night's coming?" asked Mudge.

Ultrich shook his head.

"It's never night here," he said uneasily. "Nighttime is too disturbing for already disturbed minds, but I think I know what this means."

The others looked at him expectantly.

"They are coming," he said. "The *cromadia,* the four horsemen." There was little change in the blank looks of those around him.

"The most powerful of the rebels," he continued. "The ones with enough power to break into our world, if they were given the opportunity."

The rangers looked anxiously to Ochren for direction, but he just shook his head.

"You will have to show us the way, *Accessit,*" said Ultrich, looking at Mudge. He was using the title given to the one who would next be Legatus, who would next lead the Karnatic League.

If there hadn't been so much going on in his mind, Mudge might have done some rebelling himself. He had no plans to be Legatus, and no intention of leading the throng around them anywhere, but the high probability of death for them all wonderfully concentrated his mind.

"I don't think anybody needs showing anything," he said, his voice rising above the desert winds. They were beginning to flap and tease around the giant buildings, flicking up grains of sand.

"We're going to have to make this up as we go along!" he roared to the great throng around him. He found himself turning into the giant mountain cat he had become when he faced the Empress. He looked out across the crowd.

"Don't stick to what you think you should do," he told them, "just be yourselves. Stay flexible. Find your own solutions.

"Trust your skills, and be confident. You know what you're doing! Above all, come at them with something unexpected!"

"Am I making sense! Do you understand what I'm saying!" he roared, and the crowd around him thundered back its approval.

Mudge looked down the wide street. It ended abruptly in a wall of sand. The desert had partly buried a number of stone buildings there already. The sky, now a shade of dirty green, was darkening ominously over the barren wasteland beyond.

He called the Keeper Stone to him, but it resisted his command. It wanted something from him first. It took Mudge a while to realize it was trying to rearrange his emotional state. It was demanding more flexibility, more loyalty, and a readiness to meet the unexpected. The same things he had been telling the others they needed.

He smiled. The Keeper Stone was keeping him honest. He had given that advice to the others without making sure he was living it himself. Maybe that was why it was the Keeper Stone. It was becoming his conscience, making sure his words and deeds were always the same.

So he willingly gave up his preconceived ideas. It felt good to be free from such limiting concepts as winning or losing, free to just do his best. Then the Keeper Stone unfurled. He couldn't describe what happened in any other way. It shook itself into the shape of an enormous prehistoric eagle. Its wings cast half the throng about them into shadow. Mudge found himself clinging to its back, and then it rose swiftly into the air.

He felt like he was riding a rocking horse upholstered in eiderdown. Each feather he clung to was longer than his whole arm. The street, and then the city, dropped away below them. The great bird gained height, and turned into the wind. It was heading for a distant spot where the green-shaded sky had darkened almost to black.

Four dark shapes towered over the desert far ahead of the eagle. Their outlines blurred and changed. They were covering the distance to the city at extraordinary speed.

Mudge recognized the winged creatures that soared ahead of the dark shapes on the desert air. They were more of the leathery creatures that had hunted Mudge and his companions in The Wilderness, and attacked them at the walled compound in the Scion Kingdoms. The prince dug his fingers deeper into the eagle's thick covering of feathers.

He had a score to settle, and his blood stirred. Creatures like this had sent Bear to the edge of death. Then his mount climbed higher in the sky, gaining an advantage.

Moments later the great eagle turned in the sky. It pulled its wings in, and rolled over into a dive. Mudge dropped his head down, and flattened his body against the eagle's feathered back. There was a single harsh call as one of the flying demons spotted them. Then a tearing sound as great claws shredded leather wings, and the demon spiralled out of the sky, falling toward the desert below.

The eagle rolled over and flung itself upwards. Mudge could feel himself upside down, hanging on grimly. The eagle struck again, and another demon creature fluttered downward, one of its wings trailing behind it.

Then two of the leathery creatures converged on the eagle at once. Serrated teeth scraped across its chest as it twisted in mid-air.

The protection of feathers and muscle saved the great bird from any serious harm, and its claws sent one of its attackers plummeting toward the sands below.

Mudge saw another winged shape ahead of them. He reached out with his spirit senses, and closed down its instinctive, reptilian mind. It faltered in the middle of a wingbeat, then recovered. Mudge could sense something present in its mind. It was controlled by one of the *cromadia,* the rapidly moving shapes on the desert below them.

He reached out again, clamping down on the creature's mind with all his strength. For a moment there was a struggle that tested Mudge to his limits, and then the winged demon fell away, a limp carcass of flesh and bone in the air. It struck the desert hard.

One of the dark, changing shapes below him paused, and raised an arm. The great eagle hurled itself aside as a spirit bolt the colour of dried blood seared past them. Mudge swirled a spirit shield about himself and his mount, and they blinked out of existence. He could feel the evil below searching for them, and he tightened the shield.

The eagle crippled the last of the winged creatures, and then swerved to avoid the crackling spirit bolts that probed the skies blindly for them. Mudge felt a moment of triumph. The demise of the creatures brought him a great sense of satisfaction.

Plummeting out of the sky to build up speed, and then levelling off, the giant eagle sped for the city. The buildings made a distant pattern of squares and angles among the soft, rolling dunes of the desert, and the sands blurred below them as the city approached. Then they were descending into the same wide street they had left. Mudge alighted gingerly. It had been quite a ride. The prehistoric eagle vanished once he was on the ground, and the Keeper Stone resumed its place inside him.

Then he called Ultrich and Ochren to him, and explained what he intended to do.

"Your decision," said the Legatus mildly, smiling at his son, and Mudge realized that was another strength his father had. He was able to let go of his worries and fears as soon as a decision had been made. It was the best way to prepare for a struggle. Then it was time.

The surging throng of shapes and shades sorted itself into three groups at Mudge's command. Each one contained a mixture of the different forces that were present in the gathering. Mixing them up had been Ultrich's idea. It was the way he organized the League Defence Forces.

When he thought his forces were ready, Mudge looked down the street and out over the desert. The blurring, changing shapes in the desert had begun to take on more permanent forms as they approached the city.

Mudge transported himself to a position on the roof of one of the buildings, and Ultrich masked his surprise. Spirit transportation was a rare skill among spirit walkers, but his son had shown no hesitation in attempting it.

The four *cromadia*, archdemons of the underworld, hesitated at the edge of the fallen city, and Mudge smiled to himself. The city was a monument to their fall from grace, an example of their arrogance and misplaced pride. It must seem like bitterness and gall to them to come here.

With a noticeable shudder, each of the four archdemons took on a final shape that was part animal and part human. The human part was hideously distorted, but Mudge was surprised to find he recognized the grotesque shapes before him. The pictures in the old School of Mysteries texts had been quite accurate.

It made him realize that one of his predecessors, a spirit walker like himself, had travelled here. A spirit walker who had seen the archdemons first hand. That required extraordinary bravery, and an exceptional level of skill. The thought humbled the prince.

The first of the archdemons was clearly *Usrad,* the physical horrors that followed disease, famine and war. The second was *Gilliad,* the emotional turmoil of despair, lunacy and hatred. The third was *Ungamon,* the fates that destroy the dreams of men and women and cripple their spirits, and the fourth was *Illarsis,* the destruction of community through greed, corruption, and hearts of stone.

The fourth was assuredly the Empress. It was she that had corrupted Xaan. Hers was an addiction to power, to the love of conquest, and the destruction of communities.

The loathsome creatures howled extravagant battle cries, and massive hooves, claws and misshapen feet stepped forward onto the streets of the city. The three battalions of Mudge's companions surged forward to meet them.

Some had chosen a direct frontal attack. Some, like the sprites, skittered up the sides of buildings to launch themselves at the demons from the rooftops. And some, like the shades of previous spirit walkers, rose into the air to direct spirit bolts.

Three of the archdemons were soon fully occupied, attackers swarming thickly about them. Mudge had chosen the fourth demon for himself. He landed on the scaly shoulder of *Illarsis,* pleased that the Empress was his to deal with.

The Keeper Stone transformed itself into a sword of vengeance, and Mudge drove the sword into the join where the Empress' neck met a scaly shoulder, angling it down toward her heart. But the grotesque body stiffened, and threw him off, blasting him out over the city. He controlled his fall, and landed softly on the top of a nearby building.

It appeared he wasn't going to get anywhere with a physical attack. Here, in the Empress' realm, such attacks had a limited effect. Then Jago and Luce appeared on either side of him. An old spirit walker in the heavy, home-spun clothing of much earlier times appeared in front of Mudge. The prince acknowledged the ancient spirit walker's sudden appearance with a nod. Spirit transportation was always a rare thing.

He wondered if this could be the spirit walker who had been to this place before, the one who took descriptions of the archdemons back to the Mysteries school. The ancient before him smiled, and nodded, understanding what was in Mudge's mind.

A small group of Mesoans landed on the rooftop beside Mudge. Curling sapphire tendrils reached out to touch him, and then the others who were with him. A hard, brittle light began to emanate from them all.

The prince understood at once what the Mesoans had done. This was power from the dawn of time. It was the same power the sorceress used. The Mesoans had given up their energy to help Mudge counteract hers.

He smiled his thanks. The people of the present day would need everything they had to stop her once again. The Keeper Stone reached into his mind and nudged him. He understood that all those fighting the evil they had found fought for their land and their people. They would lose this battle if they fought for themselves.

The group of four lifted into the air, and the Keeper Stone unfurled under them as the great prehistoric eagle it had been before. They rose smoothly toward the Empress, a little group that sat unwavering on the great bird's back.

As they closed on the archdemon they made an unworldly picture that few would have believed. Still figures, on a great prehistoric bird, surrounded by diamond light. Mudge felt his senses heighten, and he noticed how eerily clear and still everything was.

The Empress projected a blood-red spirit bolt at the eagle, but it was overcome by the diamond light. She clawed at them with one huge, wolverine arm, but the arm slowed as it entered the adamantine light around them. The brilliance of the light spread down her arm, turning it grey and insubstantial.

The Empress howled in fury. Her giant body sloughed away, and her essence escaped to take a spirit form. She rose toward them as a dark red ball of twisting energy.

Mudge could sense what his companions were doing. The ancient spirit walker was holding them steady in the sky while the Keeper Stone was using the Mesoan energy to shield them against the raging energies of the Empress. Jago and Luce drifted toward the spirit ball and taunted the archdemon, distracting it. Already dead, they had nothing to fear from the Empress.

Mudge knew this was the League's one chance to finish this battle, finally and forever, and he mentally prepared himself for the challenge. Then Ultrich appeared on his left, and the ancient spirit walker was on his right. Together, they left the eagle and plunged into the heart of the dark, red ball of energy.

A small bat-like shape fluttered toward them in the darkness. The shape was blacker than anything had a right to be. It was like looking through a hole into a darker, deeper world beyond. The fluttering shape must be the Empress' soul, decided Mudge, if demons had souls. Whatever it was, he and his companions had come all this way, across all the different times and places of the land they loved, to destroy it.

Mudge balled up his hopes for the Karnatic League, and all his anger at what the Empress had done to his world. He added his dreams for his own future, and the future of everyone and everything in the League, and coalesced it into a concentrated star of spirit energy.

He could feel Ultrich and the ancient spirit walker supporting him, adding to what he was doing, while the Keeper Stone gave the star shape and direction. When it seemed the star could grow no brighter, Mudge pushed it into position with his mind. It surrounded the fluttering shape at the heart of the Empress.

He motioned with his hand. It was a gesture intended, like his father's, to concentrate his mind. Then he let the star collapse onto the Empress' soul.

It imploded in a cataclysm of fire, boiling off energies that seared the space around them. It took all the effort of the Keeper Stone to shield Mudge and his companions from the gigantic explosion of fire and light. Then the brightness dimmed, and the last of the star turned red, and faded. That was when Mudge saw that the black shape still fluttered at the heart of the twisting red energy that was the Empress.

They had failed.

Mudge risked a quick glance over the city. He saw the other archdemons pressing their attackers back along the broad streets., and he realized there was only so much time left in which to do something.

On one side of him the ancient spirit walker was trying to tell him something. Then the Keeper Stone was nudging him. Mudge tried to concentrate, but his mind was distracted by fears that they would lose. At last he understood what the others were saying, and used their words to rebuild his energies in a new way.

He shut out all anger from his heart, and made himself understand that the destruction of the Empress was the only possible future for his world. Then he built another kind of star.

This time, he felt a new energy add itself to the mix. It was something much more subtle. Something without preference, and without judgement. It was something that understood the world had a purpose, and he realized it would help him fight for that purpose.

Endata, whispered Mudge to himself. First cause. He wondered if the others felt it too.

The star descended toward the archdemon again, and she seemed powerless to stop it. The starburst that followed was different to the first. In some respects it was less than before, yet it took the Empress' energies into itself and contained them, teasing them apart.

And this time the brightness of the star prevailed. The blackness at the heart of the Empress' spirit energies gave way. It became a cloud of scattering grains, each one flaming to nothing in the diamond light of the star. The last of the Empress' spirit evaporated, and then the brightness of the star was all that remained. Slowly, it began to fade.

Cheering broke out below them, and Mudge could see the remaining archdemons retreating along the streets of the city. They were being pursued by the League forces, and he felt for a moment the desire to see them all destroyed. He wanted to chase them down and make sure their evil was expunged from the underworld so it could no longer threaten the real world, but something stopped him.

He realized what the purpose of his world was. It was a training ground. A place to overcome difficulties, and to develop as a people. The world needed evil, so it could face pain and difficulties with courage and purpose. It was a hard lesson for him to learn, but it was not for Mudge to remove the evil by which the world experienced growth and change.

He sent a spirit call to bring the League battalions back from their pursuit. When he was sure they were retracing their steps, he lowered himself and his companions onto the top step of one of the giant buildings.

When the great throng was gathered before him, he stepped forward to address them. They filled the spacious street and pressed up against the steps.

"Impossible as we may have thought it to be," he roared out over them, "we have tracked the Empress back to her lair, and destroyed her." A great cheer went up from the multitude, and Mudge waited until it died away.

"And that is enough," he continued.

"The future of our world does not depend on destroying all of the evil in the underworld. Even though that evil will continue to try and make us slaves, or worse, in the real world. The truth is, the more of them we destroy, the more will come forth to replace them."

There was silence as the great crowd digested his words.

"Our strength lies in building strong communities and forging alliances. If we stand firm against those who profit from disaster and war, we can keep away the evil the archdemons feed on." Another great roar went up from the throng in the street, and Mudge let it die away.

"I don't know how we got to this world, and I'm not sure how we will get home," he said, turning his mind to the one remaining problem, "but that is something we will work on together. Put your minds to the task now. The sooner we understand how to return to our own world, the sooner we can go home."

"Legatus! Legatus! Legatus!" chanted the throng below him.

Mudge wasn't sure who the chant was for. It seemed everybody wanted to give him the top job these days, but he wanted his father to remain head of the League for a long while yet.

"Perhaps it's for all three of us," said Ultrich with a smile. "The Legatus that was, the Legatus that is, and the one to come."

"The Legatus that was?" enquired Mudge.

"Prias the First, if I'm not mistaken," said his father, turning to the spirit walker in the ancient style of clothes. The spirit walker nodded once, and turned back to look at the crowd below them. It had started to disperse as each group set up a headquarters nearby.

"The sea port of Prias was named after him," said Ultrich, turning back to Mudge, "and he started the Priatic School of Mysteries. That was over 400 years ago.

"He was also the first Legatus. In the beginning the League was only a federation of the three Marches, and that was almost lost a hundred years ago, when the Tengue Dynasty set up trading colonies along our coasts. We were a small-minded and anxious people then."

He looked out over the giant city, reminiscing.

"Uniting the Marches and throwing the Tengue back into the sea was the first thing I had to do as Legatus. I wanted to reinstate Prias' idea of a Karnatic League."

Mudge nodded, it made sense. He looked up, and was pleased to see the sickly yellow hue of the sky had turned into something like the grey and white of his own world.

Ultrich nudged him. Prias was pointing to something down in the street. Mudge couldn't see anything at first, and engaged his farsight. Then he could see a softly pulsing point of light in the middle of the street.

"The other end of the passageway between the worlds!" exclaimed Mudge. He clambered down the outsize steps and strode across the flagstones. Then he bent to examine it more closely.

It wasn't long before a small group had clustered round the softly pulsing light in the middle of the wide street. These were the most experienced of the spirit walkers, but even to them it seemed there was no obvious way to unravel the mysteries of the spirit passageway. The remainder of the great throng waited patiently along the great flagstones.

TWENTY

There was a great deal of experience working to unravel the puzzle of the spirit passageway, but Mudge didn't think it would be enough. He was beginning to understand the rules that *Endata,* the first cause, worked by. It wasn't for creatures like themselves to travel between worlds on a whim. But for a higher purpose, maybe.

The thrum of spirit power reached a new peak as the spirit passageway was twisted this way and that by those trying to unlock it. Mudge knew it was time to add his own understandings to the mix, but it was his state of mind that would count the most.

He cleared his thoughts of all self-interest. He saw instead the rightness of all these beings returning to their own world. He saw the needs of their kin, and the fulfilment of their destinies. He held in his mind the benefits of a positive future for the Karnatic League. He saw the growth and understanding humanity might still attain if things were put back the way they were.

Mudge felt a lightness enter the mix of energies. The same kind of feeling he had experienced when he fought the Empress. Without preference and without judgement. *Endata.*

A bright light burst outward from the middle of the street, overwhelming everything. There was a moment of confusion, and then Mudge found himself in the main hall of the Xaanian Royal Palace. Shades and shapes stretched in every direction, and he saw Butha and Andrian running toward him with a small shape behind them. He was relieved to see that it was Onjed.

"You are all unharmed?" he said anxiously, and Butha assured him they were fine.

"I'm sorry we were gone so long," said Mudge, but Butha looked puzzled at that.

"You were only gone a few minutes," she said uncertainly. "Barely time for us to make ourselves a base over there," she added, pointing to a far corner.

"But we were gone half a day," said Mudge, and he couldn't understand why there was such a difference.

"Powerful spirit work takes place outside of time," said Ultrich quietly. He had drifted over to stand beside Mudge. Butha and Andrian drew back at the pale, insubstantial nature of the Legatus' double.

"Ask Prias, he was one of the best," added Ultrich, but he couldn't find the first Legatus. Then he noticed the others were fading away too.

"I'll see you soon, my son," he said, as he began to disappear. "It will be good to get back to Rotor Valley Pass, and to be just one person again!" Then he was gone.

The great throng slowly disappeared. Only those who had accompanied Mudge from Shaker's Hope remained, and the hall seemed very ordinary once more. Just the rangers and Senovila, Arnima and Colma. Plus their new Xaanian friends.

"I think it's time to find a way out of here," said Mudge. He led the others toward one of the interwoven doors at the end of the hall.

"What about the bodyguards and the Gorlen?" said Ochren, looking a little doubtful.

"They won't be a problem," said Mudge. "The Gorlen will have returned to the elements they came from when the Empress created them. The bodyguards will be taking stock of the situation now their rulers are gone. I don't think they will try to stop us.

"We just have to get Butha and her people back to their home. Then we can take ourselves back to the Marches, so we can see our friends and families."

The others cheered up noticeably at the prospect, and half a continent away Ultrich was getting quite some grilling from the Lady Cinnabar.

"How was Prince Rossi when you saw him?" she said anxiously, though she was enjoying her stroll in the gardens of the Golden Palace with Ultrich.

The Legatus chuckled. "I don't think he'll ever be a 'royal prince', that one. He's too much his own man, and too close to the people.

"Which is why," he continued firmly, "he'll make a fine Legatus."

"I hope he doesn't think I'm trying to replace his mother," said Cinnabar earnestly. She looked worried.

"What makes you think I'm that interested?" said Ultrich, with a smile.

"Mmmph!" she snorted, and moved away from him. He moved smoothly with her, and slid his hand down from her waist and onto her hip. She took his hand firmly in hers and swung it at her side.

"I will tell him you have a kind heart . . . and long legs," said Ultrich mischievously.

"You haven't seen my legs," she retorted imperiously.

"I know. That's something we'll have to do something about, and soon," he said firmly. He put his arm around her waist again, and pulled her closer. This time she didn't resist.

In the office of state at the Golden Palace, Mudge was hearing about the last moments at Rotor Valley Pass from Porteous.

"The Empress' commanders in the field, these Sarkosay as you call them, just disappeared, turned themselves invisible perhaps. It left the Xaanian troops leaderless," said Porteous.

"I think those creatures knew the Empress was gone immediately. They knew she had returned to the underworld. Perhaps they knew she had been destroyed shortly after that. They must have figured out that the Xaanian forces would turn on them soon, even if those forces didn't know Ottar Bey was dead. I would have made a run for it too, if I was one of those devil creatures."

Porteous stopped for a moment, as if he was reliving an experience.

"We could tell the difference, you know, sitting up on the palisade across the pass, though we didn't know what was happening at first. It was bedlam below, with the Xaanian troops coming and going, and a lot of shouting.

"Then we noticed that all their commanders were gone. I figured the best thing to do was let them work it out among themselves. At least they had stopped attacking us!

"When the Legatus returned, well, when the other half of the Legatus returned – I don't really know how that works – he told us what had happened in the spirit world. Then the Xaanian forces just packed up and left."

Porteous shook his impressive, grey-streaked head of hair. There was so much about this he hadn't figured out yet, and Mudge suppressed a smile. The sudden collapse of the Xaanian forces must have looked preposterous if you weren't at the heart of it, watching it happen.

"The Legatus is in the gardens with Lady Cinnabar, if you want to find him," continued Porteous. "He said to tell you that."

Mudge nodded. He had heard the rumours about his father and the Lady himself. At first he hadn't been sure what he thought about the new couple, but something had made it easy for him to understand.

He had woken early in the royal apartments at the Golden Palace. Something didn't feel right about the pillows and the mattress, and he was uncomfortable. Then he realized he wasn't used to soft living any more.

After a while he had thrown a couple of blankets on the floor, and settled down on that. In the morning he had woken to find another scarf from Luce draped across his neck.

At least that answered one question. He had wondered where Jago and Luce had gone after the Empress had been defeated, and now he knew that they were still somewhere nearby. He hoped he wasn't keeping them in this world beyond a natural time, but something told him their purpose here wasn't over yet.

He still missed Luce terribly. It made him realize any chance of happiness between two people was rare, and should be grasped firmly with both hands. He and Luce had not been given a chance to see where their feelings might take them, but Ultrich and Cinnabar had survived the Empress Wars, as they were already being called, and they deserved the chance he had been denied.

He decided he wanted to go back to Shaker's Hope as soon as he could. His father had already agreed to postpone his Regency investiture for a while, and Mudge intended to take a very long holiday in his adopted town before that happened.

At some stage, when he had been Regent of the Eastern Marches for a while, he would be made Legatus, and he fervently hoped that the day it happened was also a long way off.

As he descended the stairs to the gardens, he wondered what he would say to his father and the Lady Cinnabar. Then he decided he would just hug them both, which would astonish his father. Then he would wish them every happiness in their future together.

THE END

Milton Keynes UK
Ingram Content Group UK Ltd.
UKHW020630220124
436466UK00020B/1072

9 798223 101635